The Angel Killer

Book 2 of the Watcher Saga

Lisa Voisin

The Angel Killer
Copyright © 2014 Lisa Voisin
All rights reserved.

ISBN-13: (Print) 978-1-939590-38-1

ISBN-13: (ebook) 978-1-939590-37-4

Inkspell Publishing
5764 Woodbine Ave.
Pinckney, MI 48169

Edited By Rie Langdon
Cover art By Najla Qamber

DEDICATION

For Dad and Dianne

LISA VOISIN

CHAPTER ONE

The restaurant bathroom had those mirrors that always gave me the creeps. The kind that faced each other and bounced their reflections back and forth so many times you could see yourself for infinity. When my brother, Bill, and I were kids, we used to believe mirrors like that were portals to Hell. And the thirteenth reflection would show us the Devil himself.

But those were just stories. Demons don't need a mirror to come here. All they need is fear.

Yeah. So quit freaking yourself out, Mia.

I pulled a brush from my purse and tugged it through the length of my chestnut brown hair, ignoring the many arms moving in front of me. At that moment, the silver *hamsa* I wore for protection blipped and buzzed a warning at my throat. The necklace had proven itself invaluable when I'd faced the demon Azazel and had kept him at bay—that is, until it shattered. This one was a replacement.

"Hello?" I called out. My heels clacked on the black and white tiles as I checked the dimly lit room. Usually, there'd be a blur of shadows or darkness if anything was going to materialize, and I half expected a pack of hellhounds to melt through the charcoal-colored walls. But, as far as I could tell, the room was empty.

The *hamsa* continued to pulse, sending a slither of ice along my spine, and my stomach prickled as though I'd swallowed a whole sea urchin. I returned to the sink, and all five of the taps burst on at once. I shrieked, and twisted one tap after the other, fumbling to shut them off.

The valves were stuck.

With a loud hum, the overhead lights flickered. Pipes groaned, and beneath my feet, the floor rumbled so much I thought the tiles would crack. The silver doors on the bathroom stalls flew open. Even the toilets shook. Was it an earthquake? I didn't want to wait around to find out. I charged for the exit.

"Mia!" Heather jumped back to avoid the swinging wooden door that almost clipped her in the face. "What the hell?"

The ground beneath me stilled. The lights stopped flashing and the room returned to normal. I blinked at Heather. Had she noticed? There was no way to explain what I'd just experienced. All I could say was, "Sorry."

She frowned and tapped her foot. "What's the rush? You look as though you've seen a ghost."

I motioned inside and said, "Stupid double mirrors always freak me out." It would help if another human being could see the same things as me—even once.

"Why?"

"Some story we used to tell each other as kids," I muttered.

"Well, you're not a little kid anymore." Heather was far too logical a person to believe that scary stories were sometimes real.

The *hamsa* twitched again, building in speed, so I covered its silver filigree with my hand. Heather wore an identical pendant at her throat. But hers kept still. Perhaps the twitching was something only I noticed, a private warning meant just for me.

"Did Michael arrive?" I asked, unable to hide the hope in my voice. He was supposed to meet us over an hour ago. We'd made a double date with Heather and Jesse, but he was so late we'd ordered and eaten without him.

"Not yet. Did he text?"

I shook my head. I'd never seen Michael use a cell. He didn't need to. We were connected beyond that. And the thought of him taking calls while demons chased him, or stopping to text me mid-fight, made me want to laugh. This past month, I'd been terrorized by hellhounds, attacked by one demon, and kidnapped by another. Through it all, Michael had been there, risking everything to protect me. He usually showed up whenever he was needed. Except for now.

"It's okay." Heather put an arm around my shoulder and gave me a little squeeze. "You, me, and Jesse can still make the movie. It'll be fun."

She was trying to console me, thinking I'd been stood up, but I knew better. The only reason Michael wouldn't show would be some kind of emergency. For him, that meant a demonic attack. Nobody—not even my closest friends—knew what Michael really was or the things he protected them from, and I had to keep it that way. Not because they'd think I was crazy if I told them. It simply wasn't my story to tell.

I scanned the bathroom again, locking my knees, because the memory of shaking still trembled them. I hadn't hallucinated. Those taps hadn't turned themselves on. *Hamsa* or not, being part of Michael's life again meant I wasn't safe anywhere. And I didn't know how to find him—what if something had happened? All I knew was that my home was protected by sigils, as was my school. Anywhere else might put me in harm's way.

Call me chicken if you want, but I wasn't that girl you saw in horror movies, the one who makes you shout at the screen, "Don't go down the stairs!" *Please.* I had a brain, and I wasn't going to risk any more tonight.

"I'm not feeling well," I said. "I should go home."

***

That night, I dragged myself to bed early. My limbs ached with fatigue, but as soon as I closed my eyes, the memory of what had happened in the bathroom played over and over like an animated GIF. The storm outside didn't help. Rain rattled the drainpipes. Wet tires groaned along the side streets, and headlights cutting across my neighbor's yard flickered along the bedroom walls. The bed's soft mattress swayed with my every move, reminding me of the bathroom's shaking floors. When I finally drifted off, nightmares lay in wait.

I'm standing in front of the bathroom mirror again, counting instances of my repeating reflection. At the thirteenth, my form changes and morphs, becoming a man. The Devil. Only instead of horns and a pitchfork, he's in a gray suit, and his golden hair arcs around him like an angel in a pre-Raphaelite painting. His face is a skin-colored blur, without features—not even eyes. Though he has no mouth, he laughs, and the sound sends the scratch of terror down my neck. He's heading straight for me, striding through the glass as though it's made of water. I back away from the mirror, trying to escape, but the door is gone. The walls loom closer until they press against me. There's no place to hide in this small, empty space. The glass shatters and a man's well-manicured hand reaches through. A scream catches in my chest.

Next, I am looking up at a dark sky. Red and blue lights flash off the clouds. Inhuman shrieks fill the air.

A white object plummets from above. A bird—an angel. Wings limp and broken, she somersaults to the ground. Her velocity grows with each tumble until she hits the pavement, trying to land, but her legs collapse beneath her. The white jacket she wears is covered in demon slime, and her tattered wings splay out at wrong angles. Her halo flickers, threatening to go out.

4

A blond veil of hair covers her features, but I know who it is. Arielle.

I crouch beside her, brush the hair from her face. "What happened?"

Her eyes, unfocused and wild, lock with mine. "I couldn't stop it," she says.

Before I can ask "Stop what?" she coughs, and blood from a stab wound spills from her chest. Her angelic blood seeps along the pavement, tinged with a golden light that erupts through the night the way sunlight breaks the horizon at dawn. In a wail of lament, the light sings.

I place my hands under her arms and try to lift her, but the movement is wrong. Her lithe, athletic body is too damaged, broken from the blow.

The street falls silent except for the sound of trickling along the asphalt. Everything is a blur of cement and bricks and gray. We could be anywhere. Behind her stands a huge, charcoal-skinned demon with the face of a gargoyle. Smoke rises from him as Arielle's blood sears and burns his skin, filling the air with the stench of charred rot. His right hand holds a blade. He points it at me.

I awoke trembling. By the dim orange glow of my alarm clock, I could make out the large bookshelf, the old, blue armchair beside the bed, Egyptian art on the walls. I was safe in my room—no demons. I let out my breath.

My heart raced as I untangled my legs from the blankets and leaped out of bed. Through the thin walls, I heard the faint wheeze of my mother snoring in her room. Though her presence was reassuring, I couldn't wake her. I didn't want to talk about my night, nor could I involve her in this world of demons and nightmares. Knowing what I knew would only scare her, and the more frightened people were, the more they were at risk.

I tiptoed to the bathroom and splashed cold water on my face to break the sticky web of sleep. Though Michael had been busier than usual, either he or Arielle watched over me at night to protect me. I never knew which one of them it would be, but I hoped for Michael tonight. I'd dreamed before about things that were going to happen, obscure warnings that didn't make sense until it was too late. If Arielle were the one to respond…what if I called her and had to relive that horrible dream for real?

Worry pressed at my thoughts. Though I couldn't explain what it was about, something *felt* wrong. The sooner I knew Michael was okay, the better. I switched off the bathroom light and padded carefully along the bungalow's cold wooden floors to my room.

Michael once told me he was able to sense my feelings and knew when I was in danger. Would it be possible to contact him deliberately? Wondering if he could sense me now, I focused on my erratic, thudding heartbeat, and in my mind, I called his name. *Michael!*

Pressing my forehead against the glass, I scanned the back yard, where I hoped he would land. Under the dim glow of the streetlight, a few maple branches shook off their last leaves in the wind. I turned away from the window to try again, sending all my fear and confusion to Michael as I paced the small path between my dresser and bed.

But he didn't show. No one did.

CHAPTER TWO

Michael didn't show up at school the next day either. By lunchtime, I was ready to send out a search party, but didn't even know where to start. He could literally be anywhere, so recruiting my friends and driving around West Seattle seemed pointless. Especially since I couldn't tell any of them what we were doing or why. It was bad enough to be worried about him. Worse was worrying alone.

The cafeteria lineup spilled halfway to the gym, and the din of voices, laughter, and clattering dishes echoed through the huge space and bounced off the painted concrete walls. My friends and I sat closest to the windows, where the cold damp from the rain outside fogged up the glass. Nobody asked about Michael. They must have sensed it was a touchy subject for me. Instead, Fiona's outrageous flirtation with Dean dominated our conversation.

"You're so going to ace those tryouts!" Fiona tossed her curly strawberry blond hair and smiled at him. "You were a star last year! You had more smackdowns than Paul Curtis."

"You mean *takedowns*," he corrected. At the mention of

7

tryouts, Dean's skin paled to a pasty oatmeal color, and his hazel eyes grew wide. He'd hardly touched his mac and cheese. The wrestling season was starting, and tryouts were after lunch. "I'm in a higher weight class now. It's different."

"Yeah, but you've been working out! Look at those arms!" Fiona turned to Jesse. "Doesn't he have great arms?"

Jesse shrugged, his expression more than a little awkward at being pulled into Fiona's flirting. "Nothing personal, dude, but I don't see you that way."

"Thank God," Dean said.

"Oh, please," Heather interjected. "There's nothing wrong with noticing another guy's muscles. It's primal. You see it in the wild all the time. Comes from the competition for food, territory, or even mating."

Jesse turned his grin to her. "I don't think Dean and I will be mating anytime soon."

"That's not what I mean and you know it." Heather had perfected the cool, blond stare. "Those primal instincts still rule us." She must have been reading her psychology texts again. I wouldn't be surprised if she were writing an essay for extra credit.

"Oh blah, blah, blah! You two. Enough psychobabble already!" Fiona waved her hands for emphasis. "Mia, doesn't he have nice arms?"

Dean pushed up the sleeve of his T-shirt and flexed his arm, the biceps bulging at the table. Fiona giggled as she squeezed it.

I thought of Michael's arms. They were at least ten times as strong. But what if that strength wasn't enough? For all I knew, he could've been ripped apart by a demon by now.

Someone threw a juice box across the cafeteria. It hit the wall near the exit and exploded purple drink everywhere, soaking a few nearby freshmen. Behind me, someone cheered. Pulled from my dark thoughts, I turned to find out who it was, but all I saw were the backs of two boys bolting out the doors.

"Hey Jesse," I said, ignoring Fiona's embarrassing question. "You sure this isn't the wild?"

"Poo flinging—typical primate behavior." Heather shook her head in dismay.

"No, I think *that* was just grape juice," I said dryly, making Heather smile.

Fiona caught Dean's hand between hers. "You'll do great today, babe. I know it. Hey, maybe we should go out and celebrate tonight!"

"But I haven't made it on the team yet," Dean protested.

"You will." Fiona smiled and gave his hand a squeeze. Her belief in him was unshakable.

I wished I had the same faith in Michael.

***

After school, Heather offered me a ride and suggested we shop on the way home. Outside, clouds hung dark and thick in an afternoon sky as gray as dusk. The rain had stopped, but mist shrouded the trees and wrapped me in an icy blanket. I shivered on the way to Heather's car, knowing how easily a hellhound or other creature could materialize from the fog. I touched the *hamsa* necklace for reassurance. It was silent today.

The shops on California Avenue were less than a mile away, but Heather took it slow through the fog-obscured streets. She kept the conversation light, not mentioning Michael nor his absence. But the way she left long pauses, as though she were waiting for me to bring it up, made me pretty sure she thought I was being dumped. Rush hour hadn't started yet, so we found street parking right in front of a boutique clothing store. Of course, we had to go inside. I didn't feel up to trying anything on, but when Heather filled her arms with selections, I forced myself to make an effort.

Once we'd paid and left, I followed Heather down the street to Fatima's family's carpet store. A string of ornate brass bells hanging from the door hinge announced our arrival, and, as we stepped inside, the scent of wool and incense rushed my nose. The front of the store had a furniture display for laying out carpets, with finely woven Persian rugs draped in piles on the floor. At the back, more intricate designs hung from the walls. Fatima stood behind a glass case at the cash register, helping a woman in a business suit arrange a delivery.

Heather and I browsed the back of the store, waiting. My attention caught on a display of silver tea sets with jewel-encrusted handles. And for a moment, I forgot we were in the heart of this damp city and had been transported to a warm, exotic land.

Fatima joined us when she was finished. "Looking for a tea set?"

"So this is the store." Heather grinned and motioned around the space.

"It is." Fatima straightened one of the cups so that its handle pointed in the same direction as the others lining the shelf.

"There's a lot of beautiful things here." I approached the display case filled with silver jewelry, bracelets and necklaces decorated with scrollwork I couldn't decipher. None of them were *hamsas*, though the ones Heather, Fiona, and I wore came from here. They must have run out. Fatima had given them to us when she sensed I was in danger—she was a gifted psychic who kept her abilities secret. I was one of the few people at school who knew about them.

I noticed her throat was bare. "Where's your necklace?" I'd experienced enough weirdness these past few weeks to know that demons could be anywhere. I wanted my friends to be safe.

She smiled self-consciously. "It's at home. I forgot to

put it on today."

She *forgot*? I pretty much slept in mine.

Heather left her shopping bag and purse on the glass display counter and wandered across the store. A colorful display of scarves drew her attention before she headed over to the carpets. Was she shopping for home décor now?

I stayed in the back of the store with Fatima. Noticing Heather was out of earshot, Fatima turned to me and said, "I've had a vision. We should talk."

My heart jumped with the sudden news. Fatima's visions often came true. "What about? Is it Michael?"

The door chimes rang as two women in colorful *hajibs* entered and waved hello.

"It's about both of you, I think." Fatima smiled at them and waved back. "Can't talk now though. That's my aunt and cousin," she whispered. "Tomorrow at school?"

I nodded. I needed a friend to talk to. Surely it wouldn't hurt to tell Fatima about the freaky occurrence in the bathroom the night before, and even about my nightmares. Maybe she knew where Michael was, or if he was in danger. That could have been what her vision was about.

Yeah, talking would be good. In fact, I could hardly wait.

***

The sun had already set when Heather and I left the store. The mists hadn't subsided and the lights from the shop windows diffused an eerie glow around us. Cars clogging the streets would have been invisible if it weren't for their headlights. As we waited to cross the street, the *hamsa* at my throat jumped and then stopped. I turned back to see a man in a dark suit and hat head into Fatima's store. My stomach hitched in response.

"Everything okay?" Heather asked.

"I hope so." Part of me wanted to rush in after Fatima, so I could be sure she was okay, but another part wanted to get away as fast as I could. My feet clung to the pavement, refusing to move.

"Come on. It's our light." Heather tugged my arm and dragged me across the street.

Through the fog, another tall figure approached. I tensed further, wondering if we should dart into the Husky Deli nearby, in case we were being followed. Though the idea of safety was relative these days, the deli was, at least, well lit and full of potential witnesses.

The figure came closer. I recognized the walk, the broad shoulders, and then his wavy dark hair as Michael's features came into view. I huffed out my breath and the knot in my chest released. He was *safe*. His jacket zipped up to his neck, he moved with a slow, weary-limbed determination. Thinking he might be hurt, I rushed to his side, noticing the stubble lining his strong jaw, and the remnants of a scar healing on the left side of his face. His smile erased my fear.

"There you are! I thought…" Remembering Heather was there, I stopped myself and smacked the side of his arm.

"Hey!" He rubbed the spot I'd just hit. "What's that for?"

"Not showing up last night!" I didn't need to tell him how worried I was. I couldn't hide it. Part of his being an angel meant he could feel everything I felt.

"You could've phoned," Heather scolded. Now that she knew I wasn't in danger of being dumped she was going to tell him off on my behalf. "Mia went home early."

He glanced from Heather to me. Clearly we were two against one. "I'm sorry." When I relaxed at his apology, he circled his strong arms around my waist and drew me in for a hug. "Things have been hectic. I couldn't get away until now."

My fingers brushed the scar on his cheek. Moments

ago, it had probably been bleeding and sore. He must have healed it. I'd seen his ability to do that before, both on himself and when he'd healed me.

Leaning in, he kissed my forehead, but his muscles were coiled tight, ready to spring. The sweet ozone and grassy smell of his skin was tinged with sweat, blood, and sulfur. He'd been fighting.

"Geez," Heather quipped. "When was the last time you two saw each other? Saturday?"

Friday. I was definitely counting.

"Sorry." Michael released me and took a step back. Holding my hand, he gave it a squeeze. "I was hoping I'd find you."

"How'd you even know we'd be here?" Heather asked. "You didn't call him did you, Mia?"

I shook my head and blinked at Michael, not sure how to explain.

"Lucky guess?" He smiled, the scar even less visible now. "The coffee shop around the corner is one of Mia's favorites, so I thought I'd try there."

I loved that coffee shop, but I'd never mentioned it, and we'd never actually been there together. His ability to sense my feelings meant he could always find me. But knowing all my likes and dislikes because he knew my soul? That astonished me.

"Didn't see you at school today. You skipping class?" That was Heather: direct and to the point.

Michael cleared his throat. "No. There was an emergency at the—uh—place I volunteer at. I had nothing pressing, so I said I'd help out." Not untrue, exactly. His ability to stretch the truth to keep people from knowing what he did amazed me. It was as though he spoke in code, and I was still learning how to decipher it.

"Oh? Where do you work?" Heather said.

He shrugged, unruffled by her grilling. "All over the place."

"What do you do?"

"Today, I worked with street kids." It must have meant he'd saved someone today.

"You mean handing out lunches?" She was not giving up.

"I help them make better choices."

"You mean counseling?" She was so excited, her five-foot-five-inch frame practically lunged at him. "How did you get that gig? Is it a co-op? They told me I needed a few years of university before I could even apply."

Michael shot me a curious glance. He must have realized he'd stumbled onto a topic that Heather would never let go. "Connections, I guess." He stepped in closer and ran a hand down my arm. Even through my jacket, the heat of his touch warmed me. Leaning in, he motioned to Heather's bag. "Been shopping?"

"'Course! Retail therapy." Her phone beeped. She fished it from her purse to read a text. "It's Fiona. Dean made the team."

"Great," I said.

My phone beeped too, and when I glanced down to check it, a loose strand of hair fell into my face. Michael brushed it away, his fingertips grazing my cheek, and he smiled at me as though we were the only people there.

Heather finished a reply text to Fiona and motioned to the Husky Deli. "I...um...need to get an ice cream cone."

"Isn't it a bit cold for ice cream?" I asked.

"Some candy, then." Giving me a wink, she added, "Come get me when you two lovebirds are finished doing...whatever." She waved her hand dismissively at us before she slipped inside.

Michael leaned against the building's stucco wall and rested his hands on my hips. Light from the store cast a warm gleam in his crystal blue eyes. He leaned in, and the draw to be close to him was a gravitational force. "Hello," he said.

"Hello." I had to get a grip. It'd been so long since we'd talked, I tried to focus on all the things I wanted to tell him. "We went to see Fatima." His fingers caressed the sides of my waist, sending happy tingles through me. "You know, in her store…" To my own ears, my voice sounded raspy. I trembled.

"Cold?" He drew me closer, his mouth crooking into a grin.

Lost in him, I forgot all about Fatima. "You know damn well that's not it." I twined my arms around his back and touched the spot between his shoulder blades where his wings connected. Its warmth thawed my fingers.

He leaned in and brushed his lips along my jaw line. "Thought that was just me," he whispered, and his breath tickled my neck. "I've wanted to do this for three days."

Our lips met, and I melted into him, not caring that we were on the sidewalk, outside a deli with families shopping inside. Nor did I care that, being an angel, he had to follow very strict rules about contact with humans—especially contact of the relationship variety. Angels had the ability to enthrall humans with their touch, something Michael had to constantly keep in check. But I didn't have to be enthralled to want to kiss him. That was my own doing. All that mattered right now was that he was here. With me.

He pulled me closer and the buzz of his energy filled me heart and soul, blocking out the rest of the world. My hands sought warmth under his leather jacket and found bare skin. I could feel the shiver from my touch surge through him. His mouth pressing more firmly against mine, he brushed a hand along my cheek and tangled it in my hair.

A dreamlike blur of light and color filled my thoughts. But then the image shifted to blood. His.

Michael stood in the forest, his sword raised. A large, black demon loomed over him. Though mist shrouded its features, I didn't have to see the creature's face to know it was sharp and twisted, like a gargoyle's. It was the kind of minion I'd seen with Damiel when he'd kidnapped me. Michael swung his weapon, and the demon attacked him with a sword of its own, slicing his stomach and ribs.

His yelp of pain echoed in my ears. I gasped and pulled away.

"Mia?"

When I didn't answer, Michael's palms cupped the sides of my face, his gaze seeking to connect with mine. "Hey. You all right? What's going on?"

I shook my head and unzipped his jacket. His tank was torn and stained red, still damp. "You were hurt!" I tugged at his shirt, desperately searching his stomach for damage.

He caught my wrists. "You saw that?"

"I dreamed Arielle was killed last night, but she wasn't the one in danger. You were!"

"It's nothing. I'm fine." He raised his shirt to show me. A long, pink line puckered across the hard muscles of his stomach, running from his ribs to the top of his jeans. Anyone looking at it would think the injury was months old, instead of a few hours. Soon, even that scar would be gone. "See? I heal fast."

I traced the pink line with my fingertips and he let out his breath in surprise.

I jerked my hand away. "Does it hurt?"

He swallowed and shook his head. Tiny bumps had formed along his skin. He let his shirt fall into place.

"We were attacked," he said, his voice thick. "But it was okay. I mean, it didn't get out of hand."

"Didn't get *out of hand*?" I took a deep breath to calm down. Icy mist seeped through my clothes, and the urge to shudder twitched through my muscles, though the vision I'd just had didn't help. "No wonder I couldn't reach any of you—I was trying to."

"I was out of range." He rubbed the sides of my arms and frowned. "Someone should have responded, though. What if you were in danger?"

"I wasn't. Not really," I said, not wanting him to worry. "But things got pretty strange at the restaurant last night."

He wrapped his hands around mine to warm them. "When?"

"Around seven or so." I explained what had happened in the restroom and the way my *hamsa* had buzzed even though the space was empty.

When I was done, Michael sucked his breath through his teeth, making a hissing sound. "We noticed something, as well. The ground shook, but it was no earthquake."

"That's it exactly. Heather didn't notice though."

"Nobody did. Just you." He shook his head and smiled in amazement. "The things you can see."

"What's going on?" I asked.

"We don't know. Half our wards over the Pacific Rim dropped. Arielle and the others are checking into it."

Wards were sigils, only on a much larger scale, protecting continents instead of houses or city blocks. "I'm still surprised no one came when you called. They told me they'd watch over you. Otherwise I'd never have gone." He wrapped his arms around me again and drew me against his chest. "Since you helped us save Damiel and bring him back, the others consider you an ally. You're under their protection as well."

Damiel had once been a Grigori like Michael, but he'd become ill and fallen to the sin of envy. Two weeks ago, he'd kidnapped me in an attempt to make me the mother of his demon offspring (yeah, I *wish* I were kidding!), but Michael had arrived barely in time. Together, we'd convinced Damiel to seek his own redemption. As far as I knew, Damiel was still in recovery, too weak to talk. I was still haunted by nightmares about it.

"An ally, huh?" As difficult as the memory was, I couldn't help but smile. "I like the sound of that!"

LISA VOISIN

CHAPTER THREE

Michael and I barely had time to eat dinner before he had to put himself back on watch for the night. This time, he reassured me that he wouldn't be far away if I needed him. True to his word, he picked me up the next morning and drove me to class, only to tell me he'd been called to work on another assignment with Arielle. This one was out of town. I tried to pretend I was okay with it, but really, what were they thinking? He'd just returned from a battle that got him injured, and now he was off again. What about school? What about days off? He'd been working for two weeks straight. Even God apparently rested on Sundays—why couldn't angels? I was beginning to wonder if the others were deliberately giving him assignments to keep us apart.

It didn't matter that he healed fast, or that he knew what he was doing. Demons were *always* involved. They wouldn't hesitate to kill him if they had the chance, which meant he was in danger all the time. And the one thought that rolled around in my head, the one I tried not to think, was the possibility that he might not come back. One day, Arielle could return from an assignment alone, and then where would I be?

Remembering that Fatima had wanted to talk, I sought her out at lunch, while Heather and Fiona crammed for their afternoon History test. I found Fatima in the cafeteria in a heated argument with her twin brother. Farouk was Heather's math tutor and one of our friends. I'd first met Fatima through him. I stopped a few feet away, not wanting to intrude.

As their voices grew louder, people turned their heads to watch. Since they were speaking in Farsi, nobody understood what they were saying. It hardly mattered. Arguments were the same in every language.

Seeing me, Fatima bristled. *What had I done?*

My *hamsa* necklace twitched. I scanned the room for anything unusual, but the only thing out of place was Fatima's mood. She had told me once that the necklace could be used to detect people's ill intentions toward me. I never expected she would be the one sending negativity my way.

She shoved her half-eaten tray of food across the table, knocking Farouk's carton of milk—which he caught before it spilled. Standing, she pushed past me and stormed off.

I hovered over the space her body once occupied. "Should I leave?"

When Farouk looked up, his eyes had deep rings around them. His dark, curly hair was messier than usual, his checkered shirt rumpled. "Hey, Mia," he said flatly. "Don't be surprised if I say something to piss you off. I seem to be brilliant at that today."

"I'll consider myself warned." I slid into the seat across from him, realizing I didn't know what to say, other than *"What the hell is up with her?"* Farouk was brilliant at lots of things. He had skipped a grade in most of his classes. I'd never seen him so down on himself.

After an awkward moment of silence between us, I blurted out the first thing that entered my mind. "I didn't mean to interrupt. Fatima told me she wanted to talk."

Farouk wasn't listening. Having finished his milk, he twisted the straw, his fingers working it into a knot. "My sister, she's been—"

Across the cafeteria, some girl screamed and pointed outside. Farouk and I stood at the same time. Outside the full-length windows, Jesse staggered toward the school. His face was scratched, his black leather biker jacket torn. He clutched his leg with bloody fingers and collapsed to his knees on the pavement.

I rushed outside. A crowd of people started to gather around him, but none of them approached. I pushed my way through. One girl had the sense to call an ambulance on her cell—or so she told me as I passed.

"Jesse?" I crouched beside him. His leg was gouged above the knee, and blood oozed through fingers that loosened their grip as his head lolled to the side. Instinctively, I crushed my hands against his leg, taking up the pressure.

"Dean…" Jesse's eyes rolled back into their sockets. He was passing out.

"Dean's not here," I said, resisting the urge to ask what had happened. He needed all the strength he had left.

Farouk kneeled beside me and rolled up his sleeves. Tiny goose bumps raised the hair on his arms. "It might be an artery…" His Adam's apple jumped as he swallowed back the rest of what he was about to say. Instead, his lips pulled into a tight smile. "You'll be okay," he said to Jesse. "The ambulance is on its way." He unfastened his leather belt, working it off.

"What are you doing?" I asked.

"We need a tourniquet to stop the bleeding. I'll lift his leg." He held up the belt to me. "Reach this under his thigh—above the wound. Okay?"

I nodded, sensing a twitching at my throat, and my own heart stuttered in response—was the necklace warning me? I didn't have time for monsters now. Jesse's face was beaded with sweat. He needed us.

"Ready?" Farouk asked.

"Yeah."

When Farouk lifted the wounded leg, Jesse cried out and his eyes flew open. Wincing at his obvious pain, I slid the belt under his thigh. My blood-soaked fingers slipped as I pulled the strap, and Farouk had to lean over to help. Threading the end through the loop, he cinched it tight.

"Okay. Make room," a man's deep voice said. "What's going on here?" Mr. Ballard, our gym teacher and Dean's wrestling coach, pushed his way through the crowd.

"Hold this and keep it tight," Farouk said to me. "Jesse can't. He's blacking out."

Mr. Ballard tapped Farouk on the shoulder and checked the tourniquet. He gripped the leather strap, his strong hands pulling it tighter than I ever could.

"What happened?" he asked.

"Jesse's been hurt." I moved out of the way. Sheets of rain slicked the pavement, streaming rivulets of blood everywhere. "That's all I know."

Mr. Ballard addressed the crowd that had gathered. "Who's going to tell me how this happened? If I find out one of you has a knife…" He was a huge man, well over six feet, with shoulders as broad as a truck. When he asked questions, people usually answered. But the group had dispersed to get out of the rain. I didn't see Heather among them. Somebody needed to tell her about Jesse before she heard it through the rumor mill.

"Dean's hurt," Jesse murmured. His eyes slid closed again. "By the creek…I'm sorry… I couldn't…"

Three EMTs arrived, rolling a stretcher our way. Mr. Ballard pulled one of them aside. "He says someone else has been injured in the woods."

Once we were sure the EMTs had Jesse, Farouk and I took off across the field to the forest that bordered the school grounds. As we sprinted, our feet slid across the muddy, wet grass. Rain pelted our skin, drenching our hair and soaking our clothes.

Mr. Ballard soon caught up with us. "What are you two doing?"

"Dean's our friend...he's hurt..." I said, between breaths.

"Suit yourself." He sped past us. Damn, he was fit.

Half a block into the forest, Dean lay unconscious on the bank of the small creek. Blood from a head wound streamed down his forehead, mixing with the rain. His dark shirt was torn and stained as though his stomach were slashed.

Mr. Ballard pressed his fingers to the side of Dean's neck, checking his pulse. "What the heck happened here?" he said to himself. Dean sure wasn't about to answer, and Farouk and I didn't have a clue.

The ambulance pulled up along the trail with its lights flashing and its siren off. EMTs charged through the bushes, carrying first aid equipment and a portable stretcher.

"His pulse is weak," Mr. Ballard said to one of them, a woman who had to be in her late thirties.

Her mouth formed a grim line. "What happened?" she asked.

"Don't know, but he's pretty mangled." He shook his head. "I've seen knife fights less messy than this."

My hands were sticky with blood, so I rinsed them in the icy creek. The EMTs hooked Dean up to tubes and lifted him onto the stretcher. Before they left, one of them approached. He was younger than the rest, maybe in his mid-twenties, and the rain had already plastered his dirty blond hair to his head. "You all right?" He motioned to my jeans, stained with red from the knees down.

"Fine. It's Jesse's blood. Not mine."

The EMT gave me a nod and joined his colleagues, who were loading Dean onto a stretcher.

The air cooled even more, and the *hamsa* necklace buzzed at my throat. With a jolt, I checked the area and wasn't surprised to find shadows lurking in the bushes several yards away; red eyes flashed behind the trees.

Hellhounds. Three, maybe four by my count. The urge to shudder tugged at my muscles. I stifled it. *Don't be afraid. It'll make things worse. Nobody else can see them.*

Had they hurt Dean and Jesse? Or were they trying to scavenge a free meal?

The *hamsa* buzzed more insistently. As the EMTs carried Dean off, Mr. Ballard followed to catch a ride in the already full ambulance. Farouk and I would soon be the last people there. And, with their mouths agape to scent the air, those hellhounds looked hungry.

"I'm cold. Let's head back." I kept my voice low, as though pretending to be calm and *actually staying calm* were the same thing.

One of the hounds fixed its attention on me and growled. It knew I could see them. I knew the school had been protected by sigils that kept creatures like them away, but we were outside school grounds. Though I'd seen Michael make quick work of them before, I had neither his ability nor his weapons. Would the *hamsa* alone be enough to stop them? If so, what about Farouk?

To play it safe, I armed myself with the nearest rock. Dean probably hadn't gone down without a fight, and he was way stronger than me, but I knew how hellhounds worked. First, they fascinated their victims with fear, sapping their energy, and feeding on life force until they came into form. Then they devoured their victim's flesh. Dean might not have had a chance to fight.

"What's that?" Farouk asked motioning to one of the hellhounds lurking in shadow. "A stray?"

He could see it too? It must have materialized. "We should go," I said. "It might be rabid or something."

The hellhound growled again, as if to make its point, and Farouk froze. I wondered if he'd noticed its red eyes.

"Come on," I said, tugging at his arm.

"I don't want to turn my back on it." Farouk dipped his head, averting his gaze. "If we run, it'll treat us like

prey."
But we *were* prey.

CHAPTER FOUR

Farouk crept back, positioning himself between me and the snarling hellhound, while two others flanked us along the side of the trail, poised to materialize. Their smoky forms traversed the bushes like ghosts, leaving the wet branches undisturbed. Any second now, they would solidify and cut us off. But Farouk's gaze didn't even flicker in their direction. Telling him about them would only freak him out, and make it easier for them take us down. Right now, he had no idea what we were up against.

We inched backward in the wet, muddy terrain. My foot slipped on a rock, and I grasped Farouk's shoulder for balance.

"Careful," he said, steadying me. "No sudden moves."

"Believe me, I'm trying." I wanted to get out of there alive.

Deeper in the bush, a man dressed in white slipped behind the trees. The motion startled me enough that my breath hitched, and I stopped moving. He fixed his attention on me and placed a finger to his lips. His short-cropped hair was a pure silver, and his eyes were such a startling shade of violet that I couldn't help but stare. But that only seemed to annoy him. A blue ripple shimmered in the space behind his back—the outline of his wings.

"What is it?" Farouk asked.

"Nothing," I bluffed. "Just making sure I don't trip again."

The angel drew his sword, motioning with his free hand for me to keep moving. When his halo flared, it burned brighter than a star, forcing me to turn away. The smoky hellhounds flanking us were incinerated. But the solid one growled, turning to face its new threat.

"What's it looking at?" Farouk asked. Obviously, he hadn't seen the bright flash or the angel that caused it.

"Don't know, and I don't care. Let's get out of here," I said and bolted for the school.

Once we were back inside the safety of the building itself, Farouk and I parted ways. I headed into the girls' changing rooms to shower. There was blood on my face, in my hair, in my clothes, and even under my fingernails. And it took the taps forever to give me water warm enough to remove the chill that seeped below my skin. Though it was freezing out, all I had to change into were a pair of leggings and a T-shirt from gym class. I braided my hair wet and shivered all the way down the hall to my locker. As I put my regular clothes into my bag, I realized I'd forgotten to tell Heather and Fiona about what had happened. I checked my watch; it was almost two. Their test would be over soon. With their cell phones off, there was still a chance they hadn't heard yet.

"Nice outfit." Elaine's snide comment pulled me out of my reverie. "Trying out sporty chic today?"

Her short red hair, of course, was perfectly coiffed, as though she'd come fresh from the salon, but it was always like that. She worked as the gossip columnist for the school paper—if spreading rumors and bullying everyone else could be called work. *How did she not know what was going on?*

As she took off her wet coat and hung it in her locker, I realized she must have been off school grounds. I focused on sorting my books, trying not to stare as she fished her purse from her bag and switched on her cell. It beeped furiously. Messages from her legions of spies, no doubt.

Ignoring me, she texted back.

"Where were you?" I asked.

"What?" she snapped. "Are we playing 'let's pretend we're friends' now? You wanna chat about my day?" The smile she gave me was more of a sneer. "Okay, I'll play. I was at the dentist. How was *your* day?"

"You're not texting about Jesse and Dean, are you?" I asked, my anger overruling her sarcasm. "I can't believe you're going to exploit them like that!"

"Exploit? Really? Big words considering I just found out about it. Everyone's texted me. But we don't even know if they're okay. It's a gong show. As if I'd publish it. I have ethics, you know."

I knew all about her ethics. She'd sell her soul for a piece of gossip, and from what I knew about demons, and how easily they could possess people, I wouldn't be surprised if she turned into one on the spot.

Heather. There was no way she could find out this way! Pulling out my own phone, I texted, "Call me ASAP." To Elaine, I said, "Don't you dare tell Heather or Fiona!"

"They don't know?" Elaine smirked and her eyes lit up. Damn! She had her story now.

I stepped closer, staring her down. "If you write anything about this, I will hurt you." I clenched my fists so tight the nails bit into my palms.

"Enough. I get it. Quit foaming at the mouth already, you psycho!"

"Just makin' a point." I opened my hands, and let the circulation rush into them again.

My cell rang. It was Heather. "Where are you?" I demanded.

"Geez! Not you, too! What's with everyone? People are acting really weird."

"Are you with Fiona?"

"Yeah, we're right outside class."

"Don't talk to anyone. I'll be right there." I closed my locker door and sprinted down the hall.

Though I arrived at the classroom within minutes, it wasn't soon enough. They were already gone. I checked both their lockers, the library, and the cafeteria.

Fifteen minutes later, I found them leaving the office of our guidance counselor, Ms. Callou. Heather's face was ashen as she shuffled down the hall. Fiona leaned against her, sobbing. It had been less than a month since Fiona had attempted suicide, no thanks to Damiel. This was the last thing she or Heather needed!

"You knew. You were there!" Heather lashed out at me, her arm still around Fiona. "Why didn't you tell us?"

"I'm so sorry!" I said, approaching them. "By the time I got back, you were already in the test."

"You saw Dean!" Fiona said. "Do you know what happened? How he got hurt?"

I shook my head. "He was already unconscious by the time we got there." I couldn't mention the hellhounds circling, or how their boyfriends had both been prey. There were some things they were better off not knowing. "The paramedics got there really fast. I'm sure he'll be okay."

It was the most reassuring thing I could think of.

Michael had said things were hectic. Did that mean all my friends were in danger now? Or had Jesse and Dean simply been in the wrong place at the wrong time?

CHAPTER FIVE

The next day, I sat with Fiona in the beige and green hospital visitor's room while she waited for her chance to see Dean. Patience had never been her strong suit. She fidgeted the whole time, jiggling her legs and squeezing the olive green vinyl armrests so tight I thought she'd snap a nail. She must have checked the wall clock thirty times since we'd sat down.

We left Heather with Jesse in his room, so the two of them could catch up. Though his leg needed stitches and he'd lost some blood, they would probably release him in the morning. Dean's injuries, however, had been more severe. His shoulder and stomach had been slashed—well, bitten—but at least his organs were undamaged. Even so, we were told he was in a lot of pain. Since hospitals usually only allowed immediate family to visit in cases like this, we needed my mom to get us in. And Mom was late.

Fiona got up and paced across the waiting room floor, her sneakers squeaking on the freshly-washed linoleum. Over our heads, one of the fluorescent bulbs blinked, threatening to go out.

"She'll be here soon," I said. Mom wasn't usually the type to be late.

"He's going to miss his first tournament of the season." She bit her lip. "It's less than three weeks away, and scouts from Oregon State are supposed to be there. He was so excited about it."

"They'll come again," I said, immediately regretting my words. For all we knew, he could miss the entire season.

Mom entered the waiting room, rushed. Head down, she checked her watch before she said hello. Across the sitting room, an elderly man put down his paper, thinking she had news for him. She shook her head and turned to us. "Something came up. I've only got twenty minutes."

Fiona and I followed her into Dean's room. His mom's insurance wouldn't cover a private room, so he had to share with a guy in his twenties. Though he was connected to an IV drip, he couldn't have been that sick, because he was reading a mountain bike magazine and ogled us as we walked by.

The sun had already begun to set, casting shadows across the industrial beige walls. Those same shadows hung over Dean as well, making the heart monitor and IV drip attached to him seem even more ominous. As we approached his bed, Fiona let out a little gasp. Even sleeping, Dean's face was pale and drawn.

His eyelids slid open, and for a second he seemed disoriented. I felt terrible for waking him, but this visit meant a lot to Fiona.

"Fiona and Mia are here to see you," my mom said.

Fiona swallowed hard, and blinked, before she managed to put on a tight smile.

She appeared to have gone mute, so I asked, "How are you doing?"

He gave me a crooked half smile. "Been better."

A breeze from an open window flapped the curtain beside the bed, making the shadows dance around us and over Dean. My stomach rolled like a bowling ball.

Fiona took his hand and smiled sweetly at him. "Missed you." She kissed his cheek.

His heart monitor beeped faster from her kiss. I decided it was time to leave the two of them alone, or sort-of alone, as the case may be. While mom had stepped away from the bed to give them privacy, she was close enough to still keep an eye on Fiona, which was the deal she'd made to get us in.

I headed into the hall to get myself a ginger ale from the vending machine, hoping it would settle my stomach. That was when I saw Michael. He must have come straight from "work"; the tank he wore flying was visible under his half-zipped leather jacket. It had been three days since we'd seen each other, and I'd been looking forward to it. But now that he was here, I panicked. The bowling ball in my stomach rolled up to my chest, cold and heavy. A sharp pain twinged at the base of my skull.

"I came as soon as I could," he said, answering the accusation I hadn't spoken.

Where the hell had he been? So much had happened since he left. The hellhounds came back, my friends had been injured, and I'd faced it all alone. He was always busy. First he'd stood me up, making me worry about him. Then he'd barely come around long enough to make me care before he'd taken off again and left me to deal with things. How dare he think I'd welcome him now? As if everything was fine?

"Don't hurry on my account." I pressed the button for ginger ale. The vending machine clunked but nothing came out. I gave it a shove.

Michael took a step back, frowning. I guessed I wasn't giving him the reception he'd hoped for. Ignoring him, I jammed my shoulder against the machine, throwing my weight into it.

"Hey." He grasped my arm and pointed to the DO NOT TIP sign. "Stop it."

"Dammit." I pulled my arm free and kicked the machine. He was lucky I didn't kick him.

"Back off," he said. His energy flared a brilliant white,

hurting my eyes.

A growl formed in my chest and I took a futile swing at him. He caught my arm and pulled me into the short hallway that led to a supply closet. With a flicker, his halo surrounded us, making us invisible to any passersby. He reached over his shoulder and pulled out his sword.

My throat tightened. What was he thinking? Why would he draw his weapon on me? "Leave me alone!"

"You want to tangle with me?" His icy gaze sliced right through me. The silver-blue blade of his intention sword extended with a hum. "Come on!"

Though the weapon couldn't cause me harm, I knew he'd hurt people before. He'd even killed someone. Had he relapsed? Gone insane? Instinctively, ready to flee, I shifted my weight to my toes. But he stood between me and escape. With his reflexes and speed, I was trapped.

I shoved him as hard as I could. "What kind of macho crap is this?"

With his hand on my shoulder, he pressed my back against the wall and glared at me. "Leave her alone."

Leave her alone? Referring to me in the third person? He must have gone insane. "Let me go." I kicked him in the shin as hard as I could, and he winced but didn't budge. "I'll scream."

He raised his sword. Its blue light sizzled and flared. I squirmed, pressing both hands against his chest, trying to push him off me.

"What the f—?"

"Hold still, Mia. Don't be afraid." His voice was soft, musical. "It'll be all right in a minute."

He plunged the sword through my chest, and I gasped, expecting to feel the icy pain of my heart stopping. That had to hurt, right? But it only tingled, pleasantly so, and instead of coldness, warmth seeped through my veins. My anger dropped as though it were a flamed leech, and that was when I saw what Michael had been fighting. Gray and staticky, half my size, it fell to the floor with a glutinous thud.

"A minion?" I asked, my headache lifting.

"Yeah. Place is crawling with them." He plunged his sword through it again, holding the weapon in place until the creature dissolved. "They're drawn to hospitals. It's all the pain and suffering. Anyone's fair game."

"That was *on* me?" I asked, with a shiver. "You should have said something."

"Should I? It's like telling someone who's terrified of spiders, 'Don't look now, but there's a tarantula on you.' Besides, as soon as it saw me, it plugged into your brain and you went on the attack. There was no way to know if anything I said would sink in."

"It plugged into my brain?" That hadn't been me fighting with Michael; it was a minion. Bile hit the back of my throat at the thought of that creature taking me over. What kind of ally could I possibly be if I couldn't even see these things—let alone keep them off me?

He scanned the area and flared his halo around us to make sure the space was clear before we headed down the main hall.

Noticing my silence, he added, "It's not your fault, Mia. It's how they feed." Retracting his sword, he tucked it between his shoulder blades, returning it to its invisible sheath.

"My mom works here! Can't you put up sigils or something?"

"We do, but they're not foolproof. We have to fix them all the time. Get enough minions and they simply bust through."

"But the *hamsa* usually warns…" I touched my throat, finding it bare. "It's gone!" I retraced my steps, scanning the floor.

"You lost it?"

Mentally, I played back the last twenty-four hours. "I remember it buzzed yesterday, when Farouk and I saw the hellhounds."

Michael spun to face me. "You saw hellhounds?"

"That's what attacked Dean and Jesse. They'd materialized, and Farouk saw them. If that other angel wasn't there, I don't know what would have happened."

"Other angel? Who?"

"He didn't exactly tell me his name. He's tall, not as tall as you, has silver hair."

A crease formed between his brows as he let out a long sigh. "Turiel."

An orderly passed us, pushing a cart of dirty dishes. The smell of medicine and half-eaten vegetable soup wafted through the halls.

I made a mental note to ask about Turiel later. "Whatever. Michael, look, Jesse's going to be okay, but you've got to help Dean. He's hoping to get a wrestling scholarship, and the season begins in a few weeks. "

Michael stopped to put some coins into the vending machine. When he pressed the button for ginger ale, the can dropped easily into the tray. He handed it to me.

Any discomfort I'd had around him earlier had dissipated. My friends were in danger, and the burden of that showed on Michael's face. It felt as though he'd been away forever. "Can you heal him? Would you?"

"Yes, but I can't stay long," he said.

"What do you mean? You just got here."

"The attacks we've been experiencing are unprecedented. We knew Damiel was behind them before, but when we reclaimed him, I thought things would lighten up. I was wrong. Hell's fighting back, and we're not as strong as we once were. Many of us are getting battle-weary." He hesitated as though he wasn't sure how to say the next part. His eyes sought mine apologetically. "The others think the way I feel about you is an unnecessary distraction."

I knew they'd never really approved of us. And though he was careful to say it was what *they* thought, his words stung. "And what about you? Do you think that?"

"No." He wound an arm around my waist and pulled me close, whispering, "To me, you're essential." Closing his eyes, he leaned his forehead to mine. "Just seeing you for a moment, knowing you're safe in all of this…" He didn't finish his sentence. He didn't need to.

"Me too," I said. The heat of his breath lingered on my skin. I wanted to kiss him, but there wasn't time. Lately, there was never enough time.

Letting me go, he laced his fingers with mine. "Let's go see Dean."

***

I didn't know if Michael was making it possible for me to see things, or if it was a residual effect of either being in his presence or having had a giant slug cleared off me, but I saw the shadows in Dean's room for what they were— minions that skittered away from Michael the way cockroaches escaped the light. The few exceptions were already attached to people. Raising their dark gray, linty heads, they bared their jagged, black "teeth" in warning. A few of them even hissed. Everyone in the room had at least one on them, except Fiona. Even so, a bear-sized minion hovered behind her, trying to get close, but her *hamsa* kept it away. The guy with the bike magazine had a snakelike minion on his lap. The creature hissed when it saw Michael, but the guy's eyes glazed over, as though he'd completely checked out.

Dean was the worst off. Two massive, slippery globs feasted on his stomach, draining him where he'd been wounded. A third twined around his neck as though it whispered in his ear.

As much sympathy as I had for Dean, for me, the most horrifying sight in the room was my mom. She sat in a green armchair with a huge creature draped over her shoulders like a gray, animated cloak. Another pierced her heart. Her face was pinched, the lines on her forehead etched deeper than I'd ever seen.

When she saw Michael, the lines hardened as her face pulled into a frown. "Get him out of here!"

"Mom!" I rushed between them. How could she be so rude?

Michael caught my arm and whispered, "It's the minion—not her."

Approaching her, he flared his halo so bright I couldn't look at him. But Mom didn't even squint. I had to get used to the fact that nobody else could see these things. Perhaps that was what it meant to be an ally.

Michael placed a hand on my mom's shoulder and her knees folded beneath her. He guided her to collapse back into the chair. "Shelly," he said, his voice a chord. "It's me." His halo flared brighter, and the creatures on her recoiled. She stopped in her tracks and fell silent, her green eyes flat, glassy, the light in them gone. I wondered if I'd looked this vacant before he'd helped me. *Would he have to stab her, too?* But the minions dropped to the floor and, sizzling, scurried away. "Come back to us, Shelly."

Come back? Where had she gone?

She took a deep breath, blinking as the light returned to her eyes. "Michael!" she said. "My goodness, what happened?"

Fiona gave me a puzzled look. She'd seen everything. At least he hadn't had to pull out the sword the way he did with me. We'd never be able to explain that. This was strange enough.

"You weren't yourself." He withdrew his arm and backed away. "You must be tired."

"Tired?" Mom smiled weakly and checked her watch. "I need to get back to my shift. Say your goodnights for now."

After her short visit with Dean, Fiona's face was already pinched with worry. Michael drew closer, touching her sleeve. The minion around her scattered and disappeared. She smiled up at him. If she wondered about my mom's strange behavior, it didn't show.

"I won't be long," he said. "You don't have to leave."

Fiona nodded.

"Hey, Mike." Dean forced a smile, but his face was tired and drawn.

"Heard you were attacked."

"Yeah. Stupid dog."

I let out my breath, relieved he thought it had been a dog, not a shadow—nothing supernatural. That was a good sign.

"Brutal," Michael said, but I could tell his focus was elsewhere. The light around him grew brighter and hotter, but the creatures on Dean held their grip. Dean winced.

Fiona hovered over him, bouncing nervously on her toes. "Are you okay?"

"Yeah," he said. "A bit tired is all."

Mom stood up. "The three of you should let him rest." She placed a hand on Dean's arm. "I'll send in the on-call nurse to give you something for the pain."

Once we left Dean's room, Michael told me he had to leave and gave me a quick kiss goodbye. And though I didn't ask, I already wondered when I'd see him again.

Halfway down the empty hall, he cloaked himself, until he was invisible to everyone but me, for I could always see him. And with his sword drawn, he returned to Dean's room.

CHAPTER SIX

They released Jesse from the hospital in the morning, so Heather skipped class to spend the day with him. Fiona moped through her day until Dean called at noon with good news of his own: he'd apparently made a "miraculous recovery" and was on his way home. She was thrilled. I wished I could tell her what Michael had done. He deserved our thanks.

Truth was, I envied my friends. I wanted my boyfriend back too—as if the angels would let him off duty. These past few weeks, we'd spent so little time together that I felt as though I was dating a ghost. And I worried, constantly, about him getting hurt. But when a bouquet of stargazer lilies arrived—complete with a note saying "Sorry I couldn't be there!"—my fears abated. If he had time to send flowers, things had to be okay.

While my friends reunited with their boyfriends, I spent the evening searching for the *hamsa* necklace. It wasn't exactly easy to replace. Last I'd checked, Fatima's store didn't have any, and this one had been blessed by more than one type of priest. So I scoured every corner of the house with a flashlight and was contemplating checking the field outside the school, when the light caught a sparkle under the bed. The necklace must have fallen off in my sleep. I checked the clasp, but it was fine. After seeing my mom possessed by a minion the day before, I decided she should have it. After all, I had Michael. And when he wasn't around, I spent most of my time at school or at home, both of which were protected spaces. Giving her the necklace was the only way I could think of to keep her safe.

When I handed it to her at the dinner table, the rhinestones sparkled under the dining room's halogen lights. "What's this?" Mom asked. "It's not my birthday or anything."

"It's for luck. You should wear it." I motioned to her navy blue scrubs that matched the necklace's faux sapphires. "It matches your outfit."

"It is pretty. I've seen you wear it before." She hesitated, examining the silver chain, and for a moment I thought she might give it back. She'd always put us—her kids—before herself.

"I want you to have it." I leaned forward in my seat. She had to keep it. I couldn't bear to think of my mom having minions on her ever again.

She opened the clasp with her thumb and fastened it around her neck. Relief poured through me. "Thank you." She smiled and touched my cheek. "You've got a kind heart."

I swallowed back the emotion her sentiment brought up in me and smiled back. "Thanks, Mom. Glad you like it."

***

I saw Michael again on Friday, when he slipped through the door at the start of English class. He had what was becoming a typical look for him: hair still damp from the shower, hollows of his cheeks more pronounced, a look of fatigue in his eyes. But today its volume had been turned up. When he took his seat in the row beside me, he moved slowly, his posture rigid as he folded himself into the desk. Even our teacher, Mr. Bidwell, noticed. His attention fixed on Michael, but instead of calling on him to read, he asked Jesse. We were studying one of my favorite Shakespeare poems, Sonnet 116, "Let me not to the marriage of true minds admit impediments."

As Jesse read, Michael fidgeted beside me, cracking his neck and tapping his foot. At first, I thought he was being rude. But when he didn't participate in the discussion afterward, despite how much it would contribute to our grade, I knew something was bothering him.

After class, he rushed to my side. "We need to talk." He nodded in Mr. Bidwell's direction. "Alone."

"Gee, abrupt much?" I asked, unintentionally sarcastic. His jitters in class must have rubbed off on me. "Why so tense?"

"You've no idea." Taking me by the arm, he led me into an empty classroom across the hall and eased the door shut behind us. The space was mostly used for language classes. Travel posters of Italy, France, and Spain lined the walls, and a collection of dictionaries and language texts had been stacked along the shelves.

Rising to my toes, I gave him a quick kiss on the cheek. "The flowers were a nice gesture, though. Thanks."

He caught me by the waist and the familiar heat of his touch blazed through me. "What flowers?"

"Lilies, the pink ones I like." I scanned his face for signs of recognition and found none. "You didn't send them?"

He frowned. "Wish I had."

I'd assumed they were from him, though there was no name on the card. The last anonymous gift I'd received was when Fatima had given me the *hamsa*. Perhaps she'd sent flowers to make up for her mood the other day. I made a mental note to ask her about it later.

"I've been in San Diego, fighting through the night,"

he added.

I felt a wave of sadness for him. How hard it would be to never have time off. I also remembered what his colleagues had told him about us. "Is that the real reason? You're not avoiding me because I'm an 'unnecessary distraction', are you?"

He blinked as though I'd slapped him, making me immediately regret what I'd said. "Of course not!" Sighing, he raked a hand through his hair, its crown of waves arcing in every direction. "I'm sorry, but I have about a thousand things to focus on right now." He lowered his voice. "No matter how much I'd rather be here with you."

"Yeah, well. It's been crazy around here, too," I said. When he put it that way, I felt like a selfish jerk. "What did you want to talk about?"

"It can wait." Brightening, he gave my shoulder an affectionate squeeze. "Come on, let's get out of here."

Our next class had already started, so Michael cloaked me in his halo so we wouldn't be seen. As the tingling sense of peace enveloped me, I let out an involuntary sigh of relief.

"I know," Michael said, responding to what I was feeling. "I usually prefer being cloaked."

Staying close to me, he eased the classroom door open, so that any onlookers would think it had moved by itself. We headed down the empty hallway to my locker, so I could gather my things and put on a jacket.

Once we were outside, Michael released me from his halo and staggered into me. I caught him around the waist. He groaned under his breath.

"Is everything okay?" I asked.

He smiled, but it didn't touch his eyes. "Guess I'm more worn out than I thought."

I draped his arm around my shoulder and guided him to his car, and he clicked the fob to unlock the doors. After I helped him inside, my shoulder came away bloody. He'd bled through his hoodie. I opened it to find his white shirt soaked in blood. When he couldn't sit still in class, it wasn't because he was tense. He was in pain.

"Oh my God!" I yelped. "You're hurt!" I grabbed the base of his shirt, tugging and fumbling with the buttons so I could check the wound.

He clasped my hands. "Mia. Stop. I'm fine."

"No, you're not," I insisted. "You're bleeding. Tell me what happened."

"Like I said, I was fighting all night. That, healing Dean, and the flight back hasn't given me time to recuperate. It's been non-stop. The battle was almost over, but then the wound opened. There are limits. I just forget... I used to be able to do so much more."

"You came right to school?"

"I stopped at home to rest, but..." He brushed his fingers along my cheek. "I needed to know you were all right."

"I am." His concern for me was so genuine it brought a lump to my throat. Here he was injured, and worrying about me. Unnecessary or not, we were each other's mutual distraction. "Are you okay to drive yourself home?"

He nodded, catching my hand and squeezing it. "I'd rather you came with me."

I wasn't worried about blowing off class. It was the first time he'd ever shown he needed me, that I could help him. "I'll drive."

LISA VOISIN

CHAPTER SEVEN

I helped Michael unfold himself from the passenger side of his VW Golf GTI and followed him along the stone path to his house. A few steps in, he faltered, so I rushed to his side and offered my shoulder to lean on, ignoring him when he tried to wave me off. As we shuffled inside, I guided him to the living room of his basement suite, so he could sit down. But at the click of shoes on the kitchen tiles behind us, Michael stiffened and the motion made him wince.

A middle-aged woman in a gray suit and blue blouse emerged from his kitchenette, carrying a paper grocery bag. She had the same thick, dark hair as Michael, which she wore pulled back into a French twist—only hers was tinged with gray.

"Hi, Mum," he said, flanking her from the right so his wounded side faced away from her. He gave her a quick kiss on the cheek. "What are you doing home so early?"

She smiled at him and rubbed a berry-colored lipstick spot from her kiss off the side of his face. "My hearing was postponed today, so I went grocery shopping and picked up some staples for you." She glanced at her watch. "It's early still. Why aren't you in class?"

"We've got a study period," he said.

She nodded in my direction. "Who's your friend?"

Michael introduced us, and remembering his blood was still on me, I grinned at her, slipped out of my jacket, and wiped my fingers on my jeans before shaking her hand. "Nice to meet you, Mrs. Fontaine."

I studied her face, hoping that, as a lawyer, she wouldn't read my body language as shifty.

"Katharine, please," she corrected warmly, and I let myself relax. "Will you be joining us for dinner tonight?"

I glanced at Michael, not sure how to answer.

"We haven't made our plans yet, Mum," he said.

"All right then, if you want to join us, come on up. Your father is making Thai food, and you know how he always makes more than the two of us can eat."

When she left, Michael let out his breath and trudged to his bedroom. I hovered in the living room wanting to leave him some privacy, even though all that separated us was a bookshelf.

"That was close," I said. "She could've noticed your injury, but she didn't."

"Yeah, it was lucky." He gripped the bookshelf for balance and shifted his weight from one foot to the other, as he slid out of his shoes.

"Did you keep her from seeing it?" I asked.

"You mean, did I enthrall her?" He took off his jacket and the movements made him wince. Underneath, his dark blue shirt had soaked through, and the fabric clung to his chest. I hovered in the living room, wanting to help him again, but wasn't sure if I should. "You know I wouldn't do that, right?"

"I didn't mean that." I would have noticed the shine around him that came with enthrallment. But I trusted him not to use it. "I thought maybe you'd cloaked it."

"Not specifically. I stood at an angle that hid it, but other than that, people only see what they want to, and it's become second nature to hide what I am."

I couldn't imagine hiding my true identity from everyone, and yet, here I was concealing Michael's to protect my friends and family, the same way he was. Though I understood why it was necessary, that didn't make doing it any easier. "Maybe it's because your mom treats you like an adult. She's not all nosy and stuff."

"I *am* an adult. I'm eighteen, remember? Besides..." His movements careful, he rummaged through one of his dresser drawers and then looked up at me and smiled. "I'm mature for my age."

"I wouldn't be so sure about that!" I joked. "Given how old you really are!" I truly had no idea how old that was. I'd lost count after nine thousand years.

"Details." He waved a hand dismissively and pulled a bath towel from the drawer. "Care to join me?"

"Where? The *shower*?" I froze. The idea of seeing him without his clothes on, all soapy and gorgeous, hardly freaked me out—other than being too appealing a thought. It was the idea of being *seen*. Sure. We'd been naked together before, but that was *in another lifetime*. I was in a different body. And that changed everything.

"Your expression alone made that suggestion worthwhile," he said with a wink.

I collapsed onto the huge, off white sofa. "That's got to be against the rules." Though I still didn't know exactly what the rules were, I was pretty sure it had to be a long list, possibly so old it had been carved on stone tablets.

"Nope. Don't think they thought of that one. They must lack my imagination."

His words set my insides on fire, making me blush. *My* imagination was intact, and I really wanted to take him up on his offer, but there was no way I'd risk his redemption. We had to be careful.

Draping the towel over his shoulders, he cleared his throat. "I'm going to clean the wound. You wanted to help." He raised an eyebrow at me and, despite his earlier humor, I noticed the strain around his eyes. "Or was that a ruse to get me alone?"

I got up from the couch and followed him as he limped to the bathroom. "Hey, you invited me. Remember?"

"I did, didn't I?" His lips pulled into a grin. "Must be the other way 'round, then."

In the small bathroom, he sat on the edge of the tub with slow, deliberate movements. I helped him ease out of his ruined shirt. The blood had soaked through drenched bandages and hadn't yet started to dry. I braced myself for whatever damage he had underneath, knowing it was going to be severe.

He tossed his shirt into the sink and motioned to the faucet. "Would you run the tap? Cold water works best, and the less blood my mom finds on my clothes, the better. Don't want her to worry."

"Maybe she should." Not sure whether to be impressed by his laundry skills or horrified by the fact that his knowledge of blood stains came from experience, I closed the plug and twisted the tap. Crimson clouds bloomed in the frigid water.

"I don't want to worry anyone." When I turned to him, he grazed the back of his hand along my cheek. His fingertips were stained a deep red. "Especially not you."

I swallowed the tightness in my throat. "I know."

His gauze bandages were completely sopped, so I helped him peel off the tape and wrapped them in tissue before throwing them away. I'd seen enough blood these past few days to last a lifetime. But the jagged, diagonal tear across his ribs and stomach deflated me. At least his organs hadn't been sliced. No matter how glib he'd been about healing fast, if something pierced his heart, there was no way he'd survive. I shook my head, trying to clear the thought. These past few weeks, I'd been worried about him for a reason.

He ran the bathtub faucet, but as he twisted, his cut dripped more blood. He paled, pressing his lips together as he leaned over to wet the towel. I could see why he wanted my help.

"Here, let me," I said.

I held the cloth under the stream of water and wrung it out before handing it back to him.

Dabbing his wound, he hissed air through clenched teeth. The cold, or the shock, pulled his bare skin into tiny bumps.

"What happened?" I asked. "Who did this to you?"

"A soldier demon. You've seen them before with Damiel. You know, ugly, charcoal-colored minion with red eyes. But this one had wings…" He pulled his lips tight, focusing. "And a sword, obviously. So it's higher up on the food chain. It happened a few days ago."

"You mean the incident I tuned into?"

"Yeah," he said. "It really shouldn't be affecting me this much."

I wanted to know more but didn't press it. A dark stain had seeped through the light blue towel. "It's not closing," I said. "Didn't you already heal it?"

"I did. Several times," he said. "It was fine for a few days, but then it reopened. I've never seen anything like this before."

"Perhaps the others can help? Arielle?"

He shook his head. "She's in Tucson. Let me try again." He waved his hand over his stomach. Golden light streamed from his fingertips, and the shredded flesh seamed together; the puckering skin began to heal. But within seconds, it burst open, dripping blood as though newly cut, and Michael let out a deep, guttural moan. "Dammit."

The air filled with the smell of a freshly lit match. I sniffed. "What's that?"

"Sulfur. Coming from the wound." Beads of sweat formed on his brow as he hovered his fingers over the gash. "Burns more each time."

"Something's wrong," I clasped his hands, pulling his fingers away so he wouldn't touch his injury. "You need help. Use the network."

"Mia, I—"

"If you don't do it, I'll…" I was going to say I'd do it myself, but wasn't sure I could. Though I'd inadvertently connected to the network before, I hadn't accessed it on my own since I'd used it to help Damiel. And at the time, it seemed more the network had reached for me than the other way around. "I'll tell your mom," I threatened.

With a sigh of resignation, Michael closed his eyes as the energy around him flickered and blazed through the room. A few seconds later, I heard a faint popping sound and, with a flash of light, the silver-haired angel I'd seen in the woods, Turiel, appeared in the bathroom doorway. Up close, his face was more pretty than handsome, with the same feral quality I'd seen in Arielle. Perhaps all angels had it.

Turiel's halo flared and the air crackled around him. I strained to listen via the network, but all I heard was static.

"Speak out loud, Turiel, so Mia can hear," Michael said. "She's a friend."

"She's more than a friend and you know it," Turiel snapped, then stopped himself and raised both his hands in front of him, as though admitting his mistake. "Not that I'm judging you."

"Of course not. *You'd* never do that." Michael's words dripped with sarcasm.

Turiel narrowed his eyes. "What are you insinuating?"

"How'd you…? Aren't you supposed to knock or something?" I asked, trying to redirect the growing tension in the tiny space. The idea of angels walking through walls the way ghosts did shattered any illusions I had about privacy. It was bad enough the network made it possible for them to see our every move when Michael was on duty, but appearing out of thin air? I hadn't counted on that.

The angel's mouth fell open, making him look as bewildered as I felt.

"What's with him?" I asked Michael.

"He hasn't spoken to a human in a thousand years," Michael explained.

"Yes, well…" Turiel cleared his throat and, folding his arms across his chest, answered my question, "We usually appear whenever or wherever we're needed."

"You mean teleportation?" I turned to Michael. "You can do that?"

"Not me. Arielle can, but she wouldn't intrude on you that way. It would startle you," he said, and I realized that I'd never actually noticed Arielle arrive. It was as though my attention had been directed elsewhere—usually on Michael. Lifting the now blood-spotted towel, he grimaced and bit his lip. "She has manners, you see."

"I have manners." Turiel lifted his chin and inhaled sharply, his expression registering alarm. "Sulfur dioxide. Someone's used a cursed weapon on you."

CHAPTER EIGHT

"You mean an angel killer?" Michael leaned over the bathtub to rinse out his towel and blood seeped from his wound. I rushed to steady him, to stanch the flow, but he righted himself before I got there. "Haven't seen one of those for a while. Thought they were extinct."

"No one knows for sure," Turiel said. "They're extremely rare, but one turns up every few hundred years."

Michael was still clutching the stained compress, so I grabbed a face cloth from the rack and wet it under the faucet. "Cursed weapon? Angel killer? What's going on?"

Turiel blinked his violet eyes once in my direction, his lashes the color of steel, then said to Michael, "How many times have you tried to heal it?"

"Three, I think," I answered on Michael's behalf, handing him the fresh damp cloth and taking the old one. I wasn't going to let Turiel ignore me, no matter how hard he tried.

"Five," Michael said.

My shoulders tightened up to my ears. *Five times?* It was worse than I thought. I dropped the soiled bath towel in the tub. "Is anyone going to tell me what an angel killer is? Aside from the obvious, I mean."

Turiel looked down at his white leather shoes. It was Michael who replied. "It's a sword, one of the few things that can destroy an angel. They're very rare, because they're made from one of our own swords—which is no easy feat, considering the touch of one of our weapons will incinerate a lesser demon." He nodded in my direction then locked his gaze with Turiel's. "I wouldn't ignore Mia, if I were you. She can see you as well as I can."

"So I gathered when she spotted me in the woods." Turiel turned to me, bowing his head. "Forgive me. It's been a very long time since I met a prophet."

My knees went limp. "A *what*?"

"A human who can see angels," Michael explained. Was it me, or had his face gone paler than even a few moments ago? "I said you were an ally."

Ally, I could handle, but *prophet*? I hoped it didn't involve soapboxes or sermons on the street. "You left out a few details."

Turiel slid his long arms out of his white leather jacket, keeping his focus on Michael. "Did the flesh close each time you healed it?"

"Completely. The first time, it stayed closed for half a week, then a little over a day. Now, it opens immediately. Burns more each time."

Turiel crouched in front of Michael to examine him. Not wanting to hover, I tried to keep busy, wringing out the wet towel and draping it over the shower rod, then squeezing out Michael's shirt. Bloody, rust-colored water filled the sink. I released the drain, grasped the bar of soap, and scrubbed. "Can you heal it?" I asked Turiel.

"Depends what kind of curse it is." He draped his jacket over the closed lid of the toilet and sat across from Michael. "Who did this to you?"

"Just a soldier demon, so I didn't think much of it at first," Michael said. "What I want to know is how it got a cursed weapon."

"What did the sword look like?" Turiel asked.

"It was moving pretty fast, but from what I could see, it was blackened steel."

"Any inscriptions on it?"

Squinting, Michael pinched the bridge of his nose as though the pain was making it hard to focus. "Runes on the handle, maybe. Not much different from my own."

Turiel stood again and scratched his head, his mouth pressing into a hard line. "How similar was it to your own sword? Did it have the same inscriptions?"

"I don't know. I wasn't exactly reading at the time." Michael's voice was clipped.

I moved in to check on him, but he waved me off. I needed to keep busy, to be useful, so I rinsed his shirt and scrubbed it again. The cold water from the tap chilled my fingers. "Does it make a difference?" I asked Turiel's reflection in the mirror.

"Cursed weapons are extremely rare. All of them should have been destroyed in the Great War—long before Michael fell. So I have no idea what we're dealing with, or even if this is an angel killer. Any inscription may give us a clue how to heal him, providing he can be healed at all," he explained to me, then turned to Michael. "The exact same inscriptions as your own sword might mean a targeted weapon."

"Targeted?" I butted in, reeling from the gravity of his words. "You mean for Michael personally?"

"Perhaps."

Still seated on the tub, Michael leaned against the granite-tiled stall and huffed out his breath. "Hadn't thought of that." His skin was definitely paler.

"But who would do such a thing?" The shirt now clean, I wrung it out and reached to hang it on the shower rod.

Michael caught my gaze. "I have my fair share of enemies in Hell."

"No more than the rest of us," said Turiel.

"Think I didn't make a few more while I was there?"

"Demons hate us all equally." Turiel's demeanor

remained calm, even as his hands closed into fists. "I can't imagine it being easy for you. How can you expect to uphold our laws if you don't respect them, or think they even apply to you?"

Michael's face flushed with anger. "Oh, so that's what this is about." He sprang to his feet, but the effort weakened him. He squeezed the side of the stall as he eased himself back down. "You didn't think I should be allowed a second chance."

"Enough bickering," I snapped at both of them, and spun to face Turiel. "He's hurt. Can you help him or not?"

Turiel frowned. "Not the usual way." With a sigh, he sat beside Michael on the side of the tub and ran his fingers under the tap. "The way angel killers work is to erode our souls and destroy everything angelic about us, so we can't regenerate or heal." He soaped his hands and arms to the elbow, like a surgeon scrubbing in. "Because we're essentially made of soul, when the soul dies, the angel is destroyed. Whatever shadow or imprint remains is what powers the sword. It's not uncommon for an angel killer to carry the desiccated souls of, say, a dozen angels. The more souls it takes, the more powerful the sword, and the more quickly it can kill." He twisted off the tap and shook his hands, searching for something to dry them on.

With a grimace, he settled for a wad of toilet paper. "An angel killer uses our healing abilities against us. So the more he heals himself, the more the poison from the curse spreads. But lucky for Michael, he heals differently than the rest of us."

"You said the more he heals himself?" I tried to make sense of all this—poison, curses, swords that trapped the souls of angels. I dredged my brain for some kind of loophole. "So, can you heal him?"

Turiel shook his head. "It doesn't work that way. The injury Michael has would have killed any other angel by now. The curse reaches beyond our healing ability. However," Turiel paused, turning to Michael. "Being part human must have given you some strength against the cursed sword, so what would be a death sentence for one of us might not be the case for you. This may be where your rebellion pays off. Who knows? You may recover yet."

"It could take weeks to heal that gash!" I didn't like the odds or Turiel's uncertainty, not to mention the whole condescending bit about Michael's rebellion.

"What about the poison?" Michael asked. If the thought of his own death fazed him, it didn't show. "How long do I have?"

"It's already been in your system a while, and you're doing remarkably well, considering. So it's hard to say. Perhaps a few days. Unless, we..." Turiel stood and said to me. "Do you happen to know your blood type?"

"It's O negative. I typed it in AP Bio last year. Why? What's Michael's?"

"Michael's A negative. You should be compatible."

"Oh no you don't," Michael said, but his voice was flat. His shoulders drooped, and he could hardly sit on his own. No wonder, given how much blood he'd lost, how much he was still losing.

Something had to be done. But this was beyond my ability to help, and if I didn't keep busy, I was going start screaming. I folded the towel from the shower rod and handed it to Michael. I then took the cloth covering his wound and immersed it in the sink.

"I can see you're healthy enough, Mia, but how much do you love him, really?" Turiel asked. "I can't quite sense—"

"What?" Now Turiel was sensing me? Michael knew how I felt, but it wasn't as though the other angels encouraged—or even approved of—our relationship.

"That's none of your business, Turiel!" Michael tried to stand but teetered. He would have lost his balance completely if Turiel hadn't caught him under the shoulder.

"You know there's power in blood, especially a

prophet's blood." Having steadied Michael against the wall, Turiel backed away. "I can't use my power here, so I'll need to rely on ancient magic. Love is strong magic, and the more she loves you—"

"Keep her out of it." Michael shot him a deadly look. "I'm serious."

Turiel wiped his hand across his brow. "I don't want to do this anymore than you do."

"You don't even know it'll work," Michael said. "You know blood magic opens the door to other things."

I glanced up at the two of them in the mirror. "You mean, it's like gateway magic? Will it lead me on a bender or something?"

"No, Mia." Michael shuffled to the doorframe and leaned against it. "But it's minimally unpredictable. I've never done it before. All I know for sure is that your soul is activated with the magic, which is the equivalent of giving Hell your GPS coordinates so the demons can find you."

"Don't they already have that? Considering what happened with Damiel?"

"They don't know that was you. I've been hiding you as best I can. And if anything happens, I won't be able to shield you anymore." He gestured to his wound. "Not in this state."

"I'll shield her," Turiel said. "I've been assigned to her."

Michael bristled. "Since when?"

"Since the Grigori Council made her my ward." Turiel sighed. "We really don't have time to discuss this right now."

Michael's legs buckled and he collapsed to the floor. "Does Arielle know? Is she..?"

I dropped the cloth and dashed to Michael's side, bracing myself against him. "Let me help. I'll do everything I can."

"It's the best chance you've got," Turiel said.

Michael pushed himself back up. "I think I need to lie down."

Turiel got the other side, and together we walked Michael to his bed so he could rest. The effort wore him out. As soon as we got him horizontal, his eyelids fluttered shut.

"I'll do it," I whispered to Turiel, so Michael wouldn't hear. "Whatever it is. Just tell me what you need."

"Donate a pint of your blood. That's all," he replied. "Oh, and recite a short incantation. I'll help you get it right."

"You're not going to make him drink it or smear it on his wounds or anything gross like that?"

Turiel curled his lip in distaste. "Goodness, no! While washing the wounds in virgin blood might be how they did it in ancient times, a transfusion would suffice. It's much more efficient. Since he's already lost a fair bit, it would even be helpful."

My cheeks burned from the reference to 'virgin'. Did Turiel know *that* too? "Maybe we should go to the hospital?" I offered. "Tell them I want to be your donor, that you're worried about contamination."

"No. We can't." Michael opened his eyes and motioned to the wound. "How do I explain this without involving the police? It's obviously from a blade. They'd think I was in a knife fight and keep an eye on me, and that's the last thing I need."

"No, the last thing you need is to die," Turiel corrected. "Going to the hospital won't work, because the one handling the blood needs to speak the incantation. I'll suture the wound."

"It's too late for that." As a nurse's daughter, I knew stitches had to be given within a day, and Michael's injury was over a week old.

"It's fine."

I frowned at Turiel. Though he was an angel, I wasn't sure whether to trust him or not. "Do you even know what you're doing?" I wished Arielle were here.

Turiel sniffed indignantly. "My knowledge of human anatomy is excellent. I've been a healer since the dawn of the human race."

The dawn of the human race? My mind flashed to bloodletting bowls and the ancient metal blades in my history texts, the horrors of germ-infested conditions. "Yeah, but do you know modern medicine? What about infection?"

"I know what I'm doing. I can't touch that curse, but my healing abilities can freshen the wound and lessen the risks. The spell should handle the rest."

"Fine," I said, though I still wasn't sure. "We need real equipment. Do you know where to get some?"

Turiel shook his head. "Angels don't usually need such things."

"I know a place," I said. Michael's eyes had closed again, his breathing slow and rhythmic. I checked the cloth covering his stomach and then pulled a blanket over him. "But is he going to be okay if we leave him alone for a few minutes?"

"Of course. We won't be long."

"Then let's get this over with."

CHAPTER NINE

Turiel touched my arm near the elbow and told me to think about the place I'd mentioned. And in a blink, we teleported directly into a supply closet at the hospital my mom worked at. I'd had no idea what was coming, and the immediate change of scenery left me dizzy and jarred, like waking up in a different place than where you fell asleep, only worse. My stomach hated the sensation.

Turiel immediately set to work and rifled through the boxes of equipment lining the metal racks. "We shouldn't take these things."

"It's for a good cause." I braced myself against the wall and swallowed back feelings of nausea. I wished the damn room would stop spinning.

"It's still theft." He reached into the boxes and pulled out the equipment we needed: an IV tube and bag, some needles, two pairs of non-latex gloves.

"At least we're not stealing drugs," I said. "Besides, it's the one place I could think of where we could get everything we needed."

"That's hardly consolation!" He grabbed a box of gauze bandages and tape and stuffed it into his pockets. "I'd feel better if we paid for it."

"Fine." I pulled a crumpled twenty-dollar bill from my pocket and dropped it on the shelf in front of him. "Is that better?"

He handed me back my twenty. "It wouldn't go to the right place. You'd be better off donating to a charity."

I pocketed the money. "I'll donate it to the hospital children's fund, how's that?"

"Better," he said, reaching for my arm again. "Ready to go back?"

My stomach lurched in response, but I nodded anyway.

The return trip nauseated me even more. I swallowed the bile hitting the base of my throat and braced myself against the bedpost. Turiel released me from his halo and I staggered to the kitchen to get myself a glass of water. I took slow, measured sips as I waited for the dizziness to subside. When I returned to the living room, he was leaning over Michael's sleeping form.

"How do you want to do this?" I asked, keeping my voice down.

He placed the back of his hand on Michael's forehead as though he were a concerned parent checking a child's temperature. "He's burning up. The sooner we do this, the better. Sit down and put your feet up. It'll take a few minutes to collect your blood."

Rolling up my sleeve, I made my way over to the couch. "Are you sure there's no other way?"

"There is powerful magic in human blood. Ancient magic. Michael needs to become more human in order to fight this poison. This spell should tip the scales in that direction, so he can throw it off."

I didn't like the vagueness of his words, but I helped him hook up the tubing to the IV bag, and handed him the needle. "What if it doesn't work?"

Turiel left to wash his hands in the bathroom sink. When he returned, he put on the gloves and fastened a plain black necktie around my arm. "Make a fist." He tapped for a vein with the precision of a nurse and dabbed the inside of my elbow with a sterile wipe.

"Will it work?" I asked again.

The needle stung as he slid it into my arm.

"You can let go now," he said, loosening the tourniquet. "I don't know the exact weapon, but this is his best chance. He'll need to not use his powers for a few days while we trace the curse in our records and figure out where the sword came from."

"So, basically, you have no idea."

"Do you really expect me to? Considering how experimental Michael is? His very existence in a human form paves the way for other fallen angels to return. He's strong. I don't know if I could deal with where he's been." He shook his head. "I wouldn't write him off yet."

"Is that a tone of respect I hear, Turiel?" Awake again, Michael gave him a sleepy smile. "I'm touched."

Turiel readjusted the IV bag filling with my blood and placed it on the coffee table. "Mind you," he added. "I would never choose to fall the way he did."

"I hope, one day, I can live up to your expectations of me." Michael raised himself up on his elbows. Blood had already spotted the blanket.

"You should be resting," Turiel scolded. "You're going to make it worse."

Michael propped another pillow under his neck and leaned back. "Better?"

Without answering, Turiel readied the needle and suture thread and lifted the cloth. Michael watched in silence as Turiel waved a lit hand over the wound and then dabbed alcohol on the skin around it. Once the area was clean and, presumably, fresh, he let us know it was time to proceed with the stitches.

"Without anything for the pain?" I asked, wishing I'd thought of something. Even a topical anesthetic would've been better than nothing.

"There should be a box under the couch," Michael said. "Mia, can you reach for it?"

Taking care not to move or bump the needle in my arm, I felt under the sofa, found cardboard, and pulled it out. Inside was a half-empty bottle of alcohol. I held it up. "Tequila? Seriously?"

"It's been there awhile, since before the accident." With a shrug, he added, "I don't exactly go to parties anymore." The way he said it made me wonder if he actually missed his old life.

Last spring, Michael had been just a regular guy, a senior in high school. But when he crashed his motorcycle and wound up in a coma, his soul awakened. He remembered being an angel, with full angelic powers and abilities, not to mention memories that spanned thousands of years. Though it happened months before we met, I couldn't even imagine how strange the transition must have been for him.

Turiel frowned at him. "A little unorthodox, don't you think?"

"And blood magic isn't?" Michael held out his hand. "Besides, the transfusion will sober me up soon enough."

Turiel flicked his cloaked wings with the same attitude as a cat swishing its tail. The room shimmered. He reached for the fifth of tequila and gave it to Michael, unable to hide his disgust. "Don't take this being more human thing too far."

"I'm sure I could think of better things to do than get stitches." Michael opened the cap, took a long swig, and gasped. "Tastes worse than I remember."

"I don't think humans drink it for the taste." Needle in hand, Turiel leaned closer to the wound. His eyes locked with Michael's. "Ready?"

Michael nodded. Even after a few swigs of tequila, he grit his teeth and gripped the edge of his bedside table until his knuckles turned white. I couldn't watch. The idea of him in any kind of pain brought memories of the most gruesome past-life memory I'd ever had, the one of him losing his wings. They had been cut off thousands of years ago, but the recollection was still fresh in my mind. He'd become human then, and the infection from those wounds had nearly killed him.

Though he didn't seem to hold back his disdain for Michael under normal circumstances, Turiel was a patient, kind, and very efficient healer—a one-man, or one-angel, ER. Working quickly, he paused only to disconnect me from the IV bag, telling me to press where the needle had been so I wouldn't bruise. But I think he really did it because Michael had needed a break from getting stitches. His face had gone almost gray from shock.

Turiel tugged the last stitch into a knot and cut the suture. Once he'd finished bandaging Michael, he came over to me.

"How are you?" he asked, handing me a Band-Aid.

I applied the bandage, sitting up. But as soon as I stood, my head spun. "A little lightheaded."

"There's juice in the fridge," Michael offered.

"I'll get it." Turiel headed to the kitchen.

"I'm sorry you have to do this." Michael said.

"It's nothing. I'm donating a pint of blood." Now was not the time to think about the spell being unpredictable. It was going to work. It had to.

Turiel returned with a glass of orange juice. "This should replenish a bit of what you've lost. I can heal you in a few minutes, after the spell. I promise it's short and painless."

"As painless as opening the gates of Hell," Michael grumbled.

"She'll be fine. She's under all our protection," said Turiel. "Or are you so delusional as to think that you can protect her better than anyone else?"

"I've done fine so far."

"This lifetime, yes."

Michael stared at the wall, silenced by Turiel's words. It hardly seemed fair to bring up our past like that. I wanted to speak up, but my mind was foggy. My stomach growled.

I gulped back my juice. I could have eaten a whole steak, but the drink would have to do.

At least the dizziness stopped. "Okay, what do I do?"

Turiel inserted a fresh IV needle into Michael's hand, fastening it with tape. When he was done, he said to me over his shoulder, "You'll have to come over here. Can you walk on your own or do you need help?"

"I'm fine." I eased myself up and made my way over to Michael's bed.

"I can't touch him again until the transfusion is finished." Turiel held up the IV. "When you're done, fasten the tube in here." He held it up to show me how it connected to the IV needle.

"Okay. Got it."

"Repeat after me. I'll go slowly." Turiel took a step back, as though being near Michael might contaminate him. "Holy Mother, purify this heart and Heavenly Father, purify this soul."

The words seemed strange to me, as most religions referred to God as being male, but I went with it. "Holy Mother, purify this heart, and Heavenly Father, purify this soul."

Turiel smiled and his eyes lit a brilliant purple. The gossamer outline of his wings shimmered behind him. "'Let this blood from my heart heal this soul. Make him safe and well.'"

"Let this blood from my heart heal this soul. Make him safe and well."

Turiel nodded. "Now, attach it."

I fastened the tube in silence. When I was done, I asked. "That's it?"

"That's it." Still wearing the rubber gloves, Turiel nodded and then hung the IV bag on the lamp post beside the bed.

"I expected something more—I don't know—Catholic?"

"This spell predates Catholicism by far. Your

68

pronunciation was perfect, by the way."

"Thanks," I said. "English. Been speaking it a while."

"No, Mia," Michael said. "That was Khambhatian, the old language, a forerunner of Vedic Sanskrit. It was the language you spoke the very first time I met you, over nine thousand years ago."

The memory of Michael back then swirled through my thoughts. It was bad enough to have flashbacks of what I'd remembered with Arielle. Without her or Michael's help, new memories of that life were always visceral. They pulled at something deep inside me, as though I were a ball of yarn being unraveled in the reliving of it. This time, I was several months pregnant. The sun shone hot and bright on my skin as I drew water from the well. I had just poured some into a clay bowl to give the chickens, when I had a sense of dread, a blackness that brought me to my knees. I'd collapsed, thinking I'd fainted, that I would lose the baby, knowing that something terrible was about to happen. It would, but there was no baby. What grew inside me was neither human nor angelic, but monstrous. Four months later, giving birth to it had killed me.

My knees buckled. Turiel rolled the computer chair over so I could sit down before I fell.

"This isn't the first time I've been on Hell's radar, is it?" I asked, my focus still on the past life; the memory bleached like old bones. "They knew the moment I got pregnant."

"I had no idea what was going on," Michael said. "You got sick. After you died, Damiel came and tried to take your body. He was going to use it for a ritual that would sentence your soul to Hell. Demons used to do that all the time, take the bodies of the dead before they could be buried, before the soul had a chance to go, and bind them in a ritual. He and I fought, but I didn't have enough strength. He'd taken yours, and all the other angels turned their backs on both of us."

"That's not fair!" Turiel objected. "We couldn't…"

"Interfere in my choices. I know," Michael continued. "When Damiel killed me, I had a chance to repent, but he convinced me that since I had killed my own child..." His words slowed, as though the ancient lies weighted each one. The child had never been Michael's. It was a demon born of Damiel's own assault on me. "That I should go in your place. If I did, your soul would be saved. I knew it wouldn't bring you back, but it was better than knowing you'd be in Hell."

Closing his eyes, Michael leaned back onto the pillows as though dredging up these painful memories sapped him faster than we could pump my blood into him. My mind spun as I recalled the many consequences of that life. Not only had Michael left Heaven to be with me, but he had sacrificed his own soul to save mine. Because Damiel had tricked him.

Damiel had lied so much. What was another falsehood in an existence of deceit?

"When you forgave Damiel and he accepted his redemption," Turiel said to me. "It was the ultimate act of good over evil." He guided me away from Michael's bedside, toward the couch. "You sent a message to Hell, loud and clear, that everything they did could be undone. Since then, the number and intensity of attacks have increased."

"Do you think Michael's injury has anything to do with what we did to Damiel?" I asked.

"We don't know. We suspect all the skirmishes in our region are related. Now there's a soldier demon with access to a powerfully cursed sword. Something's afoot. It's simply a matter of time before the pieces come together."

If things were getting worse, more people could get hurt the way Jesse and Dean had been. What about my other friends? My family? "There has to be something we can do. Couldn't we warn people?"

Turiel's pretty, boyish features suddenly looked ancient.

"Last time we tried that, it was total mayhem. Back then, all they had was parchment, but people still theorize the end of the world because of what was written." He shuddered. "Preaching on street corners about the end of days."

I smiled at Turiel's cynicism, in spite of myself. That answered any concerns I had about prophets on soapboxes. Clearly, Turiel wasn't a fan. "But if they knew angels existed—"

He held up his hand dismissively. "Tried that."

I sighed. It was clear this discussion was going nowhere.

Neither of us spoke as Turiel cleaned up, gathering the gloves and the cotton swabs and tossing them in the garbage. The sound of Michael's long, rhythmic breaths filled the room. He'd fallen asleep.

I sat up. "How soon will he heal?"

"I don't know. But needless to say, he won't be on duty until he's well again."

"Where's Arielle?" I wished I was talking to her instead. Though Turiel was helping, the obvious tension between him and Michael tangled my nerves.

"I'm not your enemy, Mia, nor am I unfeeling."

"Oh?" I could be blunt, too. "Michael told me the other angels think I'm an unnecessary distraction—do you? He's done everything he can to keep me safe."

Turiel sighed and took a seat on the sofa beside me. "Including sacrificing his own soul. We can't let his emotions for you lead him to his own destruction. It's reckless—a conflict of interest."

Reckless! Conflict of interest? I wished I could slap him. "So you think it's my fault?"

"No, but his humanity leads him to make foolish mistakes. He's not as detached as he should be, and he needs to focus on his recovery."

"And then what?"

He frowned down at his clasped hands. "Only time will

tell."

"Tell what?" Michael eased himself up to a sitting position, the color returning to his face.

"How you'll heal." Turiel stood. "Perhaps I should go. My work here is done. I'll keep an eye on both of you until backup arrives."

Michael nodded his thanks and, with a faint popping sound, Turiel blinked out of the room. I stared at the space he'd just occupied in front of the bookshelf and wondered if I'd ever get used to angels appearing and disappearing like that.

"How are you feeling?" I asked Michael.

Behind him, the gossamer outline of light cloaking his wings faded as he rubbed the back of his head with his tethered hand. He made a motion to stand, but noticed the line leading to the bag of blood. "I guess you'll have to come to me."

"Turiel wasn't exactly thrilled to find me here." I perched myself on the side of his bed. "He calls your feelings for me, quote, 'a conflict of interest'."

Michael shook his head and frowned. "Ignore him. Turiel filters everything he sees through a list of rules longer than my arm." Then, with a smile, he reached over a tucked a loose strand of hair behind my ear. "Hey, we're finally alone. My plan worked."

That made me laugh. "A clever ruse indeed!"

"Seriously, though." He ran his free hand along the back of my neck, and my spine ignited like a lit fuse. Leaning in, he rested his forehead against mine and whispered, "All my memories of you have been written on my soul. They spent thousands of years trying to torture them out of me—but they couldn't take them. I kept every detail."

His words stole my breath. Our last life together had been short-lived. Though I'd forgotten our story in death, the moment I saw him again, all the feelings had returned.

"And," he continued. "The one thing that kept me

going was the thought of you. The thought that someday, I would see you again. You've been good for me. There, in my heart, when nothing else was."

His eyes shone a crystalline blue as they searched mine, and I saw an ache in him so palpable and dark it reminded me how much he'd suffered, the kind of life—or afterlife—he'd had. He'd sacrificed his soul for mine. Though Arielle told me of the torture he'd endured, he never spoke of it. But every once in a while I saw traces of wounds that made the cuts he had now fade in comparison. I wished with everything I had to take that pain away.

"Too intense?" he asked.

"No." I whispered. I wasn't foolish enough to believe I could undo millennia of suffering, but maybe, just maybe, I could alleviate it.

Easing my fingers into his hair, I brought his lips to mine, gently, not sure if it was right. When he kissed me back, I sensed he'd needed this as much as I did, if not more. Twining an arm around my neck, he leaned back, turning until I lay on the bed facing him. His lips grazed my throat, the side of my neck, sending a warm rush through me, awakening feelings I'd suppressed for weeks. It seemed like forever since the last time we'd been together, and now we were in a bed. His bed. Alone. We moved in a careful yet urgent dance, my hands exploring his chest, avoiding the bandages and tubes attached to him, while he touched my cheek, the side of my neck. His energy brushed along my skin and tingled through me in a dance of its own.

Stroking the sides of my waist, his fingers inched under my shirt, and the touch of his skin on mine made me tremble. Wanting more, I pressed my fingers into the muscles of his back and kissed the side of his neck, the line of his collar bone. With a soft sound, he raised my mouth to his, kissing me again. A golden light surrounded us, around me in particular. His energy flickered and faded.

Then he sucked in his breath and pulled away.

"Sorry!" I leapt back, embarrassed. Energy thrummed through my body as my feet found the floor. "Are you okay? Did I hurt you?" He needed to recover and here we were making out. *I am a terrible girlfriend.*

He sat up, pinching the bridge of his nose with his bandaged hand. "No. It's not you. It's…" His voice broke into a grunt of pain. He shifted, leaning forward, and I tried not to stare at the sinewy muscles rippling down his back. But I couldn't help noticing the change in him. The golden flicker of light behind his shoulder blades—from wings that could be uncloaked at any moment—was gone; so was the grid of blue light. His halo no longer shimmered around him. Sadness pulled at my throat. He was human now, vulnerable. We both were.

"You're in pain! Should I call Turiel?"

"No. I'm fine. It's the blood working. The tequila's worn off is all." He pressed his lips together until they turned white. "When I go to reach for the network, I can't—not the same. I'm becoming more human… Dammit. Is it too much to ask to be alone with you for a few minutes? No battles. No network. No other angels dropping by to check in on us."

The pressure in the air changed, and with that popping sound, Turiel appeared in the living room. "Is everything all right?"

"Use the door, Turiel." Michael leaned back on the bed with a groan. "Did you call him?" he asked me.

"She's my assignment." Turiel glided across the living room. "I sensed her distress."

Turiel glanced at me and my face heated at the thought of what other feelings of mine he'd been sensing. "Michael's hurt."

"I'm fine." Michael stood, but at Turiel's scornful look, he picked up the almost empty blood bag and held it over his head. "Better?" Despite his irritation, he moved sluggishly. Dark rings had formed around his eyes. The spell was probably the only thing keeping him awake. He collapsed beside me on the couch and placed the bag on the back of the sofa, above his heart. Stretching out his legs, he rested his feet on the coffee table.

"I've called for Arielle as backup. She's surpassingly familiar with your situation," Turiel said. "There's a lot going on, and from what I can tell, it revolves around the two of you."

The heaviness of his words landed on me, weighting my thoughts. He was saying that Michael and I were in danger, and none of us knew who or what was coming. Michael's strength was waning by the minute. And from his haunted expression, I could tell he was remembering what had happened in our past life the last time he lost his strength. Damiel had attacked, and the consequences had been fatal for both of us.

Michael would do everything he could to protect me, but it was wrong to expect him to, even if he was an angel. I needed to be able to take care of things myself.

Michael focused his attention back on Turiel. "You said you'd called Arielle. Any idea when she'll be here?"

A woman's silken voice came from behind us. "About now."

I spun around to face her. With her blond hair and long, lean frame, she had all the beauty of a supermodel, and was more angelic than anyone I'd ever known—even Turiel with all his stuffiness couldn't touch her grace or dignity. Other than street clothes that left room for their wings, angels never wore uniforms, but the way Turiel changed in Arielle's presence made me think she outranked him. I knew she outranked Michael. She was his sponsor and friend, helping him earn his way back to Heaven. I wasn't sure what the deal was with Turiel.

Arielle fixed her attention on Michael and then scowled at Turiel, her energy crackling a deep violet hue. He shrank under her scrutiny.

"*Blood magic?*" Her tone was musical, but the notes cut

sharp and deep. *"You used a prophet for blood magic? You know how unstable those spells can be. How powerful a prophet's blood is."*

Her words shuddered through me as I realized I wasn't supposed to be hearing them. This conversation was taking place in the angel's telepathic network.

Turiel bowed his head. "It was the best I could do, given the circumstances."

"I tried, but he wouldn't listen," Michael replied aloud, his voice groggy and thick around the edges.

She turned on him next. *"Oh, and your free will had been taken, had it? How do I know you didn't accept this simply to be more human for a little while?"*

"Do you really think I'd do—"

Arielle's halo blinded me, so I shielded my eyes with the back of my hand. "His wounds wouldn't close, and his own ability to heal was making things worse," I said. "It was the only way."

She spoke to me in her human voice. "You can hear us again, I see. I should have known you'd have tendency toward our work, given who you are. And the spell would exacerbate it."

"He'd been attacked with a cursed sword, probably an angel killer, and was dropping fast," Turiel added. "Blood magic was the one thing I knew that could slow its effect. The purity and magic of a prophet's blood could slow the poison and allow him to heal the way a human does. It bought us much-needed time."

"I realize that," she said in her regular voice, sighing. "But it doesn't mean I like it. It's too unpredictable."

The floor tipped and whirled and a brilliant white haze filled my thoughts. I pressed my back against the sofa cushions to steady myself, then felt myself lift out of my body, as though I were a balloon inflating with helium. I squeezed my hands into fists until my nails bit my palms. A strange, dark feeling pricked my skin as an electrical current coursed through my veins. Shadows cast by a thousand black leathery wings blocked the sky. Blood filled the rivers, human blood, as these winged creatures fell upon them. Was it memory?—my body throbbed with the pain of a thousand claws—Or was it happening now? I was broken and torn, and yet unable to feel it, as though it were happening to someone else.

"Mia!" I could hear Michael's voice. Hands gripped my shoulders, and I blinked, but couldn't shake the vision. I was trapped in white haze. Screams filled my ears.

"Give her a minute." Arielle's voice sounded tinny and far away. "You'll jar her. Can't you see her energy?"

"No. I can't sense her anymore." Michael's words tumbled out of him. "It's been a long time since I've been this blind."

"Her blood didn't simply make you more human, Michael." Arielle said, closer this time. "She's inheriting your power."

Inheriting his power? The vision darkened, and their voices faded behind the sobs and cries that would never end. The muscles burned under my skin, and the sensation swirled around my back. A sharp pain stabbed between my shoulder blades, and everything went black.

CHAPTER TEN

I woke up in my own bed, wearing the same shirt and jeans I'd worn to school, with no memory of how I'd gotten home. I assumed Arielle or Turiel had brought me. Through the curtains, clouds gave way to patches of deep blue sky flecked with brilliant stars. Turning to check the alarm clock, I had to squint against its orange glare. Twenty to nine: I'd slept through dinner. It felt as though I'd been sleeping for days.

The house was quiet, but the roar of cars zooming along the main road made me wonder if I'd left a window open somewhere. I dragged myself out of bed and shuffled to the kitchen, my body heavy and spent as though I were the one who'd polished off the tequila. Where was Mom? I tried to remember her work schedule. Perhaps she was on nights again. When I switched on the kitchen lights, they almost blinded me, and the hum of the fridge roared in my ears. I reached for a glass from the cupboard and ran the tap for water.

My head buzzed and crackled like a radio tuning into a station. I strained to listen, and a choir of voices all spoke at once in a tapestry of baroque harmonies.

"You're not alone, Mia," one of the voices said so loud in

my ear it made me drop my glass in the sink. I looked around but didn't see anyone. Nor did I recognize it. *"We're right here with you."*

"We've got your back, Prophet," said another. *"How's the perimeter?"*

The perimeter? How the hell should I know?

"Clear over here." I recognized the clarion tones of Arielle's voice right away. *"How's your side?"*

What were they talking about?

"Good. She's safe."

Who had replied? Turiel?

"And Michael?" asked Arielle.

"Sleeping. He can't hear us anymore."

Who did the other voices belong to? I recalled Michael telling me once about the Host, how when one angel spoke, all their voices were heard. But this…this felt insane. Perhaps, I was still asleep. Either that or I'd cracked. What would Heather say if she could see me now?

"Don't be afraid, Mia. You've tuned to our frequency. You're in the network." Behind Arielle's voice, I could hear sounds within sounds, layered background noises: the rushing of wind, the flapping of wings, and in the distance, inhuman shrieking.

My pulse raced. I'd heard the network before, when Arielle and the other angels were communicating telepathically right in front of me, but this time, nobody else was in the room. "Are you nearby?" I asked out loud.

"Volume, Mia. You don't need to shout. We can hear your thoughts."

"All of them?"

"Yes. You're connected to the Host, like you were when you helped Damiel. But stronger. Back then, you touched into what the network is. Now, you're connected the way we are."

"Wha—How?" My knees shook so badly, I didn't think they would carry me any farther. I collapsed on one of the kitchen chairs.

"I'll be right there," Arielle said.

Within seconds, the air crackled and she appeared in an explosion of golden light. *That* was new. I rubbed my eyes.

"You're perfectly safe." She spoke softly, using her human voice.

"Report. Arielle, is everything all right?" came a commanding voice from the network.

"I believe so," was her reply. *"Remember, the Prophet can hear you."*

"Warriors, we have a breach over Tacoma," said a woman's musical voice, layered with a cacophony of sounds beneath it. *"Flyers. Over a hundred of them."*

I shuddered. What the hell were flyers? Did I even want to know?

"How many do you need?"

"Three of you would be nice. More's better."

"Be right there," said two others in unison.

When I'd studied drama in junior year, we'd listened to an old radio play. That was exactly how this sounded. Only I was hearing it in my head, as though I were listening to ear buds, with no way of taking them out.

Arielle crouched in front of me, placing her hands on both my shoulders, calming, reassuring. "Listen to me. You don't have the focus for both our world and yours. Not yet."

"You're telling me!" I said aloud.

Arielle put her finger to her lips.

"Sorry!"

"It's fine. You can shut it off. I'll show you how."

"Please!" This time, I thought the word at her.

She continued in her soft, human voice, "I want you to use your imagination. Visualize a wall between you and the others. And make it big. Think castle wall, or fortress. You don't want anything crashing through."

I remembered the castles from my medieval history texts, fortresses made of stone, and conjured an image of the Tower of London. But then another call for help shattered my focus.

"I've got a breach over Los Angeles. They're coming through. Hundreds of them."

"Sammael, is everything under control in Tacoma? Your team's needed in Los Angeles."

"Stay calm," Arielle whispered, and I tried to block the voices. It was as though I had a war zone inside my head.

"I can't hold it!" I said. "How do you do it? You said angels are only connected to this when they're on duty. How did Michael disconnect?"

Arielle dropped her hands from my shoulders and locked her gaze with mine, as though she were lending me her strength. "You're doing very well. Try to see the network itself."

I focused on a crack in the kitchen floor's old terracotta tiles and let my mind wander. Above the urgent voices, I saw a gold three-dimensional grid made of light. "Is it a structure of some kind?"

"Yes, that's it. Can you see where you're connected to it?"

I traced the filaments of golden light to the back of my head. "I think so."

"Good. Now, using your will, push it away, or pull yourself away from it. Whatever works. It'll sting a bit, but you should be able to disconnect."

I tugged and stretched my mind like taffy in an effort to free myself from the network. Each time, it snapped back. "How do you do it?"

"I never have. But, if I recall, one of Michael's thoughts right before he left the network was 'Leave me alone', so why not try that?"

"Leave me alone!" I said to the network and felt a slight prickling as it disconnected.

"Better?" Arielle asked with a smile.

I nodded, as the last vestiges of the network slipped away. I didn't realize how clenched my jaw had been, or that I'd been holding my breath, until I let it out. My eyes still hadn't adjusted to the light in the room, so the kitchen appeared ridiculously bright. Arielle's halo made it blindingly so.

"You said something last night, before I blacked out, about my inheriting Michael's power." I squinted up at her. "Is that what's going on?"

"The spell you did with Turiel was unprecedented." She stood and leaned against the counter, folding her arms across her chest. "What I believe Turiel was trying to do was make Michael more human, so he could heal. But in order for that to happen, his power had to go somewhere safe. In this case, the spell-caster's own soul has to protect it."

"So." I fumbled to wrap my head around what she was saying. "My soul is protecting his?"

"Essentially, yes. And since you're a prophet, your soul can act as a host for his angelic abilities, to keep them safe from what's affecting him. While he experiences a loss of his abilities, you will experience an increase. And given that your abilities are already great, you will see into our world in a way that no one has before." Arielle observed me the way my mother had when I'd had whooping cough as a child. Concerned, poised, waiting for the next terrible fit to consume me. "It really is his best chance. At least until we find out more about the weapon he was attacked with."

"I have Michael's angelic ability?" The words felt strange on my tongue. "That would've been helpful to know ahead of time."

"Turiel didn't know the spell would do this. None of us did."

A dull ache throbbed under my eyebrows. I pinched the bridge of my nose, trying to fend it off. "Will I be able to fly and stuff?"

"Well, no. You won't sprout wings." A half-smile rippled her mouth, quickly replaced by her usual serene expression. "But you have a halo now, which is the brightness you're seeing. Your eyes haven't had time to adjust. And you'll experience more of the network, which is why we've blocked it out. The world will seem a very different place."

"You mean I'll see those demons and minions?" Things so disgusting to look at that after the first time I'd seen one, I wondered if I'd ever be able to eat again. "I've seen those already."

"Not like this." She reached into the kitchen cupboard and pulled out two water glasses, without hesitation, as though she knew exactly where they were. "You might be surprised."

The inside of my mouth had congealed to chalk, despite the water I'd had earlier. Arielle filled both glasses from the tap and handed me one. "Here," she said. "This'll help with the headache."

I accepted gratefully with both hands and took deep gulps. The cool glass felt solid and real between my fingertips, comfortingly so.

"You should also know," she continued. "Because you've been able to see into the past before, you might be able to access Michael's memories."

"His memories?" In the past, I'd only been able to see mine, and even that was with Arielle's help. And while the idea of knowing more about his past intrigued me, I wanted him to trust me with those secrets himself. Learning about him this way was an invasion of privacy, like reading someone else's diary. And no matter how tempting it was or how curious it made me, I couldn't exploit that.

She nodded. "Given where he's been, it could be disturbing. There's no saying what you could remember."

A chill inched up my spine. What if I discovered something horrible? "Is there any way to prevent it?"

"Not that I can think of." She finished her water and put the empty glass in the sink. "In the meantime, Michael needs to rest, and you should try to go about living a normal life. Avoid thinking about the network, in case you accidentally reconnect. But if you do need it, reach and it will come."

I recoiled at the thought. "Why would I even want to do that?"

"In case you need help. Your halo will protect you now, to a point, but it isn't safe to have all that power and disconnect from the network for long. Something will find you." Her halo flared brighter and she tilted her head a moment to listen. I didn't have to be in the network to know she was being called. "I must go to Los Angeles tonight, but I can be back in a matter of seconds if you need me."

I was glad Michael couldn't teleport. If it worked the way the network did, the last thing I'd need would be to think about a place and wind up there. Dizzy and sick, with no idea how to get back. I might not enjoy taking the bus, but I didn't hate it *that* much.

She was about to leave when I asked, "How long will it last?"

"A few weeks, maybe more. Our knowledge of cursed swords is limited, so there's no way to tell."

"Would it possible for me to use these abilities while I have them? You know, to protect myself from what I'm seeing?"

"Anyone can learn to protect themselves in some way or another." She paced across the kitchen. "Most people don't want to."

"Why not?"

"People see what they want to see, so they can be easily tricked. Prophets are different. There's no halfway, Mia. In order to protect yourself, you need to face the truth. And considering you have Michael's abilities, it may be more than you anticipate."

Facing the truth seemed easy enough. Hadn't I been doing it all along? "It can't be any worse than being afraid."

"I was hoping you'd agree." Arielle smiled, her wings

shimmering behind her. "We'll start your training tomorrow after school. In the meantime, try to get some rest."

CHAPTER ELEVEN

Getting sleep proved harder than I thought. I tossed and turned, wide awake for the rest of the night. When morning finally came, I decided I'd test my halo's protection and walk to school to shake off my restlessness. Big mistake. The sun blazed in the sky. Cars roared like dragons. Worst of all, everyone had tattered black shadows hanging off of them. It might have been funny if I hadn't known what minions were, or the way they controlled people's thoughts and actions. Even children were affected, though it seemed more prevalent among adults. When I tuned into people, all I felt was sorrow and fear.

Was the world really such a miserable place?

Over the school grounds, spirals of vivid blue light had been etched into the air. Sigils. Their edges glowed with a shimmering white shield that repelled the minions and made our school a sanctuary by comparison. Shadows dropped from the students and teachers as they crossed the invisible barrier, and white or rainbow-colored light gleamed around them. Auras. Could I see those now too? While some people's energy remained gray and dingy, few staticky minions could enter the sigil-protected space. Those that did clung desperately to the people they'd possessed. Their teeth bared, they growled with hunger, while their hosts looked miserable. I wished I could help.

When people spoke to me, I hardly listened, and I caught myself being so fascinated by the lights and shadows around me that I bumped into a wall. Though Fiona's and Heather's energies shone bright, protected by the necklaces Fatima had given them, Farouk did not look well. A gray, linty cape rested on his shoulders, as though he were dressed in rags. Something burdened him. Was he still fighting with Fatima? With all that had happened over the past few days, I'd almost forgotten how angry she'd been. Surely things were better now. After math class, I tried to catch up with him, but he slipped away before I could say hello.

***

When school was finally over for the day, Arielle met me at the front entrance. Her dress slacks and long, beige wool coat made her look like a substitute teacher. Several guys ogled her as they passed; one even waggled his eyebrows as if he had a chance. Ignoring them, she stuffed her hands into her pockets and fluffed out her wings. Though veiled from human eyes, their gossamer luminescence was more visible to me than ever.

"There's a coffee shop a few blocks away," she said. "Let's go there."

We walked in silence. It wasn't raining, though the sky had developed a thick covering of bright clouds that kept a chill from the air. But once we passed through the sigils' barrier, an unnatural coldness crept through me. Giant birds swarmed over our heads. At least that was what I'd thought they were until I'd known better. Gray, shadowy creatures ranging in size from vultures to pterodactyls blanketed the sky, and their high-pitched screeching assaulted my ears. Avoiding Arielle and me, they flew low over houses in their hunt for food, and dove on the students leaving the school grounds.

A young girl walked down the road, talking with two of her friends. Her shiny aura rippled around her, until one of the creatures swooped and landed on her back. She paused barely a moment, long enough for her eyes to glaze over and her light to dim. Her face tightened with worry, then she smiled and kept walking, as though nothing had happened.

It was a war zone, a hunting ground where people were prey.

"Is it always this way?" I asked Arielle.

She clasped her hands behind her back and strode beside me, a sergeant surveying a battlefield. "It's gotten much worse lately, since the wards over the Pacific Rim came down. We're still cleaning up the mess from that."

"What are these things? Minions?"

"Yes. But 'minions' is a general term. The airborne ones are called flyers."

A senior I recognized from the football team left the school parking lot in an old Chevy truck. As soon as the tires rolled off the school grounds, a giant flyer charged the vehicle, noiselessly landing on its blue roof. The creature's ghostly claws pierced the metal, seized a handful of green light from the boy's life force, and popped it into its mouth.

Rage simmered through my veins. "They gotta be stopped!" I sprang into the street, not thinking about what I would do if I caught that thing. I just wanted it gone.

Arielle latched onto my elbow and dragged me back onto the sidewalk. "Not so fast."

Her halo erupted around her and ignited the sky in a solar flare that spread across the city block. The larger flyers scattered. The small ones were incinerated. The huge flyer on the car was at close enough range that by the time it saw the flash coming, the halo's golden flames had already turned it to ash.

For a moment, nothing in the sky moved. People

carried on the same, but the minions were gone, and it felt safe to take a breath. Within seconds, the creatures returned. They bared their gray, shadowy claws and blackened teeth and charged straight for us. Arielle flared her halo again, incinerating the few small flyers that remained and stopping the larger ones. The creatures hissed and screeched at the impenetrable bubble of space around us, before they turned and flew away in defeat.

"They're not very smart, and they don't enjoy being challenged," Arielle commented, as we continued on our walk to the café. "They'll find easier hunting grounds soon enough."

"That's terrible!" I said. "They're going to hurt people. Shouldn't you incinerate them all?"

"Any more than what I did, and I'd be declaring war. We don't want to see any soldier demons today if we can help it."

Soldier demons—the kind that had wounded Michael. I craned my neck to scan the sky for the next attack, and was relieved to find it clear.

"Not that I mind war," she added. "I've been in enough now that I choose my battles, make sure I have adequate backup. And I don't think you're ready for that yet."

"Yet?" I swallowed hard. If she thought I'd ever be able to back her up, she was giving me far too much credit. "You're right. I'm not."

"If you could hear the network, you'd know how busy the others are right now. Stepping into a battle would be foolish."

Was that a dig? Was she disappointed in me for not wanting to stay connected last night? "Should I be listening?"

She smiled at me. We were at the door to the café, but she hesitated before opening it. "Not until you're ready. When you are, the network will no longer be a nuisance. You will see it for the valuable tool that it is. Everything I can do is made possible by my connection to it."

Café Largo's baroque style reminded me of walking back through time, and yet its black, white, and silver color scheme was clearly modern chic. I'd been there many times before. But today, because I was endowed with Michael's powers, it was horrifically surreal. People sat at silver-trimmed white marble tables, unaware of the shadowy minions feeding on them as they filled their bellies with caffeine—no doubt to pick themselves up after having their energy taken. In the corner, reflected in the ornate mirror, a lethargic older woman sprawled on a stuffed black velvet chaise with polished arms. She sipped coffee idly as a huge, python-shaped minion writhed through her chest. She caught my stare with hollowed black eyes, and I gasped. No matter where I looked, we were surrounded.

Arielle touched my shoulder. "Stay calm," she whispered. "Halo or no, any fear will draw them right to you."

I bit back the urge to scream. I felt like an arachnophobe in a spider museum. "Can't we go someplace else?"

"They're everywhere. You need to get used to them."

Same as spiders, I thought. *But I think I like spiders more.*

Even the barista had a minion resting on her shoulders. Its body undulated with the slippery contractions of a moving slug. While she perked up when she saw Arielle, the shadowy creature growled.

"How are you today?" Arielle asked her after placing our order.

"Fi—could be better, actually," the girl admitted. She gave Arielle a wan smile with her change.

Arielle took it and touched the girl's hand reassuringly. "Your dad's going to be fine."

Tears filled the girl's eyes, followed by shock. "How do you know?"

A flash of light shot from Arielle's hand along the

barista's arm and dislodged the creature on her. It hissed at Arielle, but she stared it down until it slinked away and seeped through the floorboards.

Arielle turned back to her and smiled. "I just do."

We headed for a table at the back of the café and the creatures watched us. Their dark, cavernous eyes followed our movements as we took our seats, and the people they feasted on—their hosts—scowled at us as though we were pariahs. Some even got up and left.

Instead of calling us to the front to pick up our order, the barista brought our drinks to the table. She lingered close to Arielle. "Can I get you anything else?"

"No, thank you," Arielle replied.

"Is there enough chocolate sprinkles on the mocha?" she asked. "I could get more."

"It's fine. Really."

"Umm. Okay. Thanks again." It was as though she didn't want to leave. No wonder. Now that the creature was off of her, she had color in her cheeks again. Her aura shone pink and blue.

Once she finally left, I asked. "How'd you do that? Help her, I mean."

Arielle spooned some chocolate whip cream off her mocha and tasted it. "She wanted to be free, and she admitted it when she told me the truth, instead of lying and saying she was fine. Even the smallest untruths bind people and trip them up."

I blew the foam on my vanilla latte to cool it. "But how did you send light right through her arm?"

"I directed my halo."

"Can I do that?"

"And more, once you learn to focus." She took a sip of her drink. "But first, I'm going to teach you the difference between working solo and working with the network."

I cringed at the thought of having the network's loud cacophony broadcasting through my head. I wondered how Michael could stand it all the time. "How's Michael doing?" I asked, realizing that this was the first I'd thought of him all day. Though he hadn't been around, for some reason, he hadn't felt far away.

"He was up sick most of the night. His body is expelling the poison any way it can."

"Why didn't anyone tell me?" I sat forward. "I should go see him."

She shook her head. "Not yet. He's sleeping now and needs his rest. Turiel is with him."

"Really?" Turiel had to be his least favorite angel. When Arielle gave me a questioning look, I realized they must have played down their differences around her, so I added, "At least one of us can sleep."

She continued studying me. "Yes. That is to be expected. You have the part of him now that doesn't sleep."

"Great." I sighed.

"You said you wanted to do this. Have you changed your mind?"

"Of course not!"

"Good." Taking another sip of her drink, she scanned the room. "See over there?" She nodded toward the older woman stretched out on the black chaise. The minion undulating on her chest reminded me of a giant leech or an animated oil slick. The sight of it made me ill. "Flare your halo. Let's see what you can do."

"Seriously?" Trying to hide my discomfort, I took a swig of my latte and sat up, bracing myself. "How?"

"I'm always serious. Except when I'm not." She smiled at her own joke. "Close your eyes if you have to. Connect to the energy and use your will to flare it out."

"Sounds easy enough." I closed my eyes. When I tuned to the halo, a brilliant golden-white filled my mind's eye, as though I were staring at the sun. "Wow."

"That's it," she said. "Now send it out around yourself."

I pushed with my mind, trying to send the light outside

myself. It was a strain. I pushed again, trying to make it bigger, brighter. But all the light did was shine, then flicker, and a piercing pain shot through the base of my skull. "Ow!"

"Okay, stop." Arielle said with a chuckle.

"Did I do anything?" I opened my eyes and checked the minion on the chaise lounge. It hadn't budged.

"Your own energy flared out about two feet. At that distance, something would have to be right on you to be affected. Even then, it might not even flinch."

"Damn," I muttered, then realizing I was cursing, added, "I mean—"

"That's what you're trying to do. Condemn these creatures. But there's no point in cursing the power you've been given simply because you don't know how to use it yet. Be patient."

"Sorry."

She smiled, as though she were modeling the very patience she wanted me to have with myself. "Ready to try the network this time? It's a reverse of what we did the other day. Try to see it with your mind."

I closed my eyes and, as soon as I thought of the network, the golden grid of light appeared. Today, it took on a more substantive shape, like scaffolding. "Got it."

"Good. Now, invite it to come to you. Welcome it."

This part was harder, because I didn't know what to expect. Would there be more distress? Pain? Would I see more visions? My shoulders tensed, and each time I tried to invite the network closer, I flinched, inadvertently pushing it away.

"Take it easy," Arielle said. "The network has no intention of hurting you. Don't be afraid."

I took a few deep breaths and let my weight sink into the chair, relaxing, as the grid of light drew near. With a flash, it clicked into place, and a current of energy flowed through me. My skin thrummed from the strength of it.

"*There! That's good,*" said Arielle in the musical tones that

I knew to be her telepathic voice.

The chorus of a thousand voices sang in my ears. "It's not as loud as before."

"That's because you're getting used to Michael's power," she said aloud. "It will shield you from receiving more than you can handle."

The thrill of energy racing through my veins intoxicated me. But it was Michael's power, not mine, and I couldn't help but think, *he should be the one with it, not me.*

"I understand," said Arielle. "Your desire for power is only to help. You don't crave it for its own sake. That's a good thing."

"*You can hear me?*" I asked with my thoughts, ignoring everything else she said.

"You'll learn to control your thoughts. We all do." She placed her mug on the marble table with a clink and sat back, crossing her legs. "Now try connecting the network's power to the halo."

I closed my eyes again, listening through the network first to prepare myself for any startling sounds or the cries for help I'd heard the night before. But its volume was low, bearable, like a TV in the other room. When I focused on my—Michael's—halo, it shone even brighter than before. All I did was think about flaring it out, and a buzz echoed through my whole being. I opened my eyes, as the flash erupted across the room, incinerating a few minions that hadn't attached to anyone and annoying some of the larger ones that had. The older woman on the chaise blinked, dazedly. The serpentine minion writhed in pain, as though it had been wounded.

Arielle stood, and said to me with her inside voice, "*This is where we give it a final shove.*"

"*Why don't you use your sword?*" I asked telepathically.

"*Because everyone can see me. We only fight that way when we're invisible.*"

Arielle's halo brightened around her, ready for a fight. She approached the chaise and said, "Are you all right, ma'am?"

The woman looked up at Arielle and smiled back. The demon went into a kind of frenzy, as though it expected to die. Lunging at Arielle, it hit her halo and bounced off.

"My goodness." The woman touched her silver hair, self-consciously tidying it. "I was in so much pain earlier." She stood, leaving her demon to twitch and writhe on the chaise. "But not anymore."

"Good," Arielle said. "I'm glad." Then she nodded to me and thought the words, *"I'm leaving this one for you."*

Taking a deep breath, I flared the halo as big as I could, and a brilliant ochre light flashed throughout the room. The snakelike minion flailed, trying to flee, but it dissolved, enveloped by golden flames.

I let out my breath. *"Did I kill it?"*

Arielle waved goodbye to the woman and returned to our table. "Good work. You've banished it. So it won't be back. Now you can look after yourself in an emergency."

Though I didn't share Arielle's confidence in me, I gave her a nod. Who knew if I'd be able to do it again? *Is she expecting me to?*

If she heard my thought, she didn't answer it. Instead, she smiled at me and said aloud, "Let's get you home."

I followed her out of the café. "Does this mean I'm on my own now?"

"You're never alone in the network. I'll always come. But I feel better knowing you can handle these things should they attack. And now that they know what you're capable of, it's simply a matter of time before they do."

CHAPTER TWELVE

Over the next two nights, I hardly had three hours sleep. Michael's halo blazed inexorable daylight, and I suddenly knew how people without curtains must feel during an Alaskan summer. Luckily, my lack of rest was only due to being blinded and not from being attacked. Perhaps the halo didn't give anything a chance to come near me.

Arielle kept me apprised of Michael's health via the network. For a few days, he was too sick for visitors. And though I carried a very tangible piece of him with me, I ached to look into his crystal blue eyes, hear the rumble of his laughter, or simply hold his hand.

Dean had recovered enough to come back to class and, thanks to the healing Michael had given him, was able to resume his wrestling practice. He and Jesse didn't have any creatures on them, at least not at school. And neither did Heather and Fiona, who were protected by the *hamsas* around their necks.

Outside our shielded school grounds, the number of minions increased. A few hellhounds even sniffed around to join in the feeding frenzy. Their shadowy forms lurked in the damp cedars and laurel bushes of neighboring yards, but because they'd not yet materialized, it was easy enough to flare the halo and drive them away. In the network, more and more angels were called to repair the wards surrounding the Pacific Rim. Demons had breached the perimeter, and the damage was getting worse. Though Arielle had hinted that I would get more training soon, the others couldn't spare her long enough to teach me. Even so, I couldn't wait to learn how to really fight. Whether the desire to do so was my own, or if it came from Michael's soul, I didn't know, but I went with it either way.

Not surprisingly, I found it harder and harder to concentrate on school. The murmur of voices that echoed down the long corridors was loud enough on normal days. Now it was deafening, and even with its volume turned down low, the network still distracted me. I wandered from class to class, a zombie. At least Heather and Fiona were too preoccupied with their boyfriends to notice. Jesse and Dean had healed so well that everyone at school seemed to forget they'd been injured. I hadn't.

As if things weren't crazy enough. It was Elaine Carter who gave me the biggest surprise of all. Because of her temperament, I'd once suspected she had a minion on her but couldn't prove it. Now that I was tuned to see them the way a cat senses mice, the only thing that surprised me was how big the creature was. Curled around her thighs like a giant slug, it pierced the front of her hips and wove its way along her back until its shadowy, oblong head poured from her mouth. Talk about two-faced.

She sidled up to my locker after our last class, and the minion's soulless black eyes fixed a hungry gaze on me that made the hair rise on my arms. I tried to pretend everything was normal, to focus on her features, not the creature's, though I could hardly see anything but.

"Why isn't Michael at school?" Elaine asked. "Did he finally get some sense and start avoiding you for the freak that you are?"

For the first time ever, I felt sorry for her. She had no

idea this thing was eating away at her, which made me wonder if maybe, deep down, she could be a completely different person.

There was only one way to find out.

Drawing from the network, I fueled my halo, and the creature to squirmed. I couldn't believe it was stupid enough to stay so close to the light, but from what I'd seen these past few days, minions would get cocky when they had a firm grasp on their hosts. This one was no different.

"Why are you looking at me that way?" she jeered.

I flared my halo a little brighter, hoping it would encourage the minion to leave. But instead, it reared up at me, and Elaine, as though she were its puppet, jumped down my throat. "What do you think you're doing? You're weirding me out, you freak!"

Under normal circumstances, her harsh words would've startled me, but the light of the halo grew, and with it rose secrets of the life Elaine kept hidden. A young girl, about four years old, screamed in pain as her mother dragged her by her braids across the kitchen floor. The woman pulled a serrated knife from a wooden block on the counter and waved it at her.

"Don't you ever touch my things again!" she hissed.

Tugging the girl by the braids again, the woman brought the blade to her daughter's throat. Terrified, the girl stopped crying and breathing at the same time.

The next thing I saw was the same woman with a young boy. Tears streamed from his eyes. "Be brave," she said and hovered his tiny hand over the gas stove. The boy wailed.

A bright light filled me and without thinking, I opened my mouth and words poured out of me. "I'm sorry your mother used to hurt you and your father didn't believe you. Show him your little brother. She's hurting him now."

The tops of Elaine's ears reddened, not with embarrassment, but with rage. Her hands tightened into fists and the creature on her twitched and roared. For a moment, I thought she was going to hit me, so I took a step back and, with a deep breath, flared the halo again, brighter than ever. This time the demon ignited. Its shrieks filled my ears.

Elaine tensed and, for a moment, I thought she would scream, but as the singed demon dropped and melted away, the color drained out of her. Covering her face with her hands, she collapsed against her locker door and sobbed, gasping for air.

I fished a tissue from my purse and handed it to her. "Here."

She snatched the tissue from my hand and blew her nose. "I don't need your damn pity."

"No. You need to tell the police, and your brother needs your help."

Her mouth fell open in shock and for a moment, I could see that hurt four-year-old girl in her eyes. But then her mouth tightened into a line, and she squinted at me, sizing me up. "Don't you dare tell anyone about this!"

"I won't. I promise." After all, how could I explain knowing that? No wonder she gossiped so much. Anything to distract people from her own story.

"Better not," she threatened. Another round of tears spilled from her eyes. "She'll kill me if I say anything."

"Why don't we go talk to Ms. Callou?" I offered gently. "Her office is still open."

"You'll come with me?"

If anyone had told me an hour ago that Elaine would ask me to accompany her to the school counselor's office, I would've thought they were insane, but here it was: another strange incident in my super-strange reality. "Sure," I said and grabbed my purse.

Elaine's face was blotchy from crying, so I positioned myself between her and any prying eyes as we made our way down the hall. At the door of Ms. Callou's office, Elaine dismissed me and went inside, making it clear that though we'd shared a moment, it didn't make us friends.

***

As soon as I left the sanctuary of the school's protected space, two flyers hovering outside the grounds charged at me. Despite being terrified, I remembered at the last minute to flare the halo and blocked them. I'd worked harder than I was used to helping Elaine, so the halo's outer limits extended barely a few feet. All the flyers had to do was back up so they wouldn't be incinerated, but it was enough. I focused on keeping a big bubble of light around me and wondered exactly what it must take for Michael to cloak himself and become invisible. As I walked, a few shadows approached, this time on the ground, and the flyers followed. They taunted me with screeching, waiting for me to drop the light that kept them away. A few blocks from Michael's, I was angry enough to expand the halo one more time, igniting the creatures on the ground. One of the flyers took off.

Soon, I crossed the threshold of Michael's yard and the safety of its sigils. More flyers circled the neighborhood, no doubt waiting to feast on a weakened angel. I knocked on the door. When he answered, his crystal blue eyes captured mine, and a warm river of energy tingled under my skin. The sudden surge of power made me dizzy.

He smiled and a thousand megawatts of desire pulsed through me. It was all I could do to say "hi". I gripped the door to brace myself and wondered if these amplified feelings were mine or his. Had I somehow inherited his lust along with his soul?

He pulled me into a hug and exhaled. "I missed you." The grassy scent of him filled my nose.

"I would've come sooner. Arielle told me you weren't well enough for visitors." I took a deep breath, settling in, wanting more, but the last time we'd kissed he'd convulsed in pain. I wasn't about to start that again. Not until he was better.

"I wasn't." He gave me a squeeze, his lips brushing my cheek, before he released me.

He eased me out of my coat, and I followed him into the living room where he dropped onto the sofa and rested his bare feet on the coffee table. The TV was on, and he switched between British, American, and Canadian news channels with the remote, watching them all at once. I recognized some of the events from what little I'd heard through the network. As one channel focused on a low-level earthquake that had hit Los Angeles, I realized it had happened the same day the angels had a breach. Same with an inferno in Tuscon. Each world incident was tied to demonic attacks that the angels had worked to resolve.

Waves of frustration rolled off Michael, crashing into me as though they were my own. It was odd to sense his feelings, the way he used to do with mine. He was angry with himself, because he wanted to make a difference, but couldn't. Not right now.

"How's the wound?" I scanned him for pain but couldn't find anything physically wrong.

"It's healed fine." With a sigh, he lifted his shirt to show me the puckered, pink scar where the cursed sword had slashed him. But I was mesmerized by the curves of his obliques.

"What is it then?" I sat beside him. Maybe talking about it would help.

"Turiel hasn't exactly shared any news of you." Without access to the network, Michael couldn't feel me. Given everything that had happened between us, the way he always looked out for me, not having his power and not knowing things must have been torture.

"Wait. You mean he didn't tell you anything?" I said. How could Turiel be so cold? Did he have no idea what it was like to love someone?

"Apparently, you're no longer 'my responsibility'." Sighing, Michael raked both his hands through his dark, wavy hair. "What if this is permanent? What if I can't fight anymore? I'm a sitting duck. I can't go anywhere without Turiel by my side. I'm under house arrest, and the only time I get out of here is…well, never."

"I guess we should get you one of those ankle alarm cuffs then."

He groaned. "I'm seriously going crazy in here."

I stood and gripped both his hands to pull him up. "Get your coat."

He raised an eyebrow, and a mischievous grin curled his lips. "Mia, what are you thinking?" His hands brushed my waist and lit body on fire. Touching him had never been this intense before. Was his power affecting me? Did being near me used to make him feel this way? Did it still? My pulse soared.

"I'll take you." I found my voice. "We can go out for dinner or something."

He raised an eyebrow, still holding my waist. "Are you sure?"

A shiver of excitement ran through me. I wasn't sure whose it was, mine or his, but we needed to get out of there before desire burned away all rational thought. "I've been working with Arielle. One a good day, I can flare this halo of yours almost twenty feet."

"Twenty feet, huh? Together, we'd almost make a whole angel." His grin widened and he gave me a wink. "Good enough for me. I know just the place."

He headed to his room to change, and my heart rate slowed to normal.

A few minutes later, we stepped outside and got into the car. The sun had already started to set and a chill had crept into the air. Michael turned the ignition as dozens of flyers bore down on us from the darkening sky. A pack of hellhounds approached, their maddened gazes fixed on us. They paced, growling and snarling, and waited for us to leave the safety of our shielded cage.

"Ready?" He motioned to the hellhounds and grinned. "This is gonna be so fun."

Fun? Clearly, he had a different meaning for the word. Connecting to the network, I flared the halo. When the giant balloon of fire swelled around us, I gave Michael a thumbs-up, and he backed the car out of the driveway. The hellhounds charged, and the flyers screeched and dove at us. But the halo's force kept them all at bay.

"Not bad." He nodded and shifted the car into first then second gear. "Been putting my soul to good use, I see."

We drove to a steak house in Pioneer Square, one of the older areas of town filled with brick buildings and cobbled, uneven streets. The restaurant was in a nineteenth century walk-up, near the old wrought iron and glass pergola that the district was famous for. Though the place wasn't busy yet, the after-work crowd had started to arrive in chinos and suits. Even Michael had changed into a black button-down shirt with a collar, making me feel way underdressed in my red cardigan and jeans.

The hostess led us to a quiet table in the back of the restaurant. As we passed the other diners, some of the minions and lesser demons surrounding them moved away. The ones who'd already found hosts to feed on raised their heads and snarled. Though they were no longer shrieking, they emitted a high-pitched sound that traveled like bugs along my skin.

Michael took my hand and gave it a little squeeze. "Pleasant, aren't they?" he whispered and his breath tickled my cheek.

"You still see them?" I wondered if I'd ever get used to knowing they were there.

"I never stopped."

He held my chair for me and then took his seat. After the hostess left, he said, "I'm getting better. The network's starting to come back. Sometimes, when I'm asleep, I hear it. And when I concentrate, I can connect for a few minutes and find out what's going on. Soon, I'll be able to protect myself, so I won't need a bodyguard." He grinned.

"Not even one as lovely as you."

Bodyguard? Did he resent me for protecting him? When I tuned in, those weren't the feelings I detected. "Does it bug you?"

"Maybe it should bother me that you're the one protecting me right now, and not the other way around." He opened his menu, his gaze locking with mine. "But I can't help it. I think it's kind of hot."

Pretending not to feel the rush of excitement that bubbled up my spine, I bit my lip to keep myself from smiling. I was sure my face heated up. I focused on the nightly specials printed in front of me. "Is it the warrior thing? Because if it is, I'm surprised you never hooked up with Arielle."

"Arielle isn't you." He gave me a smile that made the compulsion to kiss him so strong my hands shook.

I pressed my fingertips into the table to steady them. "I'm glad you like me this way, because I want to learn how to fight, and Arielle's been so busy with everything going on right now."

He furrowed his brow. "No doubt." A mixed emotion rolled off him, probably guilt for not being able to fight at her side.

"Will you teach me?"

"You mean in case my power doesn't come back?"

"No. So I can take care of myself when it does."

"About that," he said. "I know I haven't been around these last few days—"

"It's not just the past few days... I'm afraid. All the time. And I don't want to be." My water glass had left a dent in the white tablecloth. I smoothed it with my finger. "I never want to be put in the situation I was with Damiel again."

"Then don't send me away." A heavy sadness came over him, and I realized that despite how much he'd healed, not having his full abilities was hard for him. Even though I'd dumped him and pretty much thrown him out of my life a few weeks ago in an effort to keep Damiel away, I knew Michael still blamed himself for Damiel's assault on me. For all I knew, he still condemned himself for the first time it had happened as well, and that was thousands of years before. "I need to be able to protect myself. From what you've said before, these creatures won't forget about me when you get your powers back. And I want to know how to help when the time comes, or at least not hold you back from doing what you love because you need to look after me."

"You'd never hold me back. Don't you see that?" He closed his menu, letting it drop to the table. "You matter more."

I mattered *more*? Part of me was thrilled, but I remembered Turiel's words, that Michael's feelings for me were a *conflict of interest*. Was this what he'd meant? "But the others think—"

"I know what they think. Okay? I can handle both."

"What about what *I* want?" As much as I appreciated his protective streak, now that I'd seen his world, I refused to be a weakness to him. "You shouldn't have to worry about my safety all the time. I want to be able to handle myself until help arrives. Will you teach me to do that, or not?"

He sighed and reached for my hand, causing my energy to flare again. It was one thing to know he used to be able to feel my feelings, but now they were so amplified, I was sure the whole restaurant could.

A waiter came to take our orders, giving us both a smile as he lit the candle in the center of our table. After he left, I excused myself to wash my hands and headed down a long corridor lined with burgundy damask wallpaper. Old black and white photos of the early settlers hung on the walls. In one, a family stood in front of a log cabin. Another featured a lumberjack leaning on his axe next to an enormous, fallen tree, its width higher than the man was tall. These were the old growth forests of the

Pacific Northwest. Most of them were gone now.

As I approached the door to the washroom, the skin on the back of my neck pulled into goose bumps, and an electrical feeling crept along my back, telling me I wasn't alone.

I spun around to find myself facing a large, hooded figure: a soldier demon that stood over six feet tall with red eyes, shiny charcoal skin, and the face of a gargoyle. I flared out the halo as fast as I could, and it erupted into a brilliant ring of golden fire, extending around me as wide as of one of those old-growth trees. The creature hesitated at the barrier of light for half a second before it sneered and stepped right through the flames. Its black, icy cold hands locked around my throat, blocking my air so I couldn't scream, couldn't even breathe. I pulled at its fingers, trying to break their grasp, but it slammed the back of my head against the wall. A white explosion of pain blinded me, and I felt the halo falter and dim. In an attempt to push it off, I kicked and flailed, but its strong grip didn't falter. Panic pushed at my thoughts, threatening to take over as spots formed before my eyes. I was blacking out.

Two large hands grabbed the soldier and pulled it off me. I doubled over, wheezing cool air into my lungs. With a snarl, the demon twisted to face Michael, slicing at his face with its claws. Michael stepped away barely in time and punched it in the jaw, hard enough to throw it off balance. As Michael moved in for another blow, I realized I'd dropped the fiery protection of the halo.

Other minions of different shapes and sizes drew near and watched with hungry mouths open. A large flyer landed on Michael's back, slowing him down. He reached between his shoulder blades to grasp for his sword and growled in frustration when his hand came up empty. Three smaller, gargoyle-shaped blobs with ash-colored skin nipped at his heels. And a huge serpentine creature slithered toward me. I stared into its glowing yellow eyes, fixated.

"Any time now." Michael's voice broke the trance, and I flared out the halo as brightly as I could, igniting the gargoyles at his feet. The serpent vanished like an apparition, but the creature at Michael's back didn't budge. Neither did that soldier demon.

I called forward the light and commanded it down my arm until white sparks spit from my fingertips. Not much, but it would have to do. I gripped the creature on Michael's back, and my hands passed through the ghostly form before the sparks caught. The flyer jolted, turned to face me, baring its teeth, and I froze. Beside me, Michael was taking a beating. I'd seen him fight half a dozen of these single-handedly before. Now, he could hardly deal with one.

Before I could muster the light to throw it off, the flyer bared its slimy black teeth and sank them into my shoulder. A cold pain pierced me and then lifted. I staggered. Tired, so tired. I braced my hand against the wall for support.

Michael delivered a roundhouse kick to the soldier demon's thigh and knocked it off balance. Then he reached behind my shoulder blades and pulled out the handle of his sword. His brow creased in concentration, but nothing happened.

"Dammit. It won't respond to me anymore."

The demon landed a punch against Michael's ribs and knocked the air from his lungs. In return, Michael threw an elbow in its face. The demon staggered back but the shadow feasting on my energy stirred. I'd forgotten it was there. I grabbed Michael's hands and pulled myself to my feet. Our eyes locked, and with all my will, I focused on sharing my energy—his power—with him. A white river of light shot down my arm, and the sword extended immediately. Its blue light glinted in Michael's eyes.

The creature on me roared and plunged its freezing claws through my chest. My heart seized into a knot and I staggered, fighting for air.

With a flick of his wrist, Michael sliced the creature feeding on me and my lungs released. The ghostly black form exploded into dust. The hooded demon lunged at his back, but he turned and decapitated it in one swipe. Its head and body melted and oozed down an old brass heat vent in the hardwood floors.

An icy emptiness filled my heart, radiating through me. I collapsed and slid down the wall.

Michael dropped his sword and cupped the sides of my face. His hands were warm. His breath formed clouds of steam against my cheeks. "Are you all right?"

I nodded then shook my head, unable to speak. Thin red cuts made by the demon's claws lined his face. A bruise formed over his left eye. He slid his arms around my waist and pulled me into him, lifting me to my toes. The warmth of his body seeped into me, igniting my halo. When he pressed his lips against mine, the heat of his desire sped through my veins. I sucked his lower lip, pressing against him, and slid one of my hands under his shirt to feel the tight, corded muscles of his back, the smoothness of his skin. But with one last kiss, he caught my hands and stepped away, his breath quick and hot against the side of my face.

I blinked, still drunk from kissing him. His power rumbled through me.

"Thought that might snap you out of it," he said once he'd caught his breath. "When a flyer bites, you know it for less than a second before you forget it was ever there. It's got a numbing agent, a venom that makes it hard to detect."

"I was so cold." I couldn't believe the danger I'd brought upon us. Here I was supposed to be protecting Michael's soul, and I'd let this thing feed on me. "How much did it get? Did it—?"

"Steal part of my soul?" He didn't hide his amusement. "No. It takes more than that to drain me. But you've dropped your connection to the network. Reconnect and you'll be fine."

I closed my eyes and joined the grid. Light flooded through me. It got easier to do each time. "I forgot to extend the halo when I came here. How did you keep all those creatures off you?"

"I'm not helpless," he said with a smirk. "Just…disadvantaged."

"Of course not." My hands slid to the sides of his arms. His shoulders were broad, the muscles taut and strong, and he towered over me. There was nothing about his physicality that appeared in any way helpless, even if he were completely human. But his black shirt had dark, damp spots where the angel killer sword had once sliced him. The wound must have reopened. I frowned when I saw it, trying not to show how worried I was.

Catching my look, he explained, "It's seeping a little from the blow. It'll be fine." He motioned to the cuts on his face. "But I should clean up."

The back of my head throbbed, and my fingertips discovered a goose egg forming, wet with blood. "Me too."

He turned and headed for the men's room door. "You're right. You need to learn how to protect yourself," he said. "I'll teach you."

I smiled but he couldn't see me. "Really?"

"Tomorrow. After school." Stopping, he added over his shoulder, "Don't expect me to go easy on you, though."

CHAPTER THIRTEEN

The blue-white barrier of light from the sigils tingled across my skin as I stepped into the safety of Michael's yard. A flyer that had hovered ten feet over my head for the past six blocks crashed into the shield and ricocheted off with a terrible shriek. Either its hunger had made it foolish, or flyers weren't the brightest of creatures. Probably both.

I found Michael waiting on the stone path outside his basement suite. He greeted me with a brush of his lips, lacing his fingers through mine, and led me into a large back yard, bordered by evergreens. The center of the soft, moist grass featured a rocky pond, complete with a trickling stone fountain and two Adirondack chairs. Though the yard was well kept, leaves from a giant maple lay strewn about like reddish-brown confetti, glistening with raindrops in the late afternoon sun.

Michael tugged off his old, gray hoodie and slung it over one of the chairs. Underneath was the white tank top he normally wore flying. Goose bumps raced along the length of his bare, powerful arms. Turning to face me, he shook out his shoulders, the muscles rolling as he gave them a shrug.

"Ready?" he asked.

"For?"

"Combat training." He stretched an arm across his chest and cracked his neck as though he were warming up. Was he expecting a workout?

"Combat training? Don't you think that sounds a bit intense?" I swallowed. My voice sounded tight and high. "Violent, even?"

"What did you expect? Origami?" Stretching his other arm now, he cocked an eyebrow at me. "You wanted me to teach you, right?"

"No—yes." I cleared my throat. "I mean no, I didn't expect origami and yes, I want to learn."

"Good." He smiled. Was he enjoying my awkwardness? I tuned into his energy, attempting to get a feeling off him, but hit a wall. Was he blocking me? His expression became neutral too.

Above our heads, flyers hovered at the edges of the sigils that surrounded the yard, circling a constant threat, like giant vultures. I motioned to the sky. "Can't they see us?"

"Not really. They can't see or hear anything inside the protected space." Changing the subject, he turned to me and winked. "Ready for your origami lesson? I thought we'd start with escapes."

I folded my arms across my chest. The idea of fighting Michael felt like a joke—a David and Goliath joke. "Escapes?"

"Yeah. We're gonna start with the basics. Teach you how to get out of that stranglehold the soldier demon had you in yesterday." His feet shoulder-width apart, he motioned for me to come closer. "But we can't do it if you're all the way over there."

I took a hesitant step toward him. Though I'd asked for this, the reality of it sounded painful. "Combat training," I muttered disdainfully.

"I won't hurt you."

"I know," I said, but I wasn't so sure.

"You just have to grab my throat. Doesn't have to be hard." When I didn't move, he stepped closer. "I need you to attack, so I can show you how to get out of it."

I backed up and my sneakers crunched a small twig, startling me. I didn't enjoy the idea of choking anyone.

"You won't hurt me, either. In most cases, your opponent won't hesitate to attack. It won't even be human. Either way, you have a right to protect yourself. And if you don't practice now, you'll freeze in a crisis." He wiped his hands on his jeans and his face lit with a mischievous grin. "You girls are all the same. You may talk tough, but can't back it up."

"Us *girls*?" My anger flared. "That's sexist, you know."

"It's making you mad." His smile softened and his eyes sparked a vibrant blue. "You can use that."

"You're *trying* to make me angry?"

"Whatever it takes." He shrugged. "Are you mad enough now? Or do I have to keep going?"

"Going to insult my mother next?"

"Do you need me to?"

I charged him and lunged for his neck, but all he had to do was stretch up to his full height. At five feet eight, I barely came to his shoulder.

He backed away, immediately out of reach. I clenched my fists. *What's the point of this?*

"You'll need to change your stance," he explained. "When you choke someone, you're not standing there lining up for the movies. You'll lean into them a little, one foot in front of the other, front leg bent so that no one can tip you over." He showed me what he meant with his own feet. "See?"

"But there's no way I'd choke a demon! And I'd never choke anyone as big as you."

"Good. You should never pick a fight unless you have to. The smartest thing you can do is run."

"That, I can do." I mirrored his stance.

"I've seen you run." He chuckled and shook his head sardonically. "Not so much."

"Hey!" I swung at his arm, trying to hit him.

He dodged me and studied my posture. "Put more of your weight into the front leg, so you won't be as easy to knock down." His light touch on my lower back sent a pleasant shiver down my spine.

I shifted forward. "Better?"

He nodded. "Now try again. Reach for my neck."

As soon I did, he leaned away, dropping his chin. He was so tall it was impossible to get a grip on him.

"This is stupid," I said. "You're too big! I can barely reach you!"

He ignored my complaint. "If someone gets that close, first thing you do is make your neck less of a target. Drop your chin, all right? Makes it harder for them to hold on."

"I noticed." I lowered my arms.

He caught my hands and placed them around his throat. This time, he didn't back away or tuck his chin. Instead, he held his hands over mine, the pulse at the side of his neck strong beneath my fingertips. My vision went black, as though I was going to faint. I blinked, trying to focus, and the blackness dissolved.

"Everything all right?" Michael asked.

"Fine," I said. My stomach grumbled. I was probably hungry.

Michael resumed his lesson. He lifted his arms and arced them over mine. The backs of his hands faced each other in an exaggerated diving move as he threaded them between my wrists. "Watch what I'm doing." He pressed slowly. It didn't take much to break my hold on him. "In a real situation, you'd push a lot harder, but that's the first one. Go over their arms and down through the middle. Got it?"

"I think so."

"Good." With a nod, he took my hands again and brought them to his neck. This time I gripped tighter, and he smiled. "Next one's from below, so bring your hands underneath and go up and through." He showed me, moving his long arms in an elegant arc through mine until my grip broke. "I'm going slow, but the faster and harder you go, the better."

"So I've heard," I said with a grin.

When his gaze locked with mine, a bemused smile touched his lips, and the feeling emanating from him made my cheeks flush.

He cleared his throat, serious again. "Ready to try? I'm a little taller than the average soldier demon, but they're fast and incredibly strong."

"Why do some have wings and others don't?" I asked.

"Status mostly. In the struggle for dominance, the strong ones get to keep their wings. The weak have them taken."

I remembered the soldier demon I fought didn't have wings. "The one last night…"

"Was pretty weak, all things considered."

He stepped into me and placed his hands on top of my shoulders. His thumbs caressed my collarbones. My stomach fluttered.

"If you keep doing that, I might not want to break away," I said.

With a nod, he stretched his fingers loosely around my neck to barely touch my skin. I leaned back and tilted my chin as he'd showed me. We practiced both moves, over and under, a few times, so I could learn the mechanics. Michael was patient, gently encouraging me as I got more comfortable with each move.

"Remember. Once you've broken free, you need to follow up with something, a punch or…" He paused, his hands still light on my throat as I pushed my hands under, up, and through, breaking the grip. "In your case, go for the knee, kick it here." He motioned to the outside of his own knee. "Try to break it, then reach for the network and get help."

"Can't I just kick it in the groin or something?"

He shook his head, backing away. "Don't try that unless you know your opponent is human. Soldier demons are essentially animated Ken dolls. There's nothing there to hit."

I stifled the urge to giggle at the thought of junk-less demons. "Don't I have any weapons I can use? A demon equivalent of bear spray?"

"Of course," he said. "The first thing you use is light from the network."

"I tried that, but the foot soldier rushed me right through the halo."

"Yeah, it won't stop them if you doubt yourself in any way. But you do have it. You ran it down your hands to send it to me. Fill yourself first and then aim for the solar plexus. Right here." He tapped the top of his stomach, below the heart. "When you're no longer choking, you can throw it off. But when you're startled, it's easy to forget you can do that. You'll have to reconnect, and fast."

I nodded, trying to commit his instructions to memory. "Chokehold, network, fill with light, slam the creature in the chest."

"That's it," he said.

"What about when you get your power back? I guess I won't be able to do as much."

He shrugged, sliding his hands into the pockets of his jeans. "If and when that happens, we'll see. I doubt you'll lose your ability to connect completely. I'm still able to. Just not as much." As he spoke, I knew he missed having his power about the same as I felt guilty for having it. "It's funny, I know I used to disconnect on purpose, but I sure miss it, now."

"Is that how you kept those flyers off you last night?"

"It's not hard. Connect and fill with light. It sours the milk," he said. "But it doesn't mean they won't attack or try to scare the crap out of you."

"Great! I'm pretty much freaked out all the time."

"Even I get scared, Mia. It's hard not to be, especially since I can't do what I used to. But courage isn't the absence of fear; it's moving through it to do what needs to be done. And I know you have courage. I've seen it."

Heat swelled in my chest. When he gave praise, it was never empty. "So?" I said, "Should we try again and I'll follow through and whup your ass with the big push of light?"

His mischievous grin returned. "I'd love to see you try!" Serious again, he stepped into me. "This time, it's going to seem a little more real, so you'll need to do it as though you mean it now." When he reached for me, his thumbs brushed my throat, his fingers firm on the back of my neck.

Instead of defending myself, I froze. Everything went white, and a dizzying buoyancy pulled at my limbs. A chill crept along my shoulder blades as an image collided with my thoughts, taking over my vision.

The room's walls are as black as charcoal, lit with flecks of glowing embers, as though the walls themselves had once been aflame. The air reeks of sulfur and the sickly sweetness of burning flesh. A giant, metallic structure stands before me, a circle forged of iron, laced with spikes and chains, so a body could be attached in all sorts of configurations—and it had been. Up close, its shackles are caked with dried blood. I knew some of it had been mine—or rather, Michael's. I feel his muscles struggle as though they are my own, straining against the black creatures, soldier demons, holding him in place. Around my—his—neck, they fasten a heated iron collar. Its spikes face inward, their fiery tips piercing my skin. I bite my tongue, tasting blood, but refuse to cry out. That would only please my captors more.

"It will heal," says a chilling voice that I recognize and don't. "He always heals. Drain him until he can't do it anymore. You understand me? Drain him dry."

My vision goes blank.

"Ready to try?" Michael said, breaking the memory's spell.

I gulped in the cool, damp air as though I'd just been underwater, flailing for my life. When he saw my expression, Michael dropped his hands from my neck. Acid jumped to my throat, and I ran to the bushes at the side of the yard to retch. Though my stomach heaved and roiled, it came up empty. *This was what they did to him? Thousands of years of this—this torture?*

My knees buckled and the wet grass rose up to meet me. Michael scooped his arm around my waist to catch me before I hit the ground.

"You all right?" he asked. Guiding me to a moss-covered log at the edge of the trees, he sat me down and crouched in front of me, his elbows resting on his knees. "Wanna tell me what happened there?"

When our gazes met, the vision returned. The stench of burning flesh cloyed at my nostrils. His screams filled my ears. I dug my knuckles into my eyes, trying to drive the vision away. But that only made it worse. I choked back a sob.

Michael took a seat beside me and circled me in his arms, delicately, carefully, as though I were made of porcelain. "Shh. You don't have to learn to fight if you don't want to. It's all right."

"No," I said. "It's not... I want to. Really." Words failed me. I couldn't tell him what I'd seen. How could I make him remember something so terrible? He didn't need to go through that again. He'd already lived it.

Without demanding an explanation, he curled me into his lap and held me. His arms sheltered me long after the sun tucked behind the horizon and the lights from the house cast a dim glow across the yard. Bathed in the darkness of nightfall, the flyers continued their inexorable orbit, awaiting the opportunity to feed.

CHAPTER FOURTEEN

Light from the near-full moon shimmers off the leaves of sycamore trees, and the scent of pomegranate hangs in the air. Though my footfalls are silent on the hard-packed earth, Hell is never far away. Nor is that blood-stained rack that was my prison for millennia. The memory of my master's claws still stings my throat; the poison of his hate burns below the skin. Perhaps it always will. The only reality I've come to know is that my pain satisfies him.

Anka sleeps on a grass mat, her lithe, young form curled into a fetal position on the roof of her family's mud brick house. Strands of her long, black hair are stuck to her cheekbones from the heat. The girl is old enough to be married but will be taken to the temple of Seth in the morning instead. Rumors of her prophetic dreams have secured her place as an oracle. Such a gift interests my master too, and as influential as Seth is among the Egyptian people, he's a false god, my master's rival. A demon warlord just like him.

Her father snores deeply, but the stifling air makes her mother fitful. The woman twists and turns. Does she anticipate me? I stand over the girl and contemplate how to take her without waking them. Their terror alone would sound a call to all the scavengers along the Nile, and my master wants her soul intact. More power that way. In servitude or sacrifice, souls are the fuel that builds empires.

My hand hovers over her nose and mouth, and her soft breath

119

tickles my skin. I could suffocate her while she dreams, a silent, seemingly natural death. Or I could carve out her heart, a symbolic gesture. He'd take pleasure in that. If I'm fast enough, she won't have time to cry out or wake the others. I run my fingers over the middle of her chest and extend my claws.

***

I screamed and jerked upright on the hard-backed wooden chair. Across the room, daylight streaming through the windows burned my retinas. I buried my face in my hands and, heart pounding, let the realization of my surroundings sink in.

I'm in the school library. I fell asleep during study period.

Whispers filled the silence—questions in their voices—and I uncovered my eyes to find everyone staring at me. The faces were familiar, but none of them belonged to my friends. I didn't know if it was better that way or worse.

The librarian, a dark-haired woman in her mid-twenties, rushed to my side. "Are you all right?" she asked. "Do you need help?"

"Sorry." My skin crawled with adrenaline as I tugged a loose strand of hair with my fingers and focused on the Latin verb conjugation chart in front of me. "Nightmare." Was it merely a dream? A memory? Was I the girl or the one hunting her?

I couldn't stay here now, so I gathered my books and shuffled from the library on foal legs. The voices along the network hummed like a radio with the volume on low. One clear, musical voice chimed above the rest.

"Mia, what's happening? Is everything okay?" It was Arielle.

Moments later, she met me in an empty history classroom. Her wings weren't cloaked, their feathery filaments shimmering in the fluorescent light. Her jacket was torn and she smelled of sulfur and ash, but her halo shielded us from prying eyes. A scratch was healing along her cheekbone. She'd come straight from fighting.

Guilt for tearing her away from battle pricked my cheeks. "I'm sorry." I plunked into one of the old desks, and it creaked in complaint. "I don't know what's wrong with me."

She tucked her wings into their invisible sheath, out of this dimension, so she could sit beside me. "Tell me what happened."

I told her every detail of my dream then added, "It took place a long time ago. Egypt, I think. Is this dream about me? Did I live back then, too?"

"Not that I'm aware of." Arielle pulled the band from her ponytail and shook her hair out with her fingers. "It's a memory, though. It could be one of Michael's from when he was serving Hell."

"Oh God." I fought back another wave of nausea. Those feral, predatory thoughts weren't anything like the Michael I knew! "The girl he attacked was sighted, like me."

"It wasn't him doing it. Imagine what thousands of years of torture would do—"

"I don't need to. I *remembered* some of it yesterday."

"I'm sorry," she said. "I'd hoped you wouldn't have to experience that. Even the most noble of us would cave to that kind of trauma."

"He said he was going to take her."

"Hell is full of rival packs that use people's souls as food." Afternoon sunlight pierced the skeletons of trees in the school yard, casting eerie shadows on her face and around the room. "He harvested them for one of the warlords there."

Harvesting souls? Demonic warlords? The news quaked through me. Michael had never lied about the fact that he'd done terrible things, but I'd never seen him be cruel or unkind, only good. I remembered his kiss in the restaurant the other night, the way it had brought me back from that cold, dead place, and my face warmed. *That* feeling hadn't changed. There was nothing evil there. But maybe I'd held him in a fantasy place, thinking he couldn't have done anything really bad. I'd been naïve.

"Why am I remembering this, if I wasn't there? I've never had memories that didn't belong to me before."

"I don't really know." She folded her hands in her lap and fixed her attention there. "Michael's soul may be messaging to you what it most needs to heal. Something he deeply regrets."

Michael's regrets? I wasn't sure I was ready for those. "But why? What can I do about it?"

"I can help you recall the memories, if you want." She held up her hands as though she was going to touch my head, the way she'd made me remember before.

I jumped to my feet. "No!" I'd already had an inkling of the torture he'd been through: that rack, being burned and clawed. I couldn't imagine enduring that for two minutes, let alone thousands of years.

"I understand," Arielle said. "But know this, if it's going to come, it will. In its own time."

I paced the row of desks, needing to move. "I don't know how I'm going to deal with it when it does."

"You do know." She stood and her halo shimmered around her. "When you forgave Damiel, you tuned to the network and listened to the Host. And you acted on it… Forgiving the fallen is one of your gifts, along with prophecy and sight. It's second nature to you."

I collapsed on the old, red armchair next to the teacher's desk, its corduroy arms worn smooth with age. Last year, I'd studied Ancient Civ in this room, come to class during study periods to read my homework. It was an AP class, and I was a year ahead. Our teacher, Ms. Horowitz, would delight us with tales about the past. Egypt, Sumeria, Ancient Rome: I loved them all. Last year, my biggest problem was making sure I got a good grade. God, things had been simpler then.

"Housing another soul is an intimate thing," Arielle said softly, leaning on the teacher's empty desk. "Michael's a part of you now, which means you'll come to know things about him that only he knows about himself. It could be that each time you use his power, you learn a little more."

Reliving someone else's experiences? I wasn't prepared for that kind of learning. Whatever happened to learning from books? I liked books. They were comfortable, safe. On the board a teacher had scrawled the words "Rosetta Stone" and a page number, and I recalled something Arielle had said to me a few days before. "Is this what you meant when you said I'd have to face the truth?"

Arielle studied me a long time before she nodded. "Do you remember Raguel?"

"Of course. He's the one who cut off Michael's wings," I said. At the harshness of the memory, a tight ball squeezed in my throat. Michael's screams of pain, the angry, jagged scars on his body, not to mention the ones on his soul that had taken millennia to fully heal. "He fell with Damiel, didn't he?"

"Yes." She twisted the elastic that had once been in her hair, tugging it and letting it snap. "Most demons are disorganized and hungry, a chaotic danger at best. Raguel may have fallen to the sin of pride but he moved with purpose. He organized, banded with others, torturing any who wouldn't yield to him. By swearing allegiance to him, the other angels who fell gave him all their power. His pride led him up the ranks to warlord. He set himself up as a false god, and Damiel's envy brought him along for the ride." She stood, and the gossamer grid of her wings flicked with irritation. "Michael held out longer than anyone I'd seen. But eventually, he learned to serve."

My finger started to throb. I'd twirled a long loose thread from the old chair around it until the tip turned red with trapped blood. I loosened it and shook my hand out.

Arielle crossed the classroom and selected a book from the shelf, a text on Ancient Sumeria. She flipped it open to a random page. "Have you heard of Gilgamesh?"

The last thing I wanted right now was a history lesson. I'd had enough thinking about the past. "Yeah, he was a warrior. They say he was king for over a hundred and twenty-five years."

"King? Tyrant is more like it." She focused on the textbook and leafed idly through its pages. "In some stories, it's said that Gilgamesh was born of a god. Others say a demon."

"Okay, but what does it have to do with Raguel?"

"The early civilizations were ruled by some of Hell's fiercest warlords, who pretended to be human. Gilgamesh was one of Raguel's many disguises. He mixed demon and human blood lines to create soldiers for his armies. They were stronger than humans, but unable to reproduce on their own. When they died, they continued their service in Hell."

"As...what?" I gasped, unable to finish my sentence.

"Soldier demons. Thousands of them. All the warlords had them. But as strong as they are, they're no match for an angel. So Raguel groomed the strongest of his fallen angels to lead. He paid lots of attention to Michael, gave him special assignments."

I pulled my knees into my chest and hugged them. *What horrible things had Michael done?* "Harvesting souls?"

She snapped the book shut and returned it to the shelf. "When Michael was redeemed and able to escape, Raguel saw it as the ultimate betrayal. His followers thought he'd gone soft. They rebelled against him, led by his second-in-command."

"Let me guess. Damiel?"

Arielle nodded. "Somehow, he managed to imprison Raguel, though the power that would take..." A golden light shone from her eyes as she met my gaze. "Some believe that, in his absence, another leader is rising."

My mouth went dry. I licked my lips. "Who is it?"

She ran her finger along the wooden shelf and, finding dust, she rolled it between her fingertips. "Demons hardly make willing informants," she said. "We learned a lot from Michael when he came back, but since his return, we've little more than rumors to go on."

"What about Damiel? Wouldn't he be able to tell you what's going on?"

"Perhaps he would if he were awake, but he's in limbo, a type of deep rest that's helping him recover. None of us can reach him yet."

"Will he wake soon?" The thought of Damiel being conscious again burned in my stomach like a ball of lava. Though I'd basically forgiven him for what he'd done, I had no idea what I'd do if I ever had to face him again.

"There's no way to tell. It took Michael half a century to recover. They're different, of course, but Damiel was further gone. By the time he wakes up—"

"It'll be too late."

CHAPTER FIFTEEN

For the rest of the day, my after-school training session with Michael loomed, filling my thoughts with dread. How was I supposed to face him when I knew what he'd done? I wanted to skip the whole thing, if for no other reason than to avoid triggering more memories of his horrific past. But Arielle was persistent. When she nagged me about it over the network, I thought I'd disconnected to tune her out. But right in the middle of Gov/Econ, my last class for the day, her voice blasted over Mr. Jarvie's lecture on accounting principles, and convinced me that the more I fought those visions, the more likely they would come at the most inconvenient time. As if the middle of study period wasn't bad enough.

Even so, I shuffled my feet the entire walk to Michael's, and my own thoughts argued with themselves.

Turn around and go back.

No, it'll be okay, just act normal. Things will be fine.

But he's killed people.

So did Damiel, and you forgave him. Doesn't Michael deserve the same chance?

Flyers hovered at the periphery of my halo, emitting a high-pitched whine that pierced my skull and made my head throb. At one point, I got so frustrated I stopped in the middle of the street, shook my fists and swore at them. If anyone saw me, they would've thought I was insane. But at least it made my headache go away.

By the time I reached Michael's front step, my heart pounded as though I'd sprinted all the way there. He opened the door before I had a chance to knock. My knees shook.

"Hey," he said, sizing me up. "Long day?"

I stiffened my legs to steady them and, glancing down, noticed my coat was fastened askew. "Uh-huh." I fidgeted with the buttons.

He leaned in to kiss me hello, and all I could see was that damned iron rack, covered in his blood. My nostrils filled with the tang of sweat mixed with sulfur and decay. I flinched and pulled away.

Michael didn't react, didn't ask what was wrong. I didn't want him to.

I can do this.

I found my determination and we continued the lesson where we left off, practicing the escapes from the day before—over and under—until my limbs remembered and the motions began to flow. Michael responded to my distance as though it were simply a fear of learning to fight. His touch was light and gentle, cautious even, as he paid close attention to my every move, holding back when he had to and easing me forward only when he sensed I could tolerate more. I couldn't have asked for a better teacher. This was the Michael I knew and loved. So when he suggested we try a different chokehold, I felt ready.

"Most attackers won't come at you head-on," he said. "They'll try to surprise you."

He explained that he was going to grab me from behind and hooked an arm around my neck to demonstrate. When his warm skin brushed against my throat, and his fingers gripped my shoulder, I froze. Everything went white and staticky, and with a dizzying pull, I felt my feet leave the ground. Next thing I knew, I was observing the two of us from above, watching myself stand there limp and vacant in his arms.

The memory of the dream flashed before my eyes. The mud brick house. Anka curled up on the roof. Michael's predatory thoughts as he calculated how to kill her.

His fingertips pressed into my shoulder. "Come on," he urged. "Drop your chin." His breath raised the hairs on my neck. When I didn't respond, he spun me around.

I landed back in my body with a whooshing sound, and my breath stopped when his soft gaze captured mine. I wondered how he must have looked as a harvester of souls. Was he as beautiful as he was now? Or charcoal-skinned and horrific?

In the fading light of the yard, he paled and dropped his hands, stepping away. "I-I'm only trying to help. I'm not—"

"It's getting dark." I grabbed my coat from one of the chairs and tugged it on. *Don't look at him.* "Maybe we should call it a night. I can get myself home."

I turned to leave, but he caught my arm. "Wait. Please." At my hesitation, his voice trembled. "Don't shut me out again. I don't know what you're feeling. Talk to me."

My heart jack hammered in my chest as I readied myself to bolt. Would I need to? This was Michael standing in front of me. Perfectly human, without a trace of demon on him. But all I wanted to do was run away. Going inside and talking? Hell. No.

"Besides," he said. "You can't leave now. Your fear will draw a crowd." He motioned to the black creatures circling the sky above us. "Give yourself a minute."

"I'm fine." I took a deep breath and reached for the network with my thoughts, but when I touched into it, my connection fizzled and dropped.

Turiel appeared and scanned the yard, his sword at the ready. "Everything all right?"

"She's fine." Michael's words were clipped. "I was

showing her how to break out of a choke hold."

"Don't speak for me!"

"You're right." He backed away, raising his hands in the air. "I won't."

Turiel approached me, his tone formal. "I can sense your distress. Do you require assistance?"

Michael turned away and sighed.

Turiel's presence loosened the knot between my shoulder blades—maybe it was simply knowing I had an escape if I needed one. He could teleport me directly into my living room, from one protected space to another without having to encounter a single minion, but I couldn't leave Michael. Running away wasn't going to solve anything. I needed to talk to him. Didn't he deserve that much?

"I'm okay," I said. "Can I take a rain check?"

Turiel motioned to the sky. "It's not raining."

"It's a figure of speech. What I mean is, can I call on you later if I need you?"

Michael muttered something under his breath and seated himself on the old, mossy log a few feet away, his words muffled by the trickling of the fountain.

"Of course," Turiel said with a nod and disappeared.

The sun had finished setting, the sky deepening to gradients of blue. Streetlights cast the long, eerie shadows of trees across the yard. Bathed in the darkness of nightfall, Michael's face was unreadable, but the emotions coming off him echoed right through me. I wanted to scream, hide, run away, and cry all at once. I remembered Arielle's words: *Forgiving the fallen is one of your gifts*. Perhaps this was the moment where I was supposed to do that. After all, how could I expect him to be perfect, to be untouched by the terrible things he'd faced, when even though I had some of his power, I could hardly face them myself?

I took a deep breath to steel myself and reconnected to the network. Its light tingled through my scalp and a river of warmth rushed through me, filling my arms and chest. Arielle's voice broadcast into my head immediately.

"*Is everything okay?*"

"*I think so*," I thought back to her. Whatever happened now, we weren't alone. More images from my dream: the scent of pomegranate, the sound of Anka's breathing as she slept. The scrape of claws gripped my throat. I swallowed and it faded.

"*You don't have to relive it*," she said. "*Trust your instincts. They haven't served you wrong.*"

With her words came a flood of courage and hope that filled me until I glowed with it. I lowered the network's volume in my head and strode across the yard.

Still seated, Michael leaned toward me the way a plant orients itself toward the sun. But he didn't talk. He left that to me.

"It's cold." I offered him my hand. "Can we please go inside?"

His eyes shone by the porch light and I heard the air rush from his lungs as he exhaled in relief. He lifted my hand to his lips, kissed it palm up, and we walked hand in hand to the house.

CHAPTER SIXTEEN

Inside Michael's basement suite, I perched on one of the living room chairs. He sat next to me for a nanosecond before he leaped up and snatched a green-and-white plaid shirt from the couch. He pulled it over his T-shirt and rolled up the cuffs. Nervous energy crackled off him. I waited for him to settle, but then he flipped the switch to light the fireplace and headed toward his kitchenette.

"Want something to drink?"

"Got any tequila left?" I asked, only half joking. I wished he would chill. Maybe a shot of something would slow him down.

He frowned over his shoulder. "Really?"

"Kidding!" I said. "Whatever you've got is fine."

A thin, elongated wooden box on his coffee table snagged my attention. I picked it up and unfastened its tiny, iron clasp to find a browned scroll, its edges curled and shredded with age. I'd never been so close to an artifact this ancient before. Tempted to touch it, I hovered my fingers over its reedy ridges, and a faint buzz of energy hummed through my hand. My mind prickled with curiosity, and the part of me that wanted to be an archaeologist couldn't wait to examine it. But if it were a relic, it deserved special treatment, gloved and careful respect.

Michael returned and set a glass of orange juice on the table in front of me. His presence reminded me I was there to talk, but I had no idea where to begin. It wasn't as though they taught you how to deal with your boyfriend's demonic past life in Guidance class.

"What's this?" I held up the box and then placed it back on the table, away from our drinks.

He shrugged and folded himself on the couch. "Research I'm doing on cursed swords."

"Is it Egyptian?" The mention of Egypt sent a quake of energy through me as images from his past pressed at my thoughts. I searched his face for any signs of recognition. When I found none, I pushed the memories back. *Not yet.*

"It's Aramaic." He wiped his hands on his jeans and picked up the scroll. "Wanna see?" He unrolled the papyrus to show me its faded, ancient script.

I stiffened from head to foot, involuntarily clenched my hand. "That has to be thousands of years old and you're touching it?"

"It's from our archives. It's been shielded. Handling won't damage it."

That's what had caused the buzz. I held out my hand. "Can I?"

He carefully passed it to me, and the energetic hum tickled my fingers. I examined the dark brown lettering, the spotted, stained paper. "It's amazing. What does it say?"

"It lists all the weapons that went missing in the first war. Arielle brought it to me in case I remembered any of them. We're trying to find the sword I was attacked with, in case it helps break the curse."

"Any luck?" My heart raced at the nearness of him, the grassy sweet smell of his skin.

He shook his head. "Pictures would've been more useful. I don't recognize any of the names."

The drumming of footsteps on the stairs broke the scroll's spell. Someone knocked on the door that separated Michael's room from the rest of the house. I leaped to my feet.

"Michael?" his mother said. "Can I come in?"

He closed the scroll and returned it to its box. "I'll get rid of her," he whispered then stood and called back, "Door's open."

His mother glided into the room. She wasn't in her usual business suit that she wore to court, but slacks and a powder blue sweater.

"I thought I saw you two in the back yard, strangling each other," she said with a wink.

Michael cringed.

"He's teaching me self-defense, Mrs. Fontaine," I said.

"Just Katharine," she corrected in her rich, warm voice. "That's good. Michael's been doing Tae Kwon Do since he was six, but I've always believed women should learn these things as well, especially in the city. If you know how to defend yourself, you're less prone to becoming a victim of a violent crime."

"Thanks for the criminology lesson." Michael took a swig of his juice.

"None of your cheek," she said. "I came to tell you dinner would be ready in five minutes. And we've made plenty if you'd care to stay, Mia. Michael's dad's a fabulous cook, so you're in for a treat."

"Uh, Mum—"

"That would be great," I said, cutting him off. "Thanks."

The quaking in my energy—Michael's power—returned, and I strained to keep the memories from surging forward. It was only a matter of time before I'd have to share what I saw, and I needed to collect my thoughts. Having his parents around would make him seem more human. Though I knew he wasn't, not really, I needed to remember that he wasn't a demon anymore, either.

My nerves settled as I followed Katharine upstairs. Michael dragged behind as she led me into their living room. A fire blazed in their stone hearth and a faint scent of wood smoke perfumed the air. The room was furnished in the same sleek, modern style as Michael's, but instead of a sofa, it had a massive cream-colored sectional and glass coffee table. Their floors were a dark wood, and the room's high ceilings were crossed with exposed rough-cut oak beams. The best feature was the floor-to-ceiling windows with a view of the city lights and the silhouette of Puget Sound against the evening sky.

Four places had already been set at the dining room's large, wooden table as though they'd been expecting me. Elegant white plates on gray linen placemats, silver cutlery, cloth napkins. I wondered if they ate this way every night. Michael pulled out one of the dining room chairs, and his proximity set my energy soaring again, like a perimeter alarm. I strained to ignore it.

"Thanks again for the invitation," I said to Katharine as I unfolded the gray cloth napkin in front of me and placed it on my lap. "My mom's working late, so it would've just been leftovers for me."

Michael held out the chair beside mine. Katharine thanked him and slid into it.

"Oh? What does your mother do?" she asked.

"She's a palliative care nurse at Seattle General."

Michael frowned and sat across from me. "I told you that before, Mum."

She placed her hand on mine in a friendly gesture then pulled it away. "I know, but I wanted Mia to tell me."

Michael's father emerged from the kitchen carrying a large tray of food, which he placed on the table in front of us. A blend of cream, seafood, and garlic scented the air.

"Hope everyone's hungry," he said in an English accent much thicker than Michael's. He wiped his hands on a dark blue apron that seemed tiny on his long, lanky frame.

"John, this is Mia," Katharine said.

John and I exchanged hellos, and I noticed his resemblance to Michael. They had the same build and bone structure, including the same nose and jaw, but John's eyes were brown. His graying hair was sandy-colored.

"Tuck in," he said with a smile. "Hope you don't mind pasta and seafood." The gnocchi was homemade and smothered in cream sauce. The garlic prawns were peeled and perfectly cooked, and the Caesar salad was served with shaved parmesan. Over dinner, Michael and his dad talked about football, but they were teams I'd never heard of before: Arsenal, Manchester United, West Ham. Even Katharine weighed in on the discussion. When I asked about them, Michael explained that they were English soccer teams.

Though his parents asked Michael about school, he only gave a brief account, so they wouldn't know how much he'd missed this semester. It was obvious they didn't have a clue he was an angel. I wondered how he'd hid everything from them for so long, especially without his usual powers of enthrallment. But apparently, Michael came from a family of secret keepers. John was a regional VP of some major bank and didn't discuss his work, and Katharine couldn't violate client confidentiality by talking about her cases. So the topics were sports and current events.

Partway through our meal, the energy I'd experienced before dinner buzzed and pressed at the back of my skull. Michael fell silent, his feelings muted from me, but for the occasional puzzled glance across the table. I couldn't look at him without my head starting to throb. When dinner was over, he wished his parents a clipped good night and strode downstairs. As soon as he was gone, the headache lifted instantly. I wasn't sure which would be more awkward, following him downstairs or lingering with his folks under the guise that everything was okay. I helped

Katharine clear the table and had started loading the dishwasher when she waved me off and sent me downstairs.

I found Michael pacing in the privacy of his room. His long legs cut the small space in a few strides. Not sure where to begin, I started small. "Your parents are great."

He dug his hands deep into the pockets of his jeans and leaned against the fireplace. "Tell me what's going on. First, you freak out. Then you stay. But as soon as we're alone for a few minutes, you jump at the chance for parental supervision."

"That's not fair. I've wanted to meet them for a long time. We just never get the chance to be…normal."

Frustration rolled off him. "Well, I'm pretty damned normal now, aren't I?"

Michael's power surged through me and started to hum. I was too nervous to sit. Though I wasn't sure how I was going to broach the topic of his past, this definitely wasn't how I'd pictured it. Had I stopped trusting him? I'd glimpsed into his world and didn't like where he'd been, and that was it? I was done? As though nothing we'd been through before had ever mattered.

"Maybe Turiel should take you home," he said.

"Do you want me to leave?"

He crossed the room to the closet, retrieved my wool coat, and held it up, all the while avoiding my gaze. "I don't know what I've done."

Now that we were alone, his memories from the night before slammed against my consciousness. It was time. "I don't want to go."

"Well, that's something, I guess." Still carrying my coat, he returned to his living room and draped it over a chair.

I sat on the couch and took a deep breath. "What can you tell me about harvesters of souls?"

He folded his arms protectively across his chest and leaned against the arm of the sofa. "They're powerful demons who steal people's souls. Why?"

Though his tone was flat, as he spoke, a sea of grief and remorse overtook me. It was all I could do to not drown in the undertow. I leaned into the network for support and Arielle's voice rang through my thoughts.

"*He doesn't remember,*" she said.

"*How can that be?*" I asked her.

"*You're holding the part of his soul that has the memory. He's split off from it and needs you to tell him, so he can get that part of himself back.*"

"*What about the curse? Won't getting part of his soul back simply make it worse?*"

"*Don't worry about that,*" Arielle said. "*He's ready. Tell him what you know.*"

The sharpness of Michael's voice cut through our connection. "You went away again. I can hear music, not words, so I know you're on the network. You and Turiel planning your escape?"

"I'm talking to Arielle," I said. "It seems whenever I use your power, I am shown a bit of your past."

"What does that have to do with anything?"

Oh God! He really doesn't remember. Though Michael's room was clean, my gaze fixed on a tiny rust-colored spot on the rug, dried blood from his injury the other day. Would this knowledge only wound him more?

"There was a time in ancient Egypt, where you were sent to a young woman promised to the temple of Seth. Your master wanted her soul." As I spoke, a wave crashed through my energy, a churning riptide that threatened to pull me under as the memory returned.

The wave flashed blue across the room and crashed into Michael, forcing him to his feet. His face turned the color of boiled milk, as the horror of recognition came over him. "Anka. How could I have forgotten?" he whispered. "How long have you known?" He sank his head in his hands, his long fingers rending his dark hair.

"Since last night."

Though we were safe within the sigils, a shadow

enveloped us as though I was seeing him through a gray film. He backed away. "How can you be near me, knowing this?"

As the full force of the memory came forward, grief, shame, and self-loathing rushed through me. And even though I wanted to soothe him, and I knew I loved Michael more than anyone in the world, part of me wanted to strike him dead for what he'd done. My body shook from the impulse.

"*Steady now*," said Arielle. "*That would ruin your soul and his. Those are his feelings. Let them go.*"

The feelings clung to me, a flurry of images downloading at the speed of light. I remembered everything—he'd taken souls, led people not only to their death but to eternal damnation. I didn't care if I hurt him. A storm of angry wasps churned in my gut. Fury boiled in my veins. I lunged at him. My arms flailed with clumsy punches thrown at his stomach and chest. "You bastard! How could you?"

Arielle's voice blasted me through the network. "*Mia, Stop!*"

But I didn't stop, and Michael didn't block me. He stood perfectly still and let me fight it out, until my arms wore out and my lungs were spent and heaving. I collapsed into him.

"There's no excuse," he said softly, his voice rumbling through his chest. "I should have told you." His hands hovered over my back, close but not quite touching, as though he wasn't sure what to do. "I'd been sent to take her, but her mother woke up and begged to go in her daughter's place."

I didn't remember that part. "I thought—"

"I couldn't hide it from them. No act of mercy goes unpunished. It got so bad." His fingertips settled on my shoulders. "Each time they cut and burned me, tearing what was left... I wasn't so merciful the next time."

"But you didn't hurt her." With my arms still wrapped

around his waist, I had to tilt my chin to look up at him.

"I hurt others." He pulled out of my awkward embrace. "I was a good slave."

That night in the cabin, moments before Damiel had been redeemed, I could see two parts of him struggling for dominance. One part was the angel, the other a demon. Alternating. Separate. The angel would never have done harm, but the demon part had infected him. It had grown the way cancer takes over its unwilling host. Michael had also been broken, but the demon part, the harvester of souls, had been cut and burned away by his redemption long ago. It was gone forever. All that was left now was good, but it held the memory of infection like an imprint. He'd always felt guilty. Even now.

"I'm sorry I hit you," I said.

He shook his head and gave me a sad smile. "I've had worse."

"I know, but that doesn't mean you deserved it."

Behind me, an explosion of brilliant light as far as I could perceive burst through the network, filling me until white flames pulsed under my skin. I approached Michael and though my voice seemed to come from the network itself, I knew the words I had to say.

"You are loved. You are forgiven. Everything you've done is forgiven."

The force of his power ricocheted through me in a fireworks display that burned away any shadows and engulfed his energy in an inferno of purple, gold, and blue flames. The blaze grew and grew until his halo erupted around him into a ring of colored fire. The gossamer grid of his wings shimmered again. When he unsheathed them, they stretched across the room and iridescent starlight danced along the walls.

"Thank you," he said. The deep chord of his voice rang through the network, bringing its own unique harmony to the music already there. I'd thought returning his power to him would have left me feeling empty or lesser in some way, but I was still connected to it. I hadn't lost that; he'd said I wouldn't. So I could hear the others cheering as they welcomed him back, felt the resonance of it thrumming through my whole form until my legs shook. I could hardly stand.

Michael dropped to his knees on the rug in front of me. "Can you forgive me for what I've done?" he asked, taking my hands in his. "I know the others have, or else I wouldn't be here. But can you?"

I draped my arms around his neck and leaned into the solidness of him. He clutched at my waist and, stretching out his legs, slid me onto his lap. We were on the floor, but I didn't care.

I smiled and leaned into him. "Always," I whispered against his mouth. And then he pressed his lips into mine.

CHAPTER SEVENTEEN

Though I no longer carried part of Michael's soul, the network was as available as I needed it to be, which meant I could tune in and listen whenever I wanted, like a police radio. I was just glad I didn't have to hear it droning in the background anymore. My enhanced sight hadn't changed, either, so I'd have to get used to seeing flyers and creatures on people—I wasn't sure if that was a blessing or a curse. But at least I still had a halo, albeit smaller, to flame them with.

The other angels gave Michael several full days and nights off to allow his healing to fully set. So, for the next few days, we spent every moment together. In our spare time, he continued training me to fight. Now that he'd seen me throw a punch, he said I'd need lots of practice. No longer having his memories attached to mine, I managed to learn how to block, kick, and punch without being distracted. Michael even brought out gloves and padding so I could really let go.

My mom worked every night, so after our sessions, Michael would heal my aching muscles, and I'd fall into bed exhausted, finally able to rest without disturbing dreams or flashing to wake me. Well, his halo still flashed, but he was the one attached to it, not me. When the shimmering woke me, he'd whisper an apology in my ear and hold me tighter.

I wouldn't have given up those moments with him for the world.

On Monday, Michael drove us both to school for his first day back. I realized I'd left my Latin text in his car and went to get it. As I crossed the parking lot, I caught Farouk by himself and stopped to wait for him. Heavy shadows hung over his shoulders, but as far as I could tell, they were emotions, not sentient creatures feeding on his soul, at least, not within the school grounds. I hated to think what happened to him outside the protected space.

"Where's Fatima today?" I asked, as we made our way through the throngs like salmon swimming upstream.

"She's sick," he said with a frown. The front of his T-shirt was rumpled under his jacket, as though he'd slept in it, and the deep, dark rings circling his eyes were stark by daylight.

"Since when?" I asked, but I already knew the answer. Guilt pricked my skin. Maybe she had been acting strangely the last I'd seen her *because* she was sick. Come to think of it, I hadn't seen her since I'd developed the ability to see minions on people. "Is it serious?"

"My parents have called in the *imam*."

"A priest?" His news turned my stomach into a block of ice. I drew in a sharp, involuntary breath. "Why? Is she—?" I was going to ask if she was dying, but I couldn't bring myself to say it.

"No. Our parents are just really devout." He opened the glass door leading into the school's huge foyer. I stepped through it and he followed.

"Yeah, Fatima told me." During a tarot card reading she'd given me, she said they disapproved of such things. "So what does the *imam* do?" I said.

"The doctor couldn't diagnose her, so my mother called him in to make sure it's not…" He stopped and his dark eyes scanned the hallway, making sure no one else could hear us. "An evil spirit," he muttered self-consciously. "Crazy, right?"

I shook my head, long past the idea of evil spirits being "crazy". I was so shocked to find another person I could talk to about these things that, without thinking, I blurted out, "What kind?"

If my question fazed Farouk, he didn't let it show. "My parents think she might have been possessed by a *djinn*." When I gave him a questioning look, he continued. "It's a powerful spirit from the other side. It can be good or evil, but if it possesses someone, that person gets sick. Sometimes, it makes them do horrible things."

They sounded like minions—with a different name. Having had one on myself, not knowing what it was, I could imagine how easy it would be to become its servant. The idea of that happening to Fatima was simply wrong. I lowered my voice. "She's still not wearing her *hamsa*, is she?" Neither was I, anymore, but my crew-neck sweater hid that fact.

He paused when we reached my locker. "No. We can't find it. And the store's sold out. Someone bought up our supply right after Fatima gave them to you and your friends."

My mind darted back to the day Heather and I had gone to see her at the store. Fatima'd had news for me. I remembered that guy who came in after we left, the way my *hamsa* had jittered and stopped. Something about him tugged at the back of my mind, but when I tried to catch it, the memory dissipated like smoke.

***

When I caught up with Michael, he was heading to his locker. I tossed him his car keys. He swiped them from the air and buried them in his pocket in a single arc.

"How are you feeling?" I asked, wondering how to

bring up the subject of Fatima and the *djinn*. Was he ready for this? Would he be well enough?

"Great." He scooped an arm around my waist. "An old friend of mine—and Jesse's—has a band playing Friday night. He put us on the guest list. Wanna go?"

I blinked at him. "Really?" Going out was the last thing on my mind, but his smile was so bright, so hopeful, I couldn't spoil his mood. "You can?"

"Go out?" He drew me closer, and his halo tingled around me. His mood was infectious. "It's pretty quiet right now. Quieter than it's been in weeks."

Quiet? I had to remind myself that those flyers and minions—a permanent fixture outside the school grounds—were new only to me. So was the *djinn*. And after everything he'd been through, Michael deserved a night off.

I put on a smile. "Where is it?"

"The Icebox."

The Icebox was a club downtown where a lot of up-and-coming bands played. It catered to an over-twenty-one crowd and was notorious for its strict bouncers. I'd never been inside.

"Is it all ages? Because Heather and I don't have ID." I placed my hands on his chest, trying not to be distracted by his proximity, the heat of his fingers on my lower back.

He smiled and kissed my cheek. Tingles ran down my neck. "Don't worry about that. They're allowing a few underage guests, as long as we wear wristbands."

Going to see a band with him and my friends sounded like a dream—no demons, no *djinn*, no warring forces of good and evil. A real double date. I let it sink in.

"I thought you might appreciate something normal," he said. "After what you said the other night."

"I do. It sounds fun," I said, but Fatima needed Michael's help. I'd already forgotten to mention her once before. Not this time.

He frowned, letting his arm drop. "What's wrong?"

"I just spoke to Farouk. Fatima isn't well."

"Yeah. Heard she has mono." He turned to his locker and opened it.

"No. Last I saw her she said we needed to talk, but since then, she's been off. The doctor doesn't know what it is, so they've called in an *imam*. They think it's an evil spirit, something called a '*djinn*'."

"Ahhh." He nodded knowingly and slid his books onto the shelf. "The *djinn*."

"Are they a type of minion?"

"Some people refer to minions as *djinn*, but that's not what they really are." He kept his voice low in the crowded hallway and leaned in to speak to me. "They're creatures of hellfire. It's believed that some are good, and others are evil, but even the so-called 'good' ones aren't so much good as *less evil* than the others."

"How dangerous are they?"

"For humans? Wherever there's a *djinn*, there's bound to be trouble." He shrugged, adding, "but they're usually manageable."

"Will you help her?"

He shook his head and rummaged through his knapsack until he pulled out his chemistry text.

"Why not?" My frustration flared. Why would he help Dean and not Fatima? "Her family needs the help. They've called in a Muslim priest. I know you could…" I stopped myself. Was it too soon for him to be helping anyone? Was I pushing him? "Should you be? I mean…"

"It's fine," he said. His back was turned, so I couldn't read his expression. "But I'm not the one who's going to do it." Shouldering his pack, he spun to face me and smiled. "You are."

"But—" My knees went slack. "I don't have powers anymore. You got them back."

"Nonsense. You can connect to the network. You're a prophet. You said you didn't want to be afraid anymore. And since you can still see these things, wouldn't you feel better knowing you can do something about them?"

"I would, yeah."

"Well, consider it part of your training." He closed his locker door and sealed the lock before he glanced up at me. "That is, if you still want me to teach you."

"You bet I do."

"Good. It's settled. Your first exorcism as a prophet." He brushed his soft lips against my cheek. "We'll go right after school. We can even go out for dinner after and celebrate."

He took off down the hall but his words echoed in my head. First *exorcism*? Prophet? I'd be facing a *djinn*? Good God, what was happening to me?

CHAPTER EIGHTEEN

Fatima and her family lived in a white, old-fashioned wood house with a huge, covered porch. Pruned trees loomed over the mulched garden beds. Even under the overcast sky, their yard was bright, but the roof was covered in a blanket of shadows that reminded me of the ones I'd seen on Farouk, only much bigger. Above our heads, flyers screeched and swooped. Without sigils around the area to stop them, they flew so close I could smell the sulfur wafting off of them.

We parked across the street, and my body screamed at me not to get any closer to that house. "Looks pretty awful."

Michael frowned at the scene, his lips pressed together. "I've seen worse." He pulled the parking brake and sighed. "I know I said you were going to do this, but would you mind if I checked the situation out first?"

Mind? The muscles in my neck were pulled as tight as violin strings. "Lead the way."

As soon as we were out of the car, the flyers circled faster and started to dive. Michael flared his halo around us, a huge wall of solid flame that extended farther than I could ever get mine. Drawing his sword from behind him, he stood at the ready. I drew my consciousness to the network and listened for the murmur of angels as I filled with light. The creatures orbited and shrieked, hovering around us, but none of them dared come near.

"What do you call a group of flyers?" I asked. "You know, a flock of birds, a murder of crows…"

"We usually call them 'squadron'. Some say a 'troop' or 'muster'. Why?"

"Not creepy enough." I zipped up my jacket to fend off the chill in the air. It was colder here than near the school. "They should be the ones called a murder, not crows. Or maybe a tremble of flyers, because every time I see them, something in me trembles."

He shook his head, his attention fixed on the path in front of us. "Calling them that would only make you more afraid. It'll be fine as long as you stay in the network."

"I know." The first time we'd faced a demon together, Michael had warned me that I couldn't let it frighten me. The same rules applied now. "Love, right?"

"Exactly," he said. "As ferocious as you can make it."

I tried to picture a ferocious love. I could imagine attraction, but I wasn't about to go there with demons. I cleared my throat, hoping Michael couldn't read my thoughts. "Isn't love supposed to be a gentle thing?"

"It can also be fierce. To love in the presence of your own fear requires ferocity. Think of the extent a mother bear will go to protect her cubs. She'll take on a male grizzly one and a half times her size to protect them. Now that's love."

Love? Taking on something one and a half times my size sounded plain crazy to me. "That's just survival instinct."

"That, too." He stopped at the base of Fatima's well-worn front steps and turned to me. "Love is the one thing strong enough, *fierce* enough, to stand against evil. Not even Hell can stop it. When I was there, part of me never stopped loving you. It was the thing that made me want to change." He swallowed, and his gaze linked with mine, his eyes heavy-lidded and sincere. "No matter what you say, you can't fool me. I know how capable you are."

I fought the urge to lean into him. My voice went soft. "Only with you."

"Not true." He brushed a stray lock of hair out of my eyes. "Love is what you used to forgive Damiel. You were terrified, but you connected to the network and loved right through it."

"I never loved Damiel."

"Not in a human way, but it was still love."

Ferocious love? Not human? How long would it take before I understood his world? I motioned to the brown wooden door. Shadows lurked behind its glass inset. "Any idea what we're going to say to get inside?"

"The truth."

"You're not going to talk about love, are you?"

"No, that's just for you." He sheathed his sword so no one would see it, and gave me a nod. "Ready?"

"Ferocious love," I said as we marched up the front stairs.

Farouk answered the door in sweats and a black T-shirt that read "Hello, my name is… Awesome", though he looked anything but. His face was pale and tight and his energy much darker than it had been under the protection of the school's sigils. His tattered cape, once comprised of shadows, had transformed into serpents. They writhed around his head and over his shoulders, and had fed so much they'd gained substance.

"What do you two want?" he asked.

Behind Farouk, more snakes slithered along the floor, some as big as pythons. His entire house had been overrun by shadows that lurked in the corners. Their presence raised all the hairs on my arms.

Michael's halo flared, scattering the serpents and giving us room. But the ones on Farouk merely flinched. One of them curved around his neck, piercing his skull, as another poked its head through his chest. Everything in me wanted to run.

"We can help Fatima," I said, finding my voice. *Ferocious love.*

"*Pull the light into you, Mia,*" Michael said in a low, musical voice.

I caught his glance. His voice came from the network. I filled with light until sparks spit from my fingertips. The creatures on Farouk hissed in response. Michael flared his halo again, and a few of them singed and dropped away, but the one in Farouk's head didn't budge.

"She doesn't need your help," Farouk said, attempting to close the door.

Michael stepped inside and stood so close to Farouk, he towered over him. "Do you want her to get better?"

Farouk hesitated and I thought he was going to push Michael away. "Of course I do!"

Michael's hand glowed with a golden-white light as he brought it to Farouk's shoulder, and Farouk's eyes flew open from the touch. The serpent flailed and hissed, but Michael grabbed it, and a liquid fire shot down his arm, incinerating the snake. With a nod my way, he said through the network, "*You can do this, too. Get permission and go for it.*"

"*Okay,*" I thought back. Arielle had shown me how to do it when I'd had Michael's powers. Now I'd have to do it on my own.

Farouk blinked and rattled his head as though waking from a deep sleep. With all the snakes off him, his energy brightened. His posture straightened, but he was still cautious. "What are you going to do?"

"Help. Where's the *djinn?*" Michael scanned the house as the serpents on the floor slithered to escape the light of his halo. He didn't wait for an answer before he charged up the wooden stairs.

I followed but at the banister, Farouk stepped in front of me, blocking my way. "You told him?"

"He can help. We both can."

"She was the one teaching you. She gave you a reading and the *hamsa*." He touched the collar of my sweater, searching for a chain that wasn't there. "Which you're not wearing, either, I see. How can you possibly help?"

"Things have changed." I shouldered past him.

Michael loitered in front of an old, white door. It rattled in his presence, as though someone or something was trying to open it. "She's in there."

Farouk rushed in front of us, blocking the door with his wiry frame. Even with the serpents no longer feeding on him, he was still wary. "Hey, this is my sister's room. You can't go in there!"

"We won't hurt her," I reassured him.

"No. You don't understand. The *imam* put a seal on the room. If we break it without him, the *djinn* will be freed."

At the base of the door, shadows lurked under the gap, moving but unable to get out. The snakes slithered to reach them, but something blocked them from the inside. They slithered up Farouk's legs. He didn't even flinch.

"So you've left Fatima to deal with it alone?" I said. "Farouk, how could you?"

"Not me. My parents. They found her tarot deck and think she's brought it on herself. They've been reciting the *Manzil Dua*—a prayer to protect her from magic. We all are. We're praying for her every day. They say it's the only way."

"Well, they're wrong," Michael said. "The *Manzil Dua* will keep evil out, or lock it in. But it's not enough to get rid of this thing. This is no ordinary *djinn*."

"How do you know?" Farouk asked.

"Let's just say I'm the answer to your prayers."

"Full of yourself, aren't you?" Farouk crossed his arms over his chest. "What are you, some kind of paranormal expert?"

Ignoring Farouk, Michael's hands filled with light and he ran them along the edges of the door, scanning it. I rose up on my toes to get a closer look at what he was doing.

"There." At its top right corner, ancient scrollwork lit under his fingers. "The *Manzil Dua* created a type of sigil that seals the *djinn* in the room. How long has your sister been locked in there?"

"Two days. You're right, the prayer alone wasn't working, so we had to cover the windows and lock her with the *djinn* inside."

"Locked up for two days with a *djinn* that's unable to escape." Michael shook his head sadly. "This is worse than I expected. There might not be much of your sister left."

Farouk took a step back and ran his hands down his face. "There has to be." Serpents swirled around him like black smoke.

I leaned into the network, filling my hands until I could see sparks. I could hear the other angels talking. Some were already watching, arguing over whether I should even be there.

I ran a white flame down my arm and touched Farouk's shoulder. "This is her best chance," I said to him. "Michael knows what he's doing."

The light forced the serpent minions to back away, but others approached. I wondered if we needed to call for backup.

"*Not yet.*" Michael answered my thoughts through the network. "*So far, Farouk believes the whole paranormal expert thing. I don't want to alarm him.*"

"*Surely he believes in angels,*" I thought back. "*He has faith.*" Unlike Heather.

"*Those with faith can sometimes be the worst. When his beliefs don't match what he sees, he could just as easily turn.*" Once he'd answered me, Michael broadcast to the others, "*Be on the ready, though. We may need you yet.*"

"So?" I asked him aloud. Reaching for the door handle, I braced myself for whatever was inside. "Shall we go in?"

Michael caught my arm. "Not you. Each *djinn* has its own set of abilities, and I don't know what this one can do yet. When I open that door and break the seal, I'll need you out here to make sure nothing gets out—or goes in."

I nodded, relieved. "Any pointers?"

"*The Host is right behind you.*" He thought the words to me. "*Stay connected. Use the network and flare your energy out the way you did with my halo.*"

"*But I don't have a real halo anymore.*"

He leaned in and kissed my cheek, brushing the side of my mouth with his lips. That bit of closeness between us ignited flames of a different kind. My energy flared.

"Don't you?" he whispered.

I felt myself blush. "Be careful."

"Always."

He opened the door, and an explosion of black dust filled the air with the cloying smell of burnt garbage. Sword drawn, Michael stepped inside, and the smoke billowed around him, blocking my view. Once he had gone, the infestation of serpentine creatures his halo had kept at bay returned, writhing through the floorboards and seeping through the walls. Filling with the network, I flared my energy as big and bright as I could. Though it was nowhere near the size of Michael's, it ballooned out and gave me a few feet of space.

Since Farouk was blind to all the creatures trying to attack us, I had to keep him in my sphere of protection, else he'd be covered in them and act out their will.

"What's he going to do in there?" He slammed his back against the wall of his sister's room in frustration, drumming his hands against the plaster.

"Don't worry, he knows what he's doing." My voice wavered as I struggled to focus. Talking and holding the barrier of light around both of us proved harder than I thought. I'd never held a halo using the network with my own energy before. When I'd had Michael's power, I knew he could do it, so I could do it as well. I simply lacked practice. Now, I was on my own.

"How can he?" Farouk's doubt crept over him like a wet, gray sack that deflated my energy. The snakes inched closer.

"When he had his accident, it made him interested in this stuff. He's learned a lot." It wasn't the complete truth, but it appeased Farouk's disbelief and my energy grew again, singeing the snakes that hovered at our ankles.

In my mind, I searched the network for Michael. It was different than before. Though I could hear the angels when they spoke directly to me, I couldn't see as much as I could with Michael's abilities. "*Michael!*" I called to him in my mind.

There was no response. Was I still connected? I reached out to Arielle. "*Can you see if Michael's okay?*"

"*I see him. He's fine,*" she answered. "*Don't worry.*"

No sooner had she told me not to worry than a red light flashed in my mind, and I could see inside the room. The air was filled with smoke and the creature Michael fought was huge, black and writhing, comprised of a thousand snakes—a demon. Fatima sat up in bed, her eyes glowing a deep crimson. She swayed like a massive cobra, and the *djinn* undulated behind her. Its teeth bared, it spat venom at Michael. He dodged, but the tail of the giant snake swung around. Sharp and spiked, it pierced Michael's stomach where the cursed sword had cut him. He cried out, his arm covering the wound. Blood bloomed on his shirt as he collapsed to the floor.

"Michael!" I shouted, and leaving Farouk, dashed into the room.

Smoke stung my eyes. I blinked, straining to focus. Expecting a giant snake, I filled with as much light as I could muster. Black air burned my lungs. The light of protection around me flickered and faded. The network became harder to reach.

Something grabbed my arm. I screamed and leaped to my toes, losing my balance.

In a flash of light, the room snapped into focus and the black smoke scattered to the edges of the walls.

"What are you doing here?" he asked through gritted

teeth. "I told you to stay out."

There was no giant serpent. Fatima lay on the bed in a white nightgown that was drenched with sweat. Her long, curly hair hung limp and greasy over half her face. Her coffee-colored skin was deathly pale. But one of her eyes watched us. Red flames shone from its pupil.

"Y-you were attacked! I saw."

"And you just came running in?" Michael frowned and pushed me toward the door. "Get out of here. Now."

Before I could take another step, Fatima laughed, a deep, feral howl that couldn't possibly have come from her mouth. With a maniacal look at the door, she slammed it shut. I sheltered myself behind Michael.

"This one's talented," Michael said over his shoulder. "A master of illusion. Must've used your clairvoyance against you."

Fatima's body levitated over the bed. Then, as though she were being lifted by invisible strings, she tilted and rose to a standing position. Smoke without flames billowed up the walls, and the oily serpents wound their way in. As far as I could see, none of them were on Fatima. But when she opened her eyes and mouth, flames licked out. The creature was inside her.

"Is she dead?" I asked.

"No, but it's using her soul as fuel, burning her up inside."

The thought of my friend being consumed from within was too horrific to process. I bit my lip in concentration and focused on the task at hand. "What about the snakes?"

"They're merely decoration," he said with a grim smirk as more serpents slithered toward us. "Illusion most likely, but stay away from them. Keep your halo wide."

There had to be a way out. I sprinted for the door and found no handle or knob to grasp.

"Farouk!" I yelled, pounding the door with my fists. "Open up!" I tried to reach for the network, to let the others know we were in danger, but found only blackness.

A painful screeching filled my ears.

Keeping Fatima in his line of sight, Michael backed toward me and rested a hand on my shoulder. "He can't hear you. Neither can the network. The *djinn's* disrupted the signal. When the door closed, the *Manzil Dua* sealed it again. We're trapped. Fatima must be a powerful psychic, because I haven't seen this kind of nuisance before."

"Nuisance?" I said. With an eerie cackle, Fatima twirled on the bed, her body jerking in a macabre display. The *djinn* was showing us it could control her every move.

"I may not be in the network, but I still have a few tricks up my sleeve. If the *djinn* can't get out, I won't be able to banish it." He sighed impatiently. "That's why the door needed to stay open. We can't get out and the others can't get in, so it's up to us to destroy this thing. Once the *djinn* is gone, all the seals trapping us in this room will be broken."

"What about Fatima?"

His expression darkened. "There are no guarantees. The sooner I do this, the better."

Sword raised, he rushed for the bed, and Fatima spun round to face him. Her head lolled to the side, tilted as though she were a giant, broken doll. But when he thrust his weapon, she twirled out of reach. He swung again, but this time, she escaped with a high back flip, her foot clipping his cheek. Their dance continued, each of them barely missing each other, Michael trying to connect with his blade and the *djinn* aiming to throw him off balance.

My mind rehearsed the few moves I'd learned as I scanned the small room for anything I could use as a weapon—a straightening iron, a picture frame—but everything in reach had been locked or taken down. The windows had been boarded shut, the walls stripped bare. The only furniture was the bed and her dresser, and even its drawers had been tied closed. Her closet had been padlocked. There was nothing.

All I had was the bed with a blanket crumpled on it. If

I was going to do anything, I'd have to be fast.

I ducked behind Michael as he lunged for her thigh. His sword passed right through it. His first hit, and the *djinn* hardly registered the blow. With a twirl, she landed her opposite foot on his fighting arm, and I heard a terrible crunch.

Michael cried out, doubling over, and tossed his sword to his other hand. With his right arm limp at his side, he dodged before she could strike again. His next swing missed. So did hers. They were so focused on each other, neither of them noticed me. I dove for the blanket and Fatima sent a kick in my direction. I slid to my knees, narrowly escaping a jaw-breaking smack, and slipped under the bed. Then I scrambled to the other side and rolled out. Fatima landed to the right of my hip, trying to escape Michael's sword. I seized her ankle and tugged. She stumbled forward in her weird floating stance, but before she could correct herself, Michael stabbed her from behind. The blade connected with her ribs, slicing through the body without leaving a mark. With a piercing scream, she climbed backward, up his legs, to flip and get away. I thought she was going to charge me, as I stood ready with the blanket. With freakish luck, I managed to toss it over her head. Her arms tangled. Before she could free herself, I grabbed the sides and pulled her off balance.

It wasn't much, but it slowed her down, and that was all Michael needed. Not missing this time, he stabbed her through the heart. With a terrible shriek, Fatima's body went limp and collapsed. Michael dropped his sword and caught her under one arm before her head hit the floor. The effort brought a grimace of pain.

"Good thinking," he said.

The network came back online immediately. With both of us dropping our connections, I'd expected other angels to arrive, or at least check in as soon as we were back, but they did nothing. Didn't they see how much danger we were in? Didn't they care?

I helped Michael carry Fatima to the bed. Though I was still afraid to go near her, I needed to know if she was breathing. I put my hand in front of her nose and felt air. Color returned to her cheeks.

"*We were offline for several minutes, but I'm reporting back in,*" Michael announced through the network.

"*What?*" came a male voice I didn't recognize. "*No, you weren't. We could see you. You went in, came out, and talked to that boy.*"

They didn't know?

"*I've been fighting a* djinn *for twenty minutes. This thing gave Mia visions and cut us off from the network without you even noticing.*"

"*What kind of* djinn *can do that?*" Arielle chimed in.

His right arm still limp, Michael picked up and retracted his sword with his left hand, returning it to its sheath. "*I don't know but it was fast. It spun that body around like some kind of marionette. Anyone seen that before?*"

A few voices chattered in the background, discussing the traits of the *djinn* and past experiences. I tuned them out. "We should really get Farouk to let us o—"

Before I could finish my sentence, the door flew open. Farouk rushed to his sister's side.

At the sound of his voice, Fatima's eyelids fluttered open. Her face was drenched in sweat. "Oh Farouk, it was horrible!" She choked out a sob.

Farouk pulled the blanket over her legs and gave her a tight smile. "It's over now."

CHAPTER NINETEEN

Michael and I slipped out of the room before Fatima had a chance to notice we were there. He listened to the network as we trod down the creaky, old stairs. Now that the *djinn* was gone, the serpents and shadows had disappeared. The only remnant of what had happened was a fine layer of powdery, black dust that stuck to my skin and clothes. It stank of rot.

His movements were guarded, his arm still limp as we stepped out onto the porch, and the daylight revealed a sheen of sweat covering his face. His lips were the color of paper.

"How's your shoulder?" I asked.

"It's dislocated. Needs to be put back in before I can heal it. Did your mother ever show—"

"I'll drive you to the hospital." There was no way I could fix his shoulder. I didn't know how, and I feared my clumsy attempts would injure him more.

"I should put a sigil up over the house before we go." His step faltered and he leaned against one of the wooden posts.

I couldn't stand to see him in pain, so I tapped back into the network. Michael's voice was silent amidst a long discussion about the history of the *djinn*. I didn't know how he could listen to all that chatter in so much pain.

"*Hey*," I interrupted them. "*Michael's dislocated his shoulder and needs it put back in. Should I take him to the hospital, or can somebody come fix it?*"

In a pulse of light, Arielle arrived on the front lawn. The few flyers that remained in the yard backed away from her fiery presence as she approached. Michael seated himself carefully on the bottom step and cringed as she touched his sore shoulder. She folded his arm at the elbow and worked it side to side. With a shove, she popped it back into place, and Michael let out a stream of swear words I'd never heard before. Some of them couldn't have been English.

"Better?" she asked, once he'd stopped cursing.

Michael took a deep breath, let it out, and stretched his neck. "Much." The color returning to his face, he ran a lit hand over his sore shoulder to heal it.

Arielle motioned to me. "Let him rest."

I followed her to the edge of the yard where the grass flowed into the edge of the pavement. Little stones crunched beneath our feet.

"We used to just do sigils over houses," she explained. "But we've been covering a larger space lately. We've needed to. The rest I'm going to show you in the network, so get good and connected to it."

I closed my eyes and filled myself with the golden white light. "*You're going to show me how to make one?*" I asked through the network.

"*You won't be able to do it, but it won't hurt you to watch. There might be a kickback in energy, though, so relax your knees.*"

Between her hands, she formed cone of purple and blue light laced with a silver spiral traveling clockwise from top to point. With a thrust of her arms, she drove it into the ground and it cut through the earth without disturbing it.

"That's one," she said.

We crossed to the back yard and she did the same thing there. She laid four cones in total, one in each corner of the property. Once they were done, she waved her hand and a blue force field inflated with a soft hum, covering the whole yard, including the house.

I followed her back to the front yard. My mind had become jelly, and the network blurred in my thoughts. When we rejoined Michael, he was doubled over, retching into the bushes beside Fatima's house. He staggered to an upright position, his forehead beaded in sweat. His gray shirt was spotted with blood.

I rushed to his side, guiding him back to the house. "You're sick."

"It's not that bad," he said, collapsing on the front step.

Arielle crouched before him, lifting his shirt. "When did your wound reopen?"

"After I finished healing my shoulder."

"It also reopened after we fought off a soldier demon, back when I had his powers and he wasn't using them to heal," I added.

"That was from exertion, because it hadn't quite healed," he said. "But it's closed over half a dozen times now, and reopened just as many."

"Then it's not healed," Arielle said, examining him. She scrunched her nose in distaste as a whiff of sulfur came off the wound. "The poison's still in you. It's less than before, but it's still there."

"I can't sense it," he said. "I thought Mia's blood—"

"You should go home," she said to Michael. "You'll need to take it easy for the next day or so and rest. Heal the way a human does and don't push on your power."

"I'm hardly an invalid."

"Right now, we don't know what you are. Take a few days off, but stay in contact." She turned to me. "Mia, you should drive him home. His shoulder seems all right, but you never know."

I was surprised Michael didn't object, but he had no

need to prove himself. Standing, he handed me his keys.

***

At Michael's, I splashed cold water on my face and washed the black soot from my hair, wishing I had a change of clothes. I combed and braided my damp hair in the living room, while he took a shower. When I was done, I kneeled on the sofa, tucking my feet under me the way I used to sit as a child. It seemed everyone close to me was getting hurt. Who would be next? Bill? My dad? My mom was a bit safer, living under the same roof as me, and she hadn't taken the *hamsa* off since I'd given it to her. But apart from Michael, she was the closest person I had in my life. I couldn't bear to lose her—or any of them.

"You all right?" Michael asked as he came into the room.

Startled, I glanced up at him and couldn't help but stare. His gray shirt was unbuttoned, his sculpted chest still damp from the shower. The jagged cut over his abs was freshly sealed. I wondered if it would eventually scar. He pushed back the wet hair falling over his eyes and slid onto the sofa beside me. He smelled of fresh soap and mint. I felt grimy in comparison.

"First Jesse and Dean, now Fatima," I said. "Who else is going to get hurt?"

He put an arm around my shoulder and kissed my cheek. "It's not your fault, Mia. You know that, right? Evil has nothing to do with you."

Outside his window, flyers circled over the sigils. Sick of always being able to see them—their constant, looming threat—I got up to close the blinds. "How can we possibly keep them all safe? What if they go after my mom? Bill? My dad?"

"We've been watching your immediate family since Damiel came back. They're fine."

"You have?" I spun around. "Why didn't you tell me?"

"It's what we do." He stood, and with a shrug, started to fasten the lowest buttons on his shirt. "I never gave it much thought."

The air released from my lungs. My family was safe, for now. Michael drew closer and I felt the heat emanating from him, the quiet strength of his presence. I wanted it to be just him and me. No more violence. No more people getting hurt. "What if I stayed here with you and never went outside? Do you think these flyers and stuff would forget about us and go away?"

His eyes soft and dark, he drew closer and rested a hand on my lower back, sending a fiery heat down to my toes. His other hand brushed a lock of hair away from my cheek, his thumb grazing my lip. "And how would we entertain ourselves, cooped up in here?"

"I'm sure you'll think of something." I caught his thumb with my teeth and smiled up at him. He drew in his breath involuntarily, his gaze locked with mine.

Moving his thumb away from my mouth, he slid his hand under my braid and caressed the nape of my neck. The blue gossamer grid of his cloaked wings shimmered behind him, as he inched his fingers along my throat and then my collarbone. His energy blazed around us, and his halo tingled through my skin, touching me in places his hands never dared.

How could this be wrong? How could the others deny us this?

Arms circling his waist, I leaned into him and kissed his bare chest, where his shirt lay open, and his heartbeat thrummed against my mouth. His hand at the base of my spine clenched into a fist, and with a growl, he pulled me closer, tilting my face up to meet his. This time, when we kissed, his tongue parted my lips.

With a few small steps back, he eased us down onto the sofa. His mouth pressed against mine, he grasped one thigh, then the other and I slid onto his lap, straddling him. Moving closer, I squeezed the sides of his waist with my thighs. He let out a soft, shuddering breath that scalded my neck.

His kisses deepened as his fingers, caressing my spine, lit a fire under my skin. I melted into him, and the energy pulsed stronger between us, glowing a deep, burnished gold. As I rode that intoxicating line between what we could and couldn't do, I brushed my palms down the muscles of his back, and along the hard planes of his chest and stomach, carefully avoiding his wounds. His skin puckered into goose bumps under my touch. And though I no longer carried his soul, I could feel the connection between us, reaching back for millennia. It soared with every touch, every heartbeat, every shared breath.

With soft kisses on my lips and neck, he played with the top button of my shirt. "May I?" His voice, thick and raw, was barely a rasp.

He unfastened the top button, and I did the rest. With his hands at his sides, he reclined against the back of the couch, watching me as though I were the gate of Heaven itself. Though he'd joked about showering together, and I was afraid of being seen then, I had no fear now. I leaned in for another kiss.

Shrugging out of my shirt, I reached around to unfasten my bra. "Tell me if you want me to stop."

His hands shook as they caught my waist and slid up my back. At my bra clasp, they pressed against my fingers, holding them in place. "I never *want* you to stop."

That couldn't be entirely true. He'd stopped me before and was stopping me now. He'd had to. "But?"

He said nothing, not moving, his breath labored, his eyes dark and intense. Clearly, he was torn. Part of me knew I shouldn't push it any further, that this was as far out on the edge as we could play today, but the problem was that my common sense had gone on vacation. And any self-control I had was marginal around him at the best of times. At times like this, it was practically non-existent.

"These are stolen moments. I don't want to have to

hide anything about us," he said. "I can't."

I pulled back. Were the others watching us? "You're not in the network right now, are you?"

"That's not what I mean. I want it to be right between us. No suspicion from colleagues. No having to hide the way I feel." He twined his arms around me and pulled me in for a slow, sweet kiss, before resting his forehead against mine. "You've seen a fraction of my world. There's councils, high councils, courts, more layers of legislation than you can count, and laws that, believe it or not, hold the universe in place. But I've petitioned them, as high as I can, for an exception to be made."

"What kind of exception?" I leaned into him, my skin singing to be next to his.

"I didn't tell you before because I didn't want to get your hopes up. These things take a long time. It could mean—"

His next words were cut off by my kiss. He was fighting for us. That was what it meant to me, and if there was the slightest possibility that we could have a future together, I would wait. He kissed me back more hungrily than before. His lips explored every inch of exposed skin until I trembled, and then he circled me in his arms and held me close, his own body trembling too.

CHAPTER TWENTY

Curled in Michael's arms, I lay on the couch, matching my breaths to the gentle rise and fall of his chest. My eyelids had fluttered closed, and I'd just drifted into a blissful dream of the two of us on a sunny, warm beach, when a faint popping sound jerked me awake. Though Arielle's wings remained cloaked, the light from her halo glinted around the room so bright and strong it emitted a low hum. At the sight of Michael and me together, half-dressed, she spun on her heel to face the fireplace and laced her long fingers behind her back. Her deep, musical tone was clipped.

"I'm sorry to interrupt, but I needed to see you both." She paused before addressing me over her shoulder. "I should let you know that Rhys and Zadkiel will be here soon. You might want to put something on."

I leaped from the sofa and snatched my shirt from the floor. "Who are they?"

"Colleagues from Michael's battalion," she said as I pressed my arms through the sleeves.

Michael sat up. "What do they want?" His shirt was wrinkled and open to the waist. If he felt guilty being caught with me in this state, it didn't show. With a yawn, he stretched his arms overhead. His curls arced in every direction, and the sight of him with bed head put a soft lump in my throat. So much for our time alone.

My own hair was one big knot, so I fished a brush from my purse and started working through the tangles.

With that familiar pulse of air, two tall, male, angels joined us. They were dressed in the same type of tank top I'd seen Michael wear but instead of jeans, they wore white karate pants. Other than that, they were total opposites. The wiry, thin one had the palest skin I'd ever seen, a thick mass of auburn hair, and jade green eyes. The beefier of the two had dark skin, a close-shaved scalp, and eyes the color of French Roast coffee. Even with their wings cloaked, the size of their bodies crowded the small space.

When Arielle introduced me to them, they seemed to already know who I was, and as soon as they spoke, I recognized their voices from the network.

Arielle took a seat beside the fireplace and motioned to the dark-skinned angel. "I brought Zadkiel because he's survived being cut with an angel killer before. He's the only one who has."

The auburn-haired angel, Rhys, wandered toward the bookcase to explore Michael's library, his fingertips sweeping over the spines.

Zadkiel remained in the living room. "May I see the wound?"

With a shrug, Michael opened his shirt. The angry scar had fused into a deep red groove over his tight abs.

Rhys let out his breath slowly and leaned against one of the shelves. "How many times has it reopened?"

"Seven, counting today," Michael said.

Zadkiel crouched in front of Michael and hovered his fingers over the wound. Golden light shot from his hand.

"Hey." I caught his wrist and took a seat beside Michael whose body was taut with pain. "Won't healing it make it worse?"

"I'm not, I'm checking for an imprint," Zadkiel said.

"Get anything?" asked Rhys.

Zadkiel stood and was so tall that the gossamer grid of his cloaked wings brushed the ceiling. "Nothing I recognize."

"What's going on?" I asked. Couldn't this wait? Wasn't it enough that they'd interrupted our solace? When I tried to console myself that at least they hadn't come fifteen minutes earlier, I recalled the press of Michael's lips against mine, the heat of his breath on my skin. My cheeks flushed from the memory.

"My apologies. Allow me to show you." Zadkiel pulled down the neck of his shirt. Over his heart, the skin had puckered into a long, bumpy, beige ridge. "The one that cut me was called *Zanjii.*"

"Remember, Michael's also human," said Arielle. "It'll help."

"Human or not, it has merely bought him time," Zadkiel said. "The poison in his system will continue to sap his strength until there's nothing left."

"What are you talking about? How much time?" I jumped to my feet and rushed at Zadkiel, until I had to crane my neck to see his face. "No. He's better, the blood spell helped. It made him better." I turned to look at Michael, whose expression could have been carved from marble, except for how many times he swallowed, the tightness around his mouth. He knew. My throat constricted until my voice came out a soft rasp. "But you've got your abilities back. You faced a *djinn* today without the network."

Zadkiel bowed his head. "I'm sorry. I forgot you didn't know."

"It was never a permanent solution, Mia." Arielle grabbed my arm and tried to guide me back to the sofa, but I wouldn't budge.

How could they stand there and be so damn calm? This was Michael's life we were talking about. I turned to him again, wanting him to say something. "Is this true?"

"I'm fine. It could be weeks before it gets to me, Mia." He swallowed again, blinked slowly. "We'll find a way."

He raised his hand for mine, and I laced my fingers with his. "There has to be a way to stop it."

Rhys took a step closer and spoke in a quiet voice as though he were trying to soothe a terrified child. "There is. We find the sword and destroy it."

"We need its name." Zadkiel brushed his fingers absently over his heart, where his scar was. "I can bind it if we have that."

"Which we don't." Michael's shoulders slumped forward. Despair rolled off him. I couldn't bear to see him lose hope. With his free hand, he motioned to the black wooden box on the coffee table, the one he'd shown me a few days before. "I've searched the scrolls. We've got nothing."

"It's far from over." Arielle reached for the box and tucked it into her coat pocket. "There are ways to figure out the name once we find it."

She nodded at Rhys, who seated himself on the arm of the sofa. "We think we may have a lead."

"Really?" Michael huffed out his breath and his halo brightened. He squeezed my fingers before letting them go.

"It's a small one," Arielle said.

Rhys exchanged a glance with Zadkiel. "We've seen a lot of soldier demon activity downtown this week, near Pioneer Square."

I recalled our dinner at the restaurant when Michael and I had been attacked in the hallway. The night he'd agreed to teach me how to fight.

"We've seen a few of them around, but in most cases they're not bothering humans, which tells us they don't want to draw our attention." Arielle said.

Zadkiel leaned against the fireplace and grinned. "So, of course, we're suspicious."

"We're heading to a club in that area tomorrow night—

The Icebox," Michael said.

"You want us to look around while we're there," I said. "Keep an eye out?"

"No. Not you." Michael raised both his hands in the air, as though he were a traffic cop. "It's not safe."

"Has anything been lately?" I crossed my arms in front of my chest and leaned back on the couch, glaring at him. Sure, I wasn't as tough as he was, but I knew how to protect myself. That had to count for something. Besides, my friends would be there. I couldn't let them—or Michael—go alone.

As if he read my mind, Rhys offered, "You won't be alone. We'll all be there."

"If Michael's there and I'm not, Heather and Jesse will get suspicious. This was supposed to be a double date, to make up for the one you missed last time. Remember?"

Michael winced when I played the you-stood-me-up card, and I felt guilty for it, but only for a second. If this was our chance to find the cursed sword, there was no way I wasn't going to help.

"Mia's got a point." Arielle's cool voice cut through our argument. "The two of you going to club is a perfect cover. Until now, we've been keeping our distance, watching from afar. With you in the area, we have an excuse to get closer without raising their suspicions. Rhys, Zadkiel, and I can check things out. We'll secure everything. Turiel can watch over you both."

"What if we see the sword?" I asked.

"Call us through the network. We won't be far away." Arielle stepped away from the couch. Zadkiel and Rhys followed.

"If you do see it, be careful." Zadkiel warned. "The mere presence of such evil plays on any weakness we have." He scanned his colleagues and added, "Even ones we don't know about."

Arielle's halo flamed a brilliant gold, tinged with a royal purple. The skin tightened around her face, until she appeared to glow from within, and her presence drew the attention of everyone. "Best start preparing the area. I don't want any people hurt."

They nodded and unsheathed their wings, and light danced along the walls. Every surface sparkled as though dusted with refracted starlight. They spoke together, both through the network and aloud, their voices a chorus. "See you both tomorrow."

The air snapped as they departed, leaving Arielle alone with us. Though her wings remained cloaked, the light from her halo still ricocheted around the room. She didn't lose her official tone.

"Due to the breach in the network today, we'll be changing our communications signal to the most secure frequency we have, one that should be impossible for anyone to block. Especially a *djinn*." She shook her head as though she couldn't believe a *djinn* could cause so much trouble. "You should be able to use the network to call us, Mia, for you can always access light if your intentions are pure—"

"If it's harder to reach, how do we know you'll be able to hear her?" Michael got up, jammed his hands into his pockets, and leaned against the mantle. "Or me, for that matter... When the *djinn* blocked the signal, we couldn't access the network for anything. I can handle a *djinn* on my own, but anything more and we'll be sitting ducks."

"We're all weakened if the network is compromised," Arielle said. "But this new frequency shouldn't be a problem for you. Just in case, you'll both be under close watch and have a presence invisible to human eyes."

"You mean bodyguards?" I asked.

Arielle nodded and scrutinized Michael as though she were taking his measurements. "You're at seventy percent of your strength right now?"

"Yeah." Michael straightened his shoulders. "About that."

"As long as you rest between now and then, I think

you'll be fine." She leaned against the arm of the sofa. "Turiel has offered his protection until you're back to full capacity."

"I don't need his help." Michael snapped, rubbing his brow. "Where is he, anyway?"

"Covering for Rhys and Zadkiel so they could come see you," she said. "The existence of such a weapon is a danger to us all. Don't you think it's time to put any differences aside?"

I nodded. "I agree." When Michael frowned at me, I added, "Sorry, but I do. He's been nothing but helpful so far."

"He's not the only one who doesn't understand your feelings for Mia," Arielle said. "He's just the most vocal about it. Deep down, he admires you."

"Admires me? He never wanted me to come back in the first place! He'd rather I served my punishment in Hell."

"You were so far gone he didn't believe you *could* be rehabilitated. And we've proven him wrong." Arielle lowered her voice, touching Michael's arm. "After Damiel, I can understand why it must be hard for you to trust the others. You were betrayed by someone so close—"

"I trust you."

"Good. Because what I'm about to say is not as your commander, but as your sponsor and friend. While you're petitioning the high councils for the status of your relationship, you're both going to have to play this very carefully and avoid getting carried away. We accept Mia as a prophet, and that she is a valuable ally, but she is not one of us. You have to give the others time to adjust."

"I'm not going to hide how I feel. There's nothing wrong with it. I'm human too."

"I know that," she said calmly. "As do they, but your conduct must be above reproach. Become too human and they won't trust you can do your job."

"If this gets worse"—he motioned to his wound—

"They could be right."

"There's no shame in being injured. Your humanity is what's keeping you alive." She sighed. "You know the rules, what you can and can't do. Don't flaunt your feelings for each other in front of the others."

"Does that mean Turiel will be chaperoning us all the time?" I asked.

"No. I've told Turiel to give you space and to treat your situation with the utmost discretion. He'll be watching from afar. But he's able to sense your feelings, Mia, so he'll know everything that's going on."

What she didn't have to say was that, blessing or curse, as long as Turiel could read me, Michael and I were never truly alone.

CHAPTER TWENTY-ONE

The Icebox was in an old, refurbished warehouse building, complete with bricked-in windows and wrought iron trim. A long line of people trailed down the sidewalk and curved into the alley. But by some miracle we found space in a parking lot across the street. Since it was an adult club, I'd wrestled with what to wear and decided on a short black dress with low-heeled boots. If soldier demons were around, I'd need to be able to move.

I got out of the car and the damp air cut right through my jacket, chilling me.

Above the building, a shimmering, bright blue light laced with silver filigree extended over the entire block. Beyond it, squadrons of flyers, soldier demons—and I could only imagine what else—circled overhead. "Wow! Look at those!"

Michael studied the sky as he closed the car door, and the reflection of light from the sigils made his eyes glow a brilliant blue. "They've outdone themselves. I doubt there are places in Heaven this secure." He clicked the car fob, and the locks beeped as he slid the keys into the pocket of his black jeans. "Network's good, as well. The new frequency's clear. The others aren't far away."

At his mention of the network, I tried to reach for it, but only got the slightest tingle of light. It wasn't much, but it was still comforting to know it was there. "Any news on the sword?"

"Nothing yet."

Cars trolled the busy street, their drivers in search of places to park. Though it had stopped raining, light from the globe lamps lining the sidewalk glimmered off the wet, cobbled pavement.

"You're sure you want to do this?" I asked. Given how many times Michael had been hurt these past few days, I couldn't believe we were actually allowed out, let alone performing a recon mission.

He laughed, more jovial than I'd seen him in days, maybe weeks. "I'm hardly an invalid. Besides, I need a night out or I swear I'm going to lose it."

He slid an arm around my waist and pulled me to his side. I pressed my cheek into his soft leather jacket and inhaled his warm, familiar scent. Excitement crackled off of him, and the heat of his energy running along my skin chased away the cold. He scanned the busy street before we crossed, and the effervescence of his halo enveloped me, strengthening my own.

"Should you be using that?" I asked, motioning to the golden ring of light around us. "Won't it tire you out?"

"Relax," he whispered. "I'm not taking any chances."

"Where's Turiel?" I asked. "Do you see him?"

"On the roof." Michael nodded toward the sky, and I caught a glimpse of movement, the flicker of Turiel's wings against the brightly lit night.

As we approached the club, the steady bass from inside echoed and slammed off the buildings. Two huge bouncers stood in front of the door, using flashlights in the darkness to check everyone's ID. Over the club's brick structure, I noticed another formation of blue light, laced with silver, a second set of wards, reminding me why we were there. I craned my neck to scan the long line for soldier demons.

Michael pressed his fingertips against the side of my waist. "Don't be so obvious about it."

"Right." I shrugged my shoulders, forcing them down. They'd crept up to my ears.

"Mia!" Heather waved to me from down the line. I'd been so focused on finding demons I didn't even see her. She looked great in a short blue dress, her long, blond hair curled into waves.

She greeted me with a hug as Jesse and Michael exchanged hellos. "Isn't this exciting?" she said. "A real night out! It seems all I've been doing lately is study."

"I know what you mean," I said. But, really, I didn't. This was no ordinary night out. We were decoys.

"I listened to some sample tracks last night," she said, referring to the band. "They sound great, but still." She motioned to the line. "This place is heaving with people!"

"They played our prom a few years ago at Sealth, and they were great," Michael said. "Of course, they were just starting out back then."

"Yeah, that was awesome." Jesse turned to Heather, taking her hand. "Why couldn't Fiona and Dean make it?"

"Dean had to practice," she said. "His first match is tomorrow morning."

"C'mon." Michael squeezed my hand. "We can go right in."

"Right." Jesse grinned and pushed his overgrown bangs out of his eyes. "Guest list."

As we made our way to the front, a few people in the line shot us dirty looks. One girl, a petite redhead in a tight green dress, even called out to Michael as if I wasn't there, "Hey gorgeous, did it hurt when you fell from Heaven?"

Michael's spine tightened into a column of iron. He spun to face her. "What?"

The girl recoiled. Her face turned crimson under the street lamps. "Nothing."

I gripped Michael's hand, pulling him back, and

whispered, "Talk about being obvious."

"Seriously. What kind of question is that?" he asked me, his voice low. "Of course it bloody hurt."

"It's a pick-up line." I couldn't believe I had to explain it. "It means she thinks you're hot."

Heather raised an eyebrow at us. Jesse punched Michael's arm. "Always the chick magnet."

Michael huffed out his breath and then grinned as though he were only kidding. The iron melted from his spine. He approached the larger of the two bouncers who stood outside the club's wooden door. "We're on the guest list."

"Name?" the bouncer asked.

"Michael Fontaine. There's four of us."

The bouncer gave him a nod. "Fine. Go on in."

Michael tucked me in front of him and we headed inside. The music was even louder than I expected. He took my jacket and we stopped at the booth to check it. A wall of warmth from the lights and people already inside pressed against my face. I'd heard most clubs weren't busy until after ten, but the Icebox was different. Another girl was scrutinizing IDs and handing out yellow wristbands to everyone over twenty-one. Being underage, ours were green.

"The opening act's going to start soon." Jesse surveyed the already packed room. "We should find a seat."

It was a huge club, all glass and painted wood, with a large balcony overlooking the dance floor below. The art deco-style sconces adorning the pillars must have been there since the Prohibition era. Michael guided us to a table in the back corner with a great view of the stage.

The opening act was called Blatant and they were a loud alternative rock band from Portland. As soon as they started playing, Jesse and Heather left us at the table to rush the stage. Once I got used the sound, including the occasional microphone squeal, I relaxed into the furious, driving beat, grateful I no longer had Michael's heightened senses. I didn't know how he could stand the volume. But when I looked over at him, he seemed perfectly at ease.

"What do you think?" I shouted.

He slipped an arm over my shoulder and pulled me into him. "Not my worst assignment."

"I mean about the band."

"Oh!" He chuckled and it rumbled through his chest. "Denizen's way better. You'll see."

I'd only been in a club once before and it had been an all-ages place in Denver that never served alcohol. As people packed in the Icebox tighter than the Monorail at rush hour, the air grew close. The smell of alcohol, sweat, and cologne stifled the air. Guys standing alone unabashedly checked me out, but all it took was a glance from Michael to send them away. The tall, blond waitress squeezed her way over to our table and we ordered some Cokes. I scanned the area for demons, but it was hard to see amid the gyrating bodies and the ocean of dark clothes.

When Blatant had finished, a DJ came on and played canned music that was better-known than the band. Some stayed to dance. Others replenished their drinks.

"What about Arielle?" I asked. "She find anything yet?"

"No, but the area's secure, so…" He grinned at me. "We should try to enjoy ourselves. Want to dance?"

"Sure."

On our way to the dance floor, I saw the redhead who'd tried to pick Michael up standing at the bar talking to two other girls, probably her friends. As we passed, one of them nudged her and pointed me out. I was sure the three of them were talking about us.

The dance floor was a loud frenzy of bodies and brightly colored lights. At first I didn't think we could possibly fit, but Michael found room for us off to the side; even so, we hardly had three inches between us. Not that I minded. In the small space, he matched his movements to mine, and it was easy to forget the immediate danger and lose myself in the rhythm.

We danced to a few songs and there were times when his body grazed mine, his eyes smiled, and all his seriousness subsided. Then clouds of fog from the dry ice machine billowed through the club and chilled the air, creeping up my spine. Combined with the strobe lights, it was hard to see. Michael took me by the hand and led us back to our table.

The smoke flickered, and the air smelled of sulfur. Michael's face was taut with concentration as he scanned the room. The blue and purple lights from the dance floor sharpened his features.

By the time we reached our table, our drinks were gone. An elegantly dressed man in a crisp white shirt and black suit jacket approached. No tie. Even slouched with his head down, he was taller than Michael, which had to make him at least six feet six. Thick, wavy golden hair fell over his eyes as he drew on a lit cigarette. Despite the fact that there was no smoking allowed at any bars in Seattle, no one seemed to notice. He gave us a sharp, tight smile, and his eyes shone a burnished gold. *I know those eyes.*

Michael's entire body stiffened, instantly on alert. "Raguel."

The leftover tuna casserole I'd scarfed down for dinner soured in my stomach. Here we were, prepared for soldier demons and maybe some recon work—but not this. Raguel was supposed to be imprisoned, never to be free again. From what I knew about him, he was more than powerful enough to tear all the sigils down and turn this place into a demonic feeding frenzy.

How'd he get past the others—or Turiel—without being noticed? Or were they already dead? With Michael still sick, we should never have gone out.

Raguel focused on Michael, hardly noticing me, so I reached for the network until I felt its faint tingle of light. I didn't know if any angels could hear me, or what was going on outside, but I sent the message, *"Raguel's here."*

Nothing. I tuned to my feelings of fright and thought

Turiel's name, to call him. Under the table, Michael squeezed my hand. So much for Turiel. All I'd managed to do was let Michael know how freaked out I was.

Raguel nodded his head at the faint blue gossamer grid that extended behind Michael. "Got your wings back, I see."

"No thanks to you." Michael bristled. "Aren't you supposed to be locked away somewhere?"

"I've been freed. Damiel's release broke all the curses he'd set to imprison me."

The simple truth of his words spun in my mind. Redeeming Damiel led to Raguel's return? Since I was the one who'd redeemed him, that made me responsible. It meant Raguel was free because of me. All the memories of Michael's torture came flooding in at once, the horrific things Raguel had done—and those were only the ones I knew of. The hot, sour taste of bile jumped to my throat. I swallowed it back. What would he do now that he was freed?

Raguel took a final drag off his cigarette and puffed a sulfurous cloud of smoke from his nostrils. "It took a while for the spell to unravel. When it did, half your wards over the Pacific Rim dropped."

"We noticed," Michael said. "If we'd known it was you, we would have sent a big welcome committee."

Raguel laughed and extinguished his cigarette in the center of our table. His golden eyes, fierce as a tiger's and equally as chilling, darted to me. One look and I knew I was facing a supreme predator. "Sajani?" I shivered at his use of my ancient name, my name from the life when Michael and I first met. "I heard you were back. I trust you enjoyed the flowers I sent you."

Raguel had sent me those flowers? I should have known something was wrong when Michael said he hadn't sent them, and it couldn't have been Fatima. Was Raguel messing with my head, or did he want the same thing as Damiel?

"Leave her alone!" Michael growled.

Raguel's smile grew wide and gleeful. "As I recall, it was you who couldn't leave her alone. It seems you still can't."

"What do you want, Raguel?"

"I want Damiel back," he said fiercely. "We have *business* to settle." He emphasized the word as though it were something dark and horrid, sending a shudder of revulsion through me.

"I can't do that. He made his choice," Michael said. "There are laws. Remember them?"

"Do you?" There was a glint of malice in Raguel's eyes as they raked my outfit, where the fabric clung to my curves. I suddenly wished I was wearing a parka. "This girl's a little transgression, but I'll bet she's not your only one."

On the table, Michael's hand tightened into a fist, and the combination of fear and rage boiling off him made his energy shake. Behind Raguel, two very strange, dark-haired men stood at the bar. They had sharp, pointy features and shadows around their forms. Soldier demons. I wondered if they had possessed people, or if they were barely cloaked to look human. For all I knew, no one else could see them.

"Well, if I can't have Damiel, remember there will always be a place for you. You were one of my favorites." With a leer, Raguel touched the side of Michael's face. Michael flinched and caught his wrist. "The sword took its toll. There isn't much left of you, but we'll make do."

Michael's eyes glazed over. I wondered what horrible vision he was trapped in. I recognized the cold, inhuman voice from when I'd had his memories: the dark room, the iron rack. *"He always heals. Drain him until he can't do it anymore."*

I fought the urge to shudder and found the nerve to speak. "Leave him alone."

Raguel turned back to me. I held my breath. "Rumor has it that you had something to do with Damiel leaving

Hell. I wonder what else you can do."

"You can't be serious!" Michael's laugh sounded cold, forced, and I knew how worried he was. "She's just a girl. A human."

"A girl you've got a thing for. That you've always had a thing for. Your perversity always served me well."

Michael let go of my hand under the table. His expression hardened until the lean features of his face drew tight to the bone. His jaw muscles twitched.

"You should've seen him when he was in Hell, my dear," Raguel said to me. "If there was a girl that looked even remotely like you, I could make him do anything."

Michael leapt to his feet and slammed his fist onto the tabletop so hard the wood split. "Enough!"

In the background, the announcer took to the microphone and people cheered. "Ladies and gentlemen, put your hands together for tonight's main act: Denizen!"

"I want him back. You have two days."

With a snap of his fingers, Raguel disappeared, and the stage burst into flames.

At first, people merely watched the smoke fill the air as though it were part of the show. Some even cheered. But when the lights went out and the announcer choked out a deep, guttural cough, the audience panicked. People screamed and rushed for the doors as alarms rang through the club. Spilled liquor inched toward the flames.

"Come with me." Michael launched over the table and grabbed my arm, almost lifting me off my feet.

I clutched my purse and tried to follow, but couldn't match his speed. "What about Heather and Jesse?"

"I'll find them. Let's get you out of here."

I pulled his arm, stopping. "No. Let me help."

He stood me in front of him and hooked his arm protectively across my collar bones, pulling me near as he scanned the room. His chest pressed against my shoulder blades. "Stay close."

The crowd scattered everywhere, roiling like ants

escaping an overturned anthill, only way more aggressive. They pushed, shoved, and screamed at anyone who'd listen. People on the balcony rushed down the stairs, gasping for air, and tripping over each other. The ones nearest the stage were trampled. Those who'd been hit by fire were trying to extinguish the flames. While some pressed themselves against the far wall, others were crushed up against the doors, pounding their fists against the metal, and screaming when they wouldn't open.

In the middle of the club, flames from the bar exploded. The mezzanine ignited above us and collapsed with a thunderous crack. Michael pulled me onto the dance floor, where people had fled to avoid being flattened by falling debris.

"Jesse's over there." He pointed to a fire exit that someone had managed to force open. The air cooled and dark shapes the size of large dogs darted amidst the smoke and chaos. With their glowing red eyes and huge teeth, the hellhounds rushed around the room, passing through people who, though they weren't completely aware of them, paled as they approached. I tugged Michael's hand, but he'd already seen them.

He leaned into my ear. "I've got to get rid of them before they materialize. Can you make it to Jesse?"

I nodded and kissed him roughly on the lips, before he pushed me into a chaos of bodies scrambling to escape. I searched for Jesse. Within a second, Michael took to the air, invisible, but in the panic nobody seemed to notice him disappear. He extended his halo into a ring of flame around the room. Though that would cost him in more ways than one, the hellhounds stopped in their tracks and growled, angry, no doubt, at being separated from their prey. They set their gruesome attention on him.

Michael reached for his sword and leaped onto the burning stage as the hellhounds rushed after him. The largest of the pack, the alpha, bared its teeth and attacked, but Michael's sword sliced clean through the beast's neck and the creature disintegrated to smoke and dust, midair.

I was tossed about in the crowd, a mosh pit gone wrong, unable to see the fight. Michael shouldn't be doing this, shouldn't be using his power. A squadron of flyers slipped through the walls and descended on the horrified masses. Terrified by the fire and choking on the smoke, they had no idea what was coming to feast on them. The floor was so sticky with spilled alcohol and covered in broken glass that each step I took crunched beneath my feet. Pushed by the throng, some guy bumped into me, obviously drunk, and the beer he was still carrying ran down the front of my dress. He yelled his apology as the crowd split us apart.

I coughed. Smoke burned my eyes. Where the hell were Turiel and the others?

Heather caught my wrist. "There you are!" She had a scratch on her cheek and her mascara was smudged from the smoke. "Where's Michael?"

"We got split up in the rush." I had to trust he would be okay. "You're hurt!"

"Somebody clipped me with their ring." She touched her cheek. "It's nothing."

I scanned her throat. Her *hamsa* wasn't vibrating, but the hellhounds scattering from Michael's attack avoided her. One of them charged at me. Instinctively, I filled with what light I could from the network to throw the creature off. As I pushed, my hands went right through it, as though I were pushing a black cloud. But the sparks from my fingertips snagged its shadowy form, giving me the feeling of substance, and I was able to throw it several feet away. The network wasn't as strong as before, but it was enough.

Jesse came up behind Heather and took her arm. "Let's go!"

We linked our arms together, forming a human chain and, with Jesse in the lead, inched our way to the open door. Panicked people shoved and screamed, blocking our way. Outside, sirens wailed, and, through the door, flashes of red and white lit a group of people pushing their way out. With urgent clangs, axes struck the locks of the other doors along the wall, and the crowd lurched through, gasping for fresh air. On my way out, I checked over my shoulder for Michael, but couldn't see him. Not even the glimmer of his halo, which meant only one thing.

He was down.

CHAPTER TWENTY-TWO

We squeezed through the doorway as part of the giant mass of people streaming from the club. Over the shouting and calls for help, walkie-talkies crackled, police horns blared. Girls sobbed in the arms of friends. Jesse led Heather and me away from the mob, but we couldn't go far. Paramedics pressed through the crowd to assist the injured, while police officers scrambled to barricade the area and keep the panic under control.

Ambulances, fire trucks, and police cars clogged the street. Their blinking lights flooded the night sky and made it impossible to scan for angels.

Where is Turiel? The others? Michael needs them.

Both sets of wards had come down, and the whole block teemed with flyers. Shrieking and growling, they swept down on people, feasting on the fear and chaos with their ghostly teeth and claws. Their victims paled, temporarily stupefied, and then carried on in the confusion and panic, as if unaware that their life forces had been taken. Even the emergency responders were attacked. No one was immune, except Heather. The *hamsa* protected her in ways she didn't know about. And a faint glimmer of light from the network kept the creatures away from me.

189

At least the hellhounds were gone. Michael had seen to that. But at what cost?

Now that the bolts were cut, the club's many doors lay torqued open, trickling smoke from the blazing mess inside. Firefighters rushed in to rescue anyone who couldn't get out on their own. I was so desperate to find Michael I had half a mind to run in with them.

Heather grasped my arm and held me back. "You can't go in there, Mia."

I paced instead. Sleet dripped down on us, its cold piercing my skin. I shivered and, hugging my purse for comfort, strained my eyes for any sign of Michael.

"Stay here," Jesse said. "I'll check across the street."

Behind one of the fire trucks a blue light flashed as though a neon sign were shorting out. Fearing the worst, I ran in its direction to find Arielle crumpled on the ground, invisible to any passersby. She lay on her back with her white wings dirty and splayed across the cobbled pavement. Her pale golden eyes stared blankly at the sky. One hand gripped her sword, which flickered and shorted, almost extinguished. The other hand pressed against her ribs, in an attempt to stop the bleeding. Her crimson blood, laced with gold light, streamed through her fingers and pooled into the cracks between the stones.

"Arielle?" I kneeled beside her, and the cold ground chilled my legs. Memory chilled my thoughts. *I'd dreamed this.*

She blinked and, with blood-soaked hands, gave me her sword.

My heart stuck in my throat. "No, Arielle, you need it." Though the blade was light, I had to wrap my fingers around hers to help her grasp the handle as I passed it back. Was this what my dream had been trying to tell me a few weeks ago? That a trap would be set? The Devil in the mirror—I'd dismissed my dream as an old childhood fear—*that was Raguel?* It happened around the same time he'd been freed. "Where's Turiel? The others?"

"He called for my help, but Raguel blocked... "
Coughs racked her body. Turning onto her side, she
convulsed and hacked up a gob of blood. "By the time I
found out…"

That couldn't be. I closed my eyes, screaming Turiel's
name in my mind. He had to be able to feel me. *Turiel.*
Please!

"I'm sorry. I couldn't stop it," she uttered—the exact
words from my dream!

"It's all right," I said, desperately wanting my words to
be true. "You'll be all right."

"The angel killer sword's name." She coughed again.
This time, her voice was almost a whisper. *"Nemeraii."*

I reached for the network, able to feel only a fraction of
its light. I prayed for the first time in my life. *God, please let*
him hear me.

With an eruption of gold and blue light, Turiel
appeared. His face was covered in sweat and grime, and his
white clothes were torn and filthy, as though he'd barely
escaped with his life. Noticing Arielle, he immediately
crouched before her and cradled her head in his hands.

"Where were you?" I demanded.

"I was swarmed," he said.

Arielle's eyes fluttered closed. Her blood stained his
white clothes and skin. Turiel scooped her limp body into
his arms and gave me a troubled look. "I need to take her,
immediately. Rhys and Zadkiel are on their way."

Before I could ask where he was going with her, a door
of bright light opened beside them barely long enough for
them to pop out of the air and disappear. Michael was
injured and could be dead, and now Arielle? My eyes
watered and stung. My body shook as grief and terror
overtook me. I pressed my fingernails into my palms to
fight it back. *Get a grip, Mia!*

With the sigils down, the area was a free-for-all.
Shadows filled the sky. Their presence darkened the area,
dimming the artificial lights of the emergency vehicles. But

again, no one else seemed to notice. Turiel had been fighting the soldier demons. Had he defeated them, or would they be coming now too?

"Mia?" Heather's voice came from behind me, jolting me back to reality.

I wiped my eyes with my fingertips and turned to find her holding a silver emergency blanket. I wore only a skimpy dress and it was so cold I could see my breath, but I'd been so wrapped up in the horror unfolding around me that I'd hardly noticed.

"We found Michael," she said. "He's been hurt, but he's waking up."

Michael. "How hurt?"

The blanket crinkled as she wrapped it around me. She gave my shoulders a squeeze. "Come with me."

We approached the ambulance. Jesse stood beside it, oblivious to the black, serpentine creature that slithered toward him. More snakes surrounded the area, glistening like polished obsidian in the artificial light.

A starburst of golden light erupted around us, igniting the serpents and turning the smaller flyers to dust. Some of the larger ones clung to their hosts, draped over them like cloudy black veils. Over the din of footsteps and voices, I detected a faint hum, and a blue light expanded across the sky. The sigils were back up. With his sword outstretched, Zadkiel swept over us, and his massive opalescent wings sliced through the air.

Two paramedics waved Jesse off and then lifted someone into the ambulance. As I approached. I noticed feet dangling off the end of the stretcher, barely covered by the gray wool blanket. A crown of dark hair arced in every direction.

"That's him!" I rushed the van. "Michael!"

Heather joined Jesse, who shoved his hands into his pockets and hovered outside the vehicle.

One of the EMTs, a short, stocky guy with a shaved head, held up an arm to block my approach. "Are you family?"

I hesitated. No matter how I answered, at our age, girlfriend wasn't next of kin. "I'm—"

"She's my wife," Michael said. The word "wife" tingled through me. If past lives counted, you could say I was— except for that whole 'til-death-do-us-part thing.

The EMT frowned. It was dark, but he had to know we were young. Neither of us wore rings. A faint shimmer filled the air and, Michael added, "She needs to ride with us."

The EMT let his arm drop. "Get in."

Had Michael enthralled him? "Save your strength," I whispered.

He reached for my hand. "It'll be fine."

I climbed onto the ambulance, as gracefully as I could in a short skirt, and turned back to wave at my friends.

Michael gazed sleepily at me and I kneeled on the floor beside him. His shirt lay open, soaked with blood. The blanket barely covered him to the waist. A fresh bandage had been applied to his wound, which had reopened, as it had so many times before. Though his injury looked new, his shirt hadn't been ripped. Wouldn't they suspect something?

I pressed the back of my hand to his forehead. It was burning up, but as far as I could tell, he had no other injuries. I exhaled in relief.

A sandy-haired paramedic crouched beside Michael and fastened a blood pressure cuff around his arm. "Try to relax." He squeezed the pump to fill it with air. His nametag read "Dave".

"If I relax any more I'm gonna pass out."

"Are you allergic to any medication?" Dave stuck the stethoscope buds in his ears and checked his watch. The other EMT closed the back doors, locking us inside.

"No, and I don't want any."

"Your blood pressure's fine, but that gash is pretty deep. You'll probably need stitches."

Michael let out a long sigh. "No doubt."

Dave took off his purple surgical gloves and tossed them into a wastebasket. As the ambulance lurched into gear, he nodded to me and motioned to a padded chair beside Michael's gurney. "Have a seat."

He folded down another black leather seat at the front of the van for himself and the three of us rode together in silence. Each of Michael's blinks became slower, lasting longer, as he drifted in and out of consciousness. Given the nature of his injuries, I wondered if doctors would even be able to help.

With a sudden flash of light, Rhys appeared beside a huge shelf of medical supplies. I gasped when I saw him, unable to hide my surprise.

Dave checked his patient then glanced at me. "Everything okay?"

"Yeah. Sorry," I replied. Rhys was invisible.

His halo glowed brighter while he and Michael had an exchange of some sort. I strained to listen in through the network, but it was no use. Over the wails of the ambulance and the hum of its tires on the wet road, all I heard was the usual static.

Rhys left as we pulled into the hospital driveway, and Michael smiled, squeezing my hand. "It'll be all right." His eyes fluttered shut.

***

Inside the hospital, they rushed Michael into an examining room. The nurse at the check-in asked me about Michael's medical history. When I couldn't answer basic questions about his home phone number or insurance, she frowned at me. Her eyes grazed my ring-less finger. Our married façade was over. She asked an attendant to find Michael and sent me to the waiting room.

Because we were downtown, it was a different hospital than the one Mom worked in. This one was older. Its beige walls could have used a fresh coat of paint. But considering the chaos we'd come from, there was an obvious lack of shadows, flyers, and other creatures. This hospital had to have sigils in place.

I perched on a scratchy blue chair in the middle of the horseshoe-shaped seating area and tried to sit still. To my right, a middle-aged man sat in the corner, holding his stomach and frowning with pain. On my left, an elderly couple whispered softly to each other. The man clutched his wrist, while his wife leaned her silver-haired head against his other shoulder to comfort him. Her wedding band, scratched and softened with age, hung loosely on her wrinkled finger. I wondered what it would be like to live with someone that long.

On the wall hung a laminated paper sign with tacky clip art, requesting all cell phones be powered off. I dug into my purse and set mine to airplane mode. The selection of homemaker and sports magazines on the table beside me left me unimpressed. Though the waiting room was warm, I felt underdressed. Short dress, smeared makeup, and my jacket had been lost in the fire. I probably looked a total mess. I crossed my legs and stretched my short skirt farther down my thighs, but it rode up again, so I picked at a hole in my stained, torn tights with blood-caked fingers. I stank of smoke and beer.

As soon as the first nurse came into the room, I leaped to my feet. "Any news?"

"You'll have to check with the desk." She focused on her clipboard. "Mr. Samuelson?"

The middle-aged man gave her a nod.

"This way, please." Turning, she motioned down the hall.

Too nervous to sit again, I paced the small waiting room until the elderly couple gave me worried looks. The room started to fill with people who must have come from the club. Some needed stitches; others were like me, with torn clothes and smudged makeup, waiting to hear about people they cared about.

If his parents were on their way, they'd be panicked enough. Seeing me in this state would only make it worse. I headed to the women's washroom to clean up. Its chipped white tiles were a throwback from the last century. The porcelain sink had rust stains from an old leak.

I washed the dried blood from my hands and discovered my reflection in the mirror was worse than I'd thought. I had raccoon eyes from the smoke, and my nose had started to shine red through my uneven foundation. Using hand soap and a paper towel, I washed my face. I had to really scrub, but wearing no makeup at all was a definite improvement. When I looked up, I discovered Rhys's reflection in the mirror behind me, and let out a yelp.

I spun around to face him. "What are you doing here? This is a women's bathroom!"

"Are you concerned what I might see? Nothing I haven't seen before. Besides…" He motioned to the row of pink metal doors. "There are stalls."

Rhys was different than Arielle or even Turiel, a complete stranger to me. Why was he here? From what I knew of angels, it had to be official business. His wings were uncloaked, arched close to his back. Definitely official business.

"Where's Turiel?" I asked.

His green eyes burned right through me and it dawned on me where Turiel was. Helping Arielle fight for her life.

This night had gone so wrong. No one had suspected Raguel would be there, but if it weren't for me, he would still be imprisoned. Arielle would be all right. Michael wouldn't be injured, not to mention my friends. Did Rhys know? He must blame me for everything.

Unable to face him, I turned away. Shame burned my cheeks, and my eyes still stung from the smoke, blurring his reflection in the mirror. "Look, I know why you're here. I know it's my fault. If Damiel—"

"Stop." He raised his hands in the air. "Just. Stop."

Not sure what I was supposed to do, I froze.

Rhys drew closer, leaning on the sink so he could face me. "I'm here because I needed somewhere we could talk. After what happened back there in the ambulance, simply appearing before you in a hospital waiting room…"

"Yeah. Good plan." With my luck, I'd make a scene or answer him out loud, and people would think I was talking to myself. And that was the last thing I needed, considering the hospital psych ward wasn't that far away.

"I'm not here to admonish you." His halo brightened until it almost hurt my eyes, his wings shimmering and reflecting a pinkish glow from the walls. Even in the dull gray hue cast by the fluorescents, his light danced around us. "You're not responsible for what happened tonight, Raguel is."

"But Raguel got free because I helped Damiel."

"So did Michael, and Arielle. It was the right thing to do. Besides, considering Raguel was there tonight, the damage could have been worse. We deal with attacks of this scale all the time. This is what we do."

"How can you say it could have been worse? Arielle was—"

"I know what happened to her." He cut me off, his voice cold. "These are the risks we take." He reached a hand to my shoulder, and the movement was graceful, softer than Michael's. While Michael's physicality was warm and solid, Rhys's was as cool and ethereal as Arielle's—made of solid light. "She's stable right now and getting the best possible care. That's what matters."

The air caught in my chest as though a metal vise had clasped my ribs, holding them tight. I knew what he wasn't saying. She was going to die. "What about giving her my blood? Or making her human for awhile?" I grasped desperately for a solution to an unsolvable problem. Arielle had to get better. "It worked for Michael."

Rhys shook his head. "It only worked because

Michael's part human. Arielle's not."

"But we've got to try something." *Or it will kill her.* "We know the name of the sword, '*Nemerai*'. Doesn't that mean anything?"

"*Nemerai*?"

"You recognize it?"

He shook his head. "It must be new. But it's something. I'll let Zadkiel know." Rhys's expression tightened. What happened to Arielle couldn't be easy for him, for any of the angels. He stood a bit straighter. "I'm here to take you home."

"But we can't leave. What about Michael? Won't his parents—?"

"They never got the call. We blocked it." He leaned in, his expression serious, as though he needed me to remember everything he was about to say. "Michael's getting stitched up right now. When he's done, Zadkiel will take him home and keep an eye on him while he rests. We don't need his enhanced healing ability on any hospital records. He already raised their suspicions once, when he recovered from his coma last spring. They'd have questions and would look for answers, and the fewer loose ends tonight, the better."

"Is he going to be okay?"

"His humanity is proving itself useful. The worst it can do to Michael is drain him, over and over, eventually leaving him powerless."

Drain him dry. It was what Raguel did best.

CHAPTER TWENTY-THREE

Michael paced his tiny living room, tugging a faded black T-shirt over his head. A corner of the bandage on his stomach had already sprung loose, revealing the black stitches binding his pink, inflamed skin. He was so preoccupied he didn't notice the pop of air as Rhys and I teleported into the suite. The fact he'd changed into an old pair of ripped jeans, frayed around the cuffs, told me that despite his injuries, he had no intention of going to bed or even resting anytime soon.

Turiel and Zadkiel stood at opposite corners of the room observing Michael, their white uniforms covered in demon grime and angel blood—probably Arielle's. Neither of them had had time to clean up. But compared to Michael's wiry agitation, they were statues of calm.

Still reeling from the teleportation, I swallowed back a wave of saliva. "You're up and about. How are you?"

Michael stopped pacing and rushed to hug me. "Arielle's hurt." He ran a hand down my spine, slowly, casually. It was meant to be comforting, but his touch burned through the thin fabric of my filthy dress. I wanted to press myself against him.

Aware of how many eyes were on us, I quickly backed

away. "I know. I'm sorry."

Turiel stepped forward. The collar of his white jacket was ripped. "All three of us will remain on watch tonight. With Arielle down, the other battalions will be handling any emergencies, and I'll look after Arielle's duties."

So Turiel was in charge now? That made the reality of Arielle's absence hit home. Not only was I missing a friend, one of the few angels who defended my relationship with Michael, but the battalion also stood to lose the best leader they had.

"How's Arielle?" I asked. "Can I see her?"

"Not now," Turiel said. "She needs to rest."

Michael brushed my arm. "We were just discussing how Raguel could have interrupted the network signal."

"First a *djinn*, now Raguel." Turiel cleared his throat. "He must have jammed it somehow, because everything seemed fine on our end."

"We had no idea we couldn't hear Michael," said Zadkiel in deep low tones. "We'd relied on Turiel to keep the closest watch. Speaking of which…" He spun on Turiel. "Where the hell were you?"

Turiel raised his chin to meet Zadkiel's stare. "Trying to repair one of the sigils. I called. You never came. Couldn't hear anything, either. I was about to go inside for a visual check when I was ambushed by soldiers."

"Raguel must have made quick work of the sigils, because things looked fine until he arrived." Michael folded himself onto the couch and beckoned me to join him. As much as I wanted to curl up in his arms and pretend none of this was happening, I remained standing. More than ever, we needed to honor Arielle's request, and not flaunt our relationship.

Zadkiel rubbed the back of his close-shaved head. "Rhys and I were nearest and we couldn't sense anything wrong." He paused, shaking his head. "If only we could have reached Arielle."

"Do we know who stabbed her?" Michael said.

"She says it was a soldier demon. Possibly the same one that attacked you," answered Turiel.

"I don't know how she could tell. They all look the same to me," Rhys said.

"Can she be helped?" I asked.

Rhys and Turiel glanced at each other with furrowed brows. Zadkiel was the only one who spoke. "If we find the sword, *Nemeraii*, and destroy it."

"That will heal Michael too, won't it?" I dropped onto the couch beside him, a formal distance away.

"It will," Michael said. "But—"

"It could be anywhere," Rhys said. "And if he's keeping it with him in Hell, none of us can get it."

"What do you mean?"

"Well, angels can't enter Hell without falling, the same way that demons can't enter Heaven without being redeemed. There are laws in place."

No one said anything to that, and we all froze where we were, each lost in private thought. My cell phone buzzed and broke the silence, so I lunged for my purse and pulled it out. I ignored the latest message from Heather, but the time leaped out at me—midnight.

I sighed. The last thing I wanted right now was to leave Michael. He'd been through so much, but my mom would be home from work in a few minutes.

"I've got to get home before Mom. If I'm still out or she sees me like this…" I motioned to my torn dress, still damp with Arielle's blood, as though it were self-explanatory.

***

Rhys took me home, landing me in my room at quarter past twelve, giving me barely enough time to wash up and change out of my club clothes before Mom got home. Once I'd had a hot shower, the evening's shock set in and sent icy tremors through me. All the teleporting tonight had left my stomach queasy, but at least it was faster, and less scary, than flight. Besides, since the night Michael had flown me over the harbor, I didn't know how I'd feel about soaring through the air in anyone else's arms.

I changed into my navy flannel pajamas, the warmest bedclothes I owned, and smothered myself in my feather duvet to stave off the night's chill. I took my phone off airplane mode and checked my texts. Heather had sent me two. One asked which hospital we were at. The other told me to call her as soon as I got the message, no matter how late it was. I quickly dialed.

She picked it up on the first ring. "There you are! How's Michael? Is everything okay?"

"He's back home," I said. My voice sounded tight. Things were far from okay.

"Really? So soon?"

"He needed stitches. That's all."

"Thank God! Jesse and I were so worried. I couldn't sleep without knowing. He could have been... I mean, when Jesse was hurt, there was nothing I wouldn't do to help him, so think I might know how you feel. It hurts."

It would have been easier if Heather had given me her usual psychobabble. A huge lump formed in my throat. I swallowed it back. "Thanks."

"I know you've got a lot on your mind right now, but if Michael's still sleeping in the morning, or his parents won't let you come over, or you just don't want to be alone, or whatever it is... Jesse and I are going to go watch Dean compete. We want to support him, you know. He had to train really hard to catch up. It means a lot to him."

"Thanks." I was so tired I could barely focus. "I'll think about it."

"Okay. Call if you want a lift," she said and hung up.

By the time my mom got home at 12:30, the lights in my room were out, but I was nowhere near sleep. My body twitched with leftover adrenaline and my mind replayed the evening's events. Now that I could see into Michael's world, a reality superimposed over my own, the hellhounds and flyers were horrifying, yes, but I knew how to protect myself from them. What made them truly terrifying was the damage they could do to other people, and I couldn't stop it. Michael wore himself out trying to keep them at bay. I knew what had happened tonight wasn't because of me; Rhys had made that clear, but I still felt guilty.

If it weren't for tonight, Arielle wouldn't be mortally wounded. No one knew what she did, how she worked day in and day out to keep people safe. And although Rhys hadn't said it, I knew if we didn't find *Nemeraii* and destroy it, Arielle was going to die, and soon.

***

The rain pounded down the next morning and transformed my front lawn into a swamp. Birds dug through the grassy mud, their beaks tugging at wriggling, fat worms. I was amazed they could even fly with wings so wet. I wondered about Rhys up there in the sky. Did the rain even hit him?

After tossing and turning most of the night, I'd hauled myself out of bed and called Heather. A few minutes later, she picked me up in her mom's blue minivan and greeted me far too cheerily for having had so little sleep. Our short ride was filled with her humming along to the radio and chattering about how lucky we'd been to escape. My limbs still ached from the night before. All I could think about was Michael, Arielle, and what Raguel wanted. Had saving Damiel been worth it?

Heather parked close to the school's main doors and we made a dash for shelter to avoid getting soaked. Inside, the school was crowded for a Saturday morning, the halls filled with strangers, and a ball of dread hit my stomach as I remembered the panicked crush from the night before. What if something were to go wrong? This meet was a big deal. Wrestling teams from three other schools competed against ours. So many lives at risk.

Cheers echoed down the corridors as we approached the gym. Clenching my hands into fists, I braced myself for another crowd. When we reached the door, and the stench of sweat caught in my throat, gagging me. Maybe I wasn't ready to be around so many people yet.

"There's Fiona," Heather said, pointing. Nothing ruffled her. Then again, she thought last night's fire was simply a freak accident, not a planned attack. It wouldn't make sense to encounter another disaster so soon. For her, such a coincidence was unthinkable.

"I need a minute," I said. "Meet you inside?"

I dashed down the hall to the first private place I could think of, the girls' washroom, and bumped right into Fatima along the way. The last time I'd seen her, she'd been a creepy, floating marionette, so my first instinct was to run. But the episode with the *djinn* was nothing compared to what I'd been through last night.

"Hi," I said. She was psychic. I hated to think she could sense my awkwardness. "Here for the match?"

"No, getting some textbooks from my locker. My dad's waiting in the car." Her curly hair draped over half her face, and her eyes darted around as though she were expecting another attack. "I wanted to thank you and Michael for what you did."

And Arielle. I thought of how she'd put up the sigils and a lump formed in my throat. I swallowed hard. "I didn't think you'd remember."

"Oh, I was in there. Unable to stop it." Her eyes widened, and she played nervously with a new *hamsa* necklace. At least she was protected again.

I lowered my voice. "How did it happen?"

She pressed her lips together and glanced down the empty hall, as though making sure no one could overhear us. "I can talk to you, right? You saw it too. You won't think I'm crazy?"

"I saw it. I know it's real."

A couple of guys burst into the hall, talking loudly about the match. She let them pass before she said, "This man came into the store one day and offered to teach me how to use my psychic gifts."

"Was it that night Heather and I were there?" I asked, remembering the stranger who'd set my *hamsa* off. But other than the fact he was wearing a hat, the memory of him had slid from my mind.

She nodded. "I'm not foolish. I'd never trust someone like that, but he had this way about him that was so compelling. I couldn't say no. He did this weird ritual that he said would help me know what real power was, and that night, the *djinn* started to take over." Her skin paled, and she licked her lips. "I could feel it talking to me, telling me what to do. At first, I thought it was me, but then it took control of my body, and I couldn't do anything to stop it."

She couldn't say no? Had she been enthralled? "I'm sorry. My *hamsa* went off that night. I should have checked on you."

"No, I'm sorry!" Fatima's voice pulled me out of my brooding thoughts. "Please tell Michael." She reached into her bag and pulled out a small box. "I don't know if you still need this, but I noticed you lost yours. It took forever to find. Our supplier's run out."

I accepted the box and opened it. It was another *hamsa*, the same kind she'd given me twice before. Guilt burned my cheeks. "I didn't lose it," I said carefully, not wanting to upset her. "I gave it to my mom. I was worried about her and thought she'd need it more." Mom had been wearing it every day since. "What about your family?"

"They've all got one, or something similar." She closed my hand around the necklace. "Keep it. It's the least I can do."

"Thank you. I really did miss having one." I unfastened the clasp and slipped the silver chain around my neck. "That day in the store, you said you wanted to talk about something. What was it?"

She slumped against one of the lockers. "I'd had a dream about you, that you were in danger. Michael too."

"What was it about?"

"All I know was that Michael was badly injured, and your friends were in danger." She shook her head. "I'm sorry. The rest is gone."

Both those things had already happened. If she knew more, the rest of her memories were missing. Fatima had been attacked before she could deliver the message to warn me. "That man—what did he look like?" I dredged my mind, trying to conjure an image, to remember something distinctive about him.

"He was tall and pleasant looking, I think. Blond hair, well-dressed. Said his name was Raguel."

"Raguel?" I repeated dumbly. Hot bile rose to my throat. Raguel had bound Fatima to a *djinn*? Right after she'd told me she had a warning for us.

She grabbed my arm, gently shaking me. "Are you okay?"

I nodded, not knowing what to say.

After we said goodbye, I ventured into the gym to find my friends in the flurry of activity. Our cheerleaders, the Westmont Warblers, shook their butts and waved their burgundy and gold pompoms to the music's loud, thumping beat. Cheerleaders from the other teams met their challenge, shouting and clapping the names of their star players. I dragged myself up the bleacher stairs to where Heather and Fiona had saved me a seat. It was such a loud, raucous event for so early in the morning I had to yell my hellos to Fiona and Jesse. I really needed a coffee.

Dean did surprisingly well, beating out two other competitors in his weight class. Fiona was ecstatic, but as happy as I was for Dean, for both of them, I couldn't get the events from the previous night, or what Fatima had told me, out of my head. The *djinn* had been able to bring down the network, because it had been working with

Raguel.

I was so preoccupied I didn't notice Heather leaning into me until she asked, "Worried about Michael?"

"Huh? Oh. Yeah." I looked up to see one of our team's wrestlers flip his opponent, who landed with a loud thud. Cheers and clapping exploded through the gym, ricocheting off the walls.

"Last night was really awful." She dug in her purse for her lip gloss and gesticulated with it instead of putting it on. "But the newspaper this morning said there weren't any fatalities. That's something, right? I know it's a small comfort, given that Michael was one of the injured, but it could have been worse."

She had no idea how much worse, or how bad things really were. Sure, she knew how it felt to have her boyfriend in the hospital, but she had no idea about Arielle, or what had really happened. She didn't even know angels existed. Could I tell her? If I did, would it blow her mind?

"Hey. You don't think Elaine will put something about it in our school paper, do you?" Heather punctuated her question by unscrewing the cap of her gloss and applying it to her lips.

"Not if we don't tell her about it." Truly, Elaine was the least of my worries, and since the day I'd taken her to Ms. Callou's office, she'd been pretty decent. She'd never published a thing about Jesse, either. Perhaps I'd misjudged her. I hoped her mother was getting help.

Dean came to visit us between sets and Fiona, Heather, Jesse, and I all congratulated him on how well he was doing. While the four of them joked and made light conversation over the sound of Westmont's brass band, a piercing pain bit between my eyes. The room went dark. This time, I knew better than to scream.

The skies are filled with black and blood red clouds, and the air smells of sulfur. Flyers circle the sky, led by huge soldier demons with black skin and leathery wings. They descend upon the crowded city streets, fighting each other for food, while people argue with each other in sudden bursts of anger. Strange accidents break out. A bus driver stops paying attention to the road and swerves into a cyclist. The passengers scream. Instead of stopping to help, the driver speeds off in a hit-and-run.

As havoc breaks out among the people below, a soldier demon separates from the fray. It lands in a brick-lined alley and darts through an old wooden door with cracked green paint. Down a broken, abandoned staircase, he follows passageways of brick and stone, on wooden walkways under the city streets. Eventually he comes upon an old, rounded, black metal door guarded by two more soldier demons. With a nod, they let him into an expansive room with brick walls and a high, arched ceiling. Behind an ornate wooden desk, in a gray pinstripe suit, sits Raguel.

The demon bows and draws out a long object that had been carefully concealed beneath his wings. It is cloaked in black cloth. He hands it to Raguel. "My Lord. The angel Arielle has been stabbed, as you requested."

Accepting it, Raguel stands and crosses the room to an old iron safe. "Thank you, Garlakra," he says. "Nemeraii was forged at a great cost. I appreciate your taking time to return it promptly." Turning the brass handle, Raguel opens the safe and places the wrapped object inside. "Last night went very well. You've earned your freedom, but I may still call on you later if I need you."

"Of course," Garlakra says.

"Mia!" Heather's voice called me back to reality. "Are you okay? You're as white as a sheet!"

"I-I…" I struggled to focus, not wanting to forget what I'd seen. Another vision. At least I was awake this time. If this was happening now, I needed to talk to Michael and fast. "Yeah. I'm kinda tired after last night." Still lightheaded from the experience, I rose carefully to my feet. The room spun. "Maybe I should head home."

"I can drive you," Heather offered.

"It's okay. It's a nice day. I think I'll walk." I gathered my bag, preparing to leave. "I need the fresh air."

"But it's raining!" said Fiona, twisting a lock of hair with her fingers. Dean had returned to his team, and I hadn't even noticed.

"I'll be fine. See ya." I turned to Heather. "Talk later?"

Before she could reply, I stumbled down the bleachers, winding my way through the crowds, knowing that my friends were watching me, and that they were probably worried, but I didn't care.

CHAPTER TWENTY-FOUR

I pressed through the gym's exit doors and called out for Rhys with my thoughts. He arrived in the hall behind me instantly, as though he'd been there all along and I simply hadn't noticed. Two sophomore girls brushed between us, completely unaware of him. They walked so slowly it took forever for them to get out of earshot.

"I've had a vision," I whispered, knowing I couldn't use the network for this. "Raguel—"

Rhys raised his hand for silence and ushered me into an empty biology lab, where a skeletal pterodactyl hung from the ceiling, looming over our heads in impossible flight. Past the rows of desks, a plastic human skeleton dangled from its stand, as a kind of macabre marionette. Rhys tightened his grip on my arm and teleported me off the school grounds.

We stepped right into a different hall, a bright crystalline corridor made of frosted glass. To settle my stomach post-teleportation, I took a few gulps of fresh air that was tinged with the sweet taste of orange blossoms. As I followed Rhys down the hall, its opaque ceilings curved high above us into gothic points, allowing room for angels to spread their wings. A labyrinth of corridors with arched entrances branched off the hallway. We turned down one, then another, each lined with countless doors.

At the next corner, Michael appeared beside us in a pulse of air. Rhys gave him a nod. "You made it."

"I can always get here." Michael wore the same jeans and T-shirt from the night before, now loose and rumpled from wear. He'd obviously come straight from his room. His wings were no longer cloaked. Even folded, they stretched out several feet behind him. Their feathery filaments shimmered and reflected the light from the walls. He walked straighter this way, his posture more formal, and yet he was completely at ease, as if the injuries he'd sustained had never happened. This was who he was, and it had been forever since I'd seen him so comfortable in his own skin.

When his arm brushed against mine, driving shivers all the way up my neck, I remembered another part of him, the part of him that craved my touch. Not wanting to think about that here, I fixed my attention on the ground. Even the floors seemed to be carved from glass, etched with strange, ornate glyphs. I soon learned that focusing on these symbols turned the area around them clear, dissolving the halls until they didn't exist, and we were walking on air. Cerulean sky surrounded us from every direction.

My body jerked away from the open space. "What the...?"

Michael caught me by the waist and chuckled softly into my hair. "It's all right, you're safe here."

"Where are we? What is this place?"

"This is the Luminarium, one of our outposts."

"Luminarium, from the Latin word for light?" I asked.

He nodded. "It's an observation area built to monitor your world."

"It's at the perimeter of both our worlds," Rhys said. "Only angels can walk these halls." After a sideways glance from Michael, he added, "*Usually.*"

I motioned to the frosted, radiant substance beneath my feet. It felt firm, yet yielded from my weight as though I were standing on damp earth. "But what are we walking on?"

"Light," said Rhys.

"That's impossible!"

"Not here." Michael gave me a reassuring smile. "This is where we are at our strongest. We're protected here, so we can heal faster. But if we're wounded by an angel killer sword, that very healing can work against us."

"Which is why we have Arielle in another chamber," Rhys explained. "She's suspended from the healing powers of this place. It's the only way we can keep her alive."

"What about you?" I asked Michael. "You were injured."

He shrugged. "They've blocked the healing for me as well."

Turiel and Zadkiel joined us in one of the corridors, and Turiel led us into a private room, making a point of going in first. His clean uniform was crisp and white, and he acted even stiffer and more formal than he had before. I wondered if he was upset about Arielle, or if it was something else. The room itself resembled a boardroom. Dimly lit, its walls were comprised of solid blue light. The crystalline floor beneath us didn't look strong enough to support the huge, black stone table at its center. The high-backed wooden chairs had splits down their spines to allow room for the angels' wings.

Rhys stood beside me and motioned for the others to take a seat. "Thanks for joining us. We're here because Mia's had a vision."

Anxiety tickled the back of my throat as I caught their questioning glances. Even now, with everything I'd been through, the idea that I was a prophet, that the angels needed my help, still unnerved me. "The *djinn* that possessed Fatima was working with Raguel," I blurted out, hoping my information was useful. "She told me." Now that all these angels had gathered, I worried that what I'd seen was just a daydream, a side effect of last night's ordeal.

Michael held out a chair for me and I eased into it before any of them could tell my legs were shaking. "When did you see her?" he asked.

"A few minutes ago," I whispered. "She says thanks, by the way."

Michael smiled and took a seat to my right; Rhys sat at my left.

Rhys looked up at Turiel. "It makes sense."

"It does." Turiel sat last, taking the chair across from me. He clasped his hands on the table in front of him and sighed. The opalescence of his wings reflected the same royal blue as the walls. "We need to know about your vision, Mia. What exactly did you see?" He smiled and nodded at me, but his encouragement made me more nervous.

I closed my eyes, trying to remember everything, and told them what I could. What Raguel had said, where Garlakra had landed, and how he'd gone through those underground tunnels. All the while, Turiel prodded me for details, until I'd given him Raguel's exact words and described the location in the most tedious detail.

"Sounds like those tunnels in the Seattle Underground," Michael said. "My parents took me on a tour of them once, years ago."

"Of course. In Pioneer Square!" I'd wanted to go with Mom when we first moved to Seattle, but as much as I'd tried to persuade her, she'd refused to go down into any "moldy, old tunnels". She didn't share my love of historic sites. Of course, I could have gone by myself. I wished I had. It would've helped to know more about the area. "The club wasn't far from there, was it?"

"Neither was the restaurant," Michael added.

Zadkiel pushed himself away from the table, standing. "How did you manage to see this when we can't?"

Agitation rolled off him. "We have seers in Heaven as well."

"She's a prophet, Zadkiel," said Rhys. "Sometimes our kind can't see the things of this world as well as a human can. We can see the future, or the larger plan, but knowing the exact whereabouts of *Nemeraii*? Can't you see it for the blessing that it is?"

With a derisive snort, Zadkiel clasped the back of his chair and slid it toward the table. "Perhaps. My experience with these swords has taught me otherwise. I'll count my blessings when it's been destroyed."

"Enough, you two." Turiel rubbed his forehead, as though he were trying to focus. "We have to get the sword back. Clearly, having it on Earth has given us an advantage. Mia, can you draw us a map of what you saw?"

"I think so."

Rhys reached into the sheath between his wings and, with a flourish, procured a leather-bound notebook and pen. "Here."

"What else do you keep in there? *Lunch?*"

"My sword." He frowned, not getting the joke. Nor did anyone else. Perhaps other angels didn't eat the way Michael did.

The silver fountain pen was cold and slim in my fingers. The dark blue ink etched crisp lines onto the smooth, white notebook paper. I sketched the landscape of the vision as best I could, but I was no artist. My work resembled a child's treasure map more than anything useful.

"He's got it protected," I said, making Xs by the door. "Three or four guards at least."

"From what you said, they're soldier demons," said Rhys. "Nothing to be concerned about. One of us should go check it out."

"Not without backup," Zadkiel insisted.

"No," Turiel said. "Rhys is right. Only one of us. I'll go."

"Shouldn't we go to the council first?" Michael asked.

"Informing the council would be wise. Raguel's actions are a blatant declaration of war," Zadkiel said with a nod.

Turiel slapped his hand, palm down on the table's smooth surface, making me jump. "There's no time. Not when Arielle's life is at stake."

"I agree we should move quickly," said Rhys. "Raguel gave us two days. If we don't bring him Damiel, he'll retaliate. We must strike now, disarm him while we can."

Zadkiel leaned his hands on the far end of the table and flicked his wings out behind him. Silvery white lights danced along the walls. "If anyone should go, it should be me. I've faced a sword of this caliber before—"

"So have I," Michael said.

"You're not at full capacity. Sending you would be folly," said Zadkiel.

"No, Zadkiel." Turiel stood. "It should be me. Arielle asked me to take her place. As your interim commander, I cannot put any of you at risk."

"You don't know what it's capable of, or the ritual to destroy it," Zadkiel said. "I do."

"When the time comes, I'll bring it back here, and you can destroy it. In the meantime, both you and Rhys should keep an eye on Mia and Michael as part of your watch."

Rhys and Zadkiel exchanged resigned looks and in unison said, "Understood."

"Be sure to guard your thoughts. We don't know how closely Raguel is listening outside these walls." Turiel led them to the door. "Now, if you'd excuse us, I have a request of Mia."

My heart skipped a beat. What else could Turiel possibly want? Was he going to reprimand me for Michael hugging me last night? Give us a lecture? Under the table, Michael caught my fingers between his, just enough of a touch to let me know he was there, that he wasn't leaving. I squeezed his hand before I let it drop, hoping Turiel couldn't see us. He wasn't omniscient, was he?

Without a second glance our way, Turiel closed the door and returned to the seat across from me. "Would you show me your vision? Let me access your memory?"

I recalled the way Arielle had helped me remember my past life with Michael, how she could feel my feelings, but not really see what went on, or so she said. The thought of Arielle tightened in my chest. "I didn't think that was possible."

"It is, here. We can set up close telepathic links without using our network, if you let me."

It was bad enough that he could feel my feelings, which meant he already knew a lot about Michael and me. And after Arielle's warning not to display our feelings for each other, I didn't want to invite Turiel to know more. What if he saw too much?

I turned to Michael. The room's blue light emphasized the dark circles around his eyes. "Would you do it?"

He nodded, but Turiel shook his head. "He really shouldn't waste an ounce of his strength right now."

"He'll only see what you show him." Michael leaned his shoulder against mine and smiled. "I'll be with you the whole time."

I squeezed my eyes shut and tightened my fingers around the chair's armrests in anticipation. The last time I'd let an angel access my mind it had hurt. A lot. I took a few deep breaths to brace myself, before giving him the nod to let him know I was ready.

Turiel's hands lit with buzzing white flames. He placed his glowing fingertips on my temples, and the burning sensation of sheet lightning burst through my mind, an explosion of white-hot pain for a fraction of a second, followed by stillness.

"It doesn't hurt as much as before." My fingers loosened their grip.

"You only have to recall something recent this time, not like with Arielle." Michael's voice rasped when he said her name. When I opened my eyes, he swallowed and looked away.

"Think of your vision, Mia," Turiel continued. "Just remember it."

Relaxing, I replayed the images in my mind for what had to be the fiftieth time that day. When I was done, I couldn't look at Turiel. It was as if I'd shared my deepest secrets with him. When Arielle had done it, she felt safe. Warmth had shone through her. But Turiel was so cold and scientific.

He removed his hands from my head. "I know exactly where it is." He gave me a kind smile, more of an afterthought, and his violet eyes glowed. "Thank you."

CHAPTER TWENTY-FIVE

Michael showed signs of fatigue when we were done, so Rhys brought us back to Michael's place and left us alone for a while. I knew we were being watched over, and with the way Rhys could pop into a room, our privacy was limited. But it still felt good to be "alone" together for even a few minutes. We avoided the subject of Arielle as though we sensed each other's worry and knew that talking about it would make things worse. To keep my thoughts from notifying Raguel and his minions, I made a point of staying far away from the network. Michael seemed to be doing the same. Though he moved stiffly, so he wouldn't rupture his stitches, he gave no indication of being in pain. That was something, at least.

"I know we can't talk about it." I took a seat on the couch beside him. "But how will we know if it happens? Or if it even works?"

"I'm sure someone will tell us." Michael propped his feet on the coffee table and picked up the phone. "I'm ordering a pizza. I'm starving, and all this house arrest is driving me batty. What do you want?"

"Pizza? It's morn…" I glanced at my cell phone. It wasn't morning anymore, it was already noon. "Uh—

pepperoni?"

"Another reason to love you." He brushed his fingers along my arm, not realizing the way his words, or his touch, had warmed my skin.

With a radiant flash of light, Turiel appeared in the living room. Michael hung up the phone and placed it on the table.

"I can't get into the room," Turiel said. His wings were tucked behind him, covered in the dusty ash of slaughtered demons, his white jacket spotted with slime. Across his chest hung a thin leather strap attached to a satchel at his hip. "I've killed the soldier demons. I've even busted the lock, but the room has a ward on it that appears to block angels from entry."

"Of course." Michael unfolded himself from the couch. "He'd have to expect we'd come."

"A human might be able to get in." Turiel said. The look he gave Michael was apologetic. "We have to try."

"All right." Michael crossed the living room, heading for the closet. "I'll go."

"No," Turiel said. "You're still angelic, even in your current state. We need Mia."

"No way!" Michael spun around. "It's probably a trap."

"Once she crosses the ward, it should break the seal and I should be able to go in after her."

"That's a whole lot of 'shoulds'." Michael pulled a leather jacket from the closet and shrugged it on over his shirt. "Do you actually *know* what will happen?"

"I won't deny it's a risk." Turiel turned to me. "Would you help us?"

"Of course. Anything I can do." I leaped to my feet, slid into my coat, and grabbed my purse. "Shouldn't we tell Rhys and Zadkiel?"

Turiel shook his head. "There's no telling when Raguel will be back, or who's listening. Any long-range communication I do with the other angels could be tracked."

"So, it's just us," Michael said. "Then you'll definitely need my help."

***

Jammed between two huge angels, the first sensation I had of my new surroundings was lack of space. Straining my eyes in the darkness, I realized we were on the same wooden walkway where the demon had been in my vision, surrounded by aged brick and wood beams. Something dripped in the distance, and the sound of Michael's and my breathing was almost deafening. Turiel made no sound whatsoever, as though he were an apparition. Beside the wooden boards we stood on, the ground was wet, and the dense wall of air carried the tang of damp metal and mildew.

At least I wasn't queasy. Perhaps I'd teleported so many times now that my stomach was getting used to it.

"I couldn't bring us any closer," Turiel whispered. "We'll have to go by foot."

Turiel strode to the front, while Michael brought up the rear, keeping me close to him, the heat of his body the only warmth in the chilly space. The two of them moved silently, but the sound of my footsteps on the wood echoed down the narrow passageway. Surely I was going to get us all killed. We followed the same turns that I had seen in my vision, forking left, then right, then left again, until we came upon the corridor leading to a green metal door.

"I'll get it open," Turiel said to me. "Then you go inside. Once you're in, the seal on the room should be broken, and Michael and I can join you."

Michael gave him a sidelong glance. "Are you sure it won't work for me? I know my powers aren't what they used to be. What if I give it a try?"

With a flourish, Turiel motioned to the entrance and said, "Be my guest."

Michael stepped forward, and Turiel opened the door. In contrast to the dark hallway, the room seemed bright. I squinted at the brick walls inside, the ornate mahogany desk and two old-fashioned, wooden chairs. In the corner stood an ancient cast iron safe.

I couldn't even detect a hum of warding, but when Michael attempted to cross the threshold, a green spark of energy bounced off his halo and threw him across the corridor. He slammed against its opposite wall and slid to the floor, winded from the blow.

"See?" Turiel cocked an eyebrow.

Michael picked himself up and shook out his limbs, as though it would help him release the charge. "Gee, thanks for the warning."

I rushed to his side, checking his wound for any seepage.

"I'm fine." Michael covered my fingers with his, and beneath the thin fabric of his shirt, I could feel his pulse racing. His gaze linked with mine. I swallowed.

"How do you know it won't do that to me?" I asked Turiel.

Turiel cleared his throat and focused his attention into the room, obviously uncomfortable around the two of us. "It seems to use our halos against us. I tried it several times to be sure. Pretty clever, really."

"I wouldn't call trying *that* several times 'clever'," Michael said.

Ignoring him, Turiel asked me, "Will you try it?"

"Do you promise to put me back together if it throws me?" I asked in return.

"Of course," said Turiel. "I would never expose you to an uncalculated risk."

"Yeah. It's your calculations I'm worried about," Michael muttered. Pulling a quarter from his pocket, he tossed it into the empty room. The coin flew through the door, landed with a soft clink, and rolled along the old hardwood floors until it finally stopped under the desk.

Turiel leaned against the side of the door and said to Michael, "It might have been clever to do that *before* you tried to go through."

"It could be a matter of size." Michael motioned to my purse. "Can I try your bag?"

I handed it to him, and he swung my purse by the strap across the threshold. It came back unharmed. "Well, it works for inanimate objects. We know that."

Folding his arms across his chest, Turiel tapped his foot impatiently. "We're running out of time."

"You don't have to do this, Mia," Michael said. "A demon could still be hiding in there."

What if there's a demon and they can't get to me? I swallowed my fear. "Turiel's right. We don't have much time left to help Arielle. And if there were a demon, my *hamsa* would warn me." I touched the necklace for reassurance. "But it's silent. Which is a good sign, right?"

Turiel nodded, but Michael's expression was solemn. He stepped behind me. "I'll be right here just in case—to either catch you or break your fall."

"Thanks. I think."

And, before Michael could object again, or I could lose my courage, I pressed my hands across the threshold, feeling a tickle of heat but that was all. On the other side of the invisible barrier, the room was the same temperature as the corridor.

"Seems okay," I said.

I stepped through the doorway, and the warmth of the barrier dissipated with my approach.

Drawing his weapon, Turiel tested the threshold with his free arm and nodded at Michael. "It's down."

Not wasting any time, Michael and Turiel rushed inside.

The room was bigger than I expected, lit from above by a droning, angry bee of an exposed incandescent bulb. It hung from a wire and swung in the breeze of the air vents. A green banker's lamp and an old, cork-colored desk blotter stained with ink sat on the desk. Behind it, a brown leather armchair with metal rivets waited for its owner. Two hard-backed wooden chairs faced the desk as though visitors were never meant to be comfortable. I shuddered at what work Raguel must do in this place.

The safe had to be at least four feet tall and a hundred years old. Its once shiny black surface was covered in gold scrollwork that had scratched and faded with age. In the center of the door, a large, brass combination lock glinted in the dull light.

"So what's the plan?" Michael brushed his fingertips along the rusted hinges. "Want to guess the combination? Or were you planning to teleport out with it? It must weigh a few tons, at least."

Turiel opened the leather satchel at his hip and pulled out a drill. "These old safes aren't that hard to crack."

"So, you're a safecracker now?" Michael said with a smirk. "Oh, how the mighty have fallen."

Turiel crouched in front of the safe. "If I recall correctly, there's a specific angle we need to drill for this particular model." With his eyes closed, he pressed an ear to the cast iron door and tapped around with his fingertips. "Should be about..." He stopped an inch away from the lock, to the right. "Here."

The drill whirred as he switched it on and its bit pierced the metal in a matter of seconds. Once he'd made three holes around the lock, he rotated the knob, and the safe opened.

"Not bad," said Michael.

I kneeled beside him. "It should be on the top shelf."

Turiel reached inside the open safe and pulled out the wrapped object. He removed the cloth cover to reveal a blackened steel sword with a Japanese-style blade. Its hilt had been carved with symbols, some kind of ancient lettering, and the blade glistened and shimmered with a fiery red light that danced across it. Its presence sent a chill across my skin.

Turiel turned the weapon over in his hands, admiring it. His features tightened as the object's glimmering light cast red speckles in his violet eyes. He hardly blinked. "It's quite beautiful," he said with a gasp. "You'd never know it was so deadly from looking at it."

Michael helped me to my feet. "It's going to be all right now." His voice was rough. His eyes glazed over as though a shadow had taken his focus, and he didn't care that we weren't alone. With a soft, lazy, smile, he brushed his fingertips along the side of my cheek, sending a tingle of heat into the base of my stomach that eradicated any chill. When he brought his lips to mine, his kiss was both gentle and deep, and my heart tugged into my throat from the intensity of it. He slid his hands to my hips and lifted me on top of the safe. Deep down, I knew this wasn't the place to be making out, especially not in front of Turiel—which was so inappropriate—but I couldn't find the words to protest. I didn't want to. It had been so long since he'd kissed me this way. I leaned into him and pressed against his warmth with a breathless urgency.

Behind him, Turiel was speaking, something about getting out of there, but in my mind's eye, his words melted into the red, orange, and purple energies swirling around us. They shimmered and blended together like fire.

I was so bewitched by Michael's kisses I didn't notice Turiel actually leaving until the door slammed. Michael was oblivious. I pulled my face away. "Turiel's gone."

Michael snapped out of his stupor, startled awake as though I'd slapped him. Taking a step back, he scanned the room and checked the door.

That was when the lights flickered and everything went black.

Fear clutched my throat, and my *hamsa* necklace vibrated its tiny, terrified heartbeat. I tried to scream, but all that came out was a whisper. "Michael!"

"I can feel it," he said. "Run!"

He grabbed my wrist and charged the door, dragging

me along with him.

CHAPTER TWENTY-SIX

The old metal door was stuck on its hinges. Michael drew his sword. It bathed his features in a cold, eerie blue as he struggled with the bolt, trying to pry it open.

I stepped back to give him room. He threw his shoulder and then his full weight into it. The effort made him groan. "Stupid thing won't budge."

"It slammed shut when Turiel left," I said.

"Yeah, well. It's been magically sealed."

"By Turiel?"

"Doubt it."

The prickling of a hundred tweezers tugged the hairs along my neck. Something was coming. A sulfurous, rotten onion smell filled the air. Through the cracks in the bricks, where the walls and ceiling met, a slimy substance trickled down the walls. It glimmered wet in the sword's faint blue glow.

Michael threw a cone of purple-blue light that erupted through the door, and the magical seal fizzled and shorted out, dissolving to dust. His teeth gritted with determination, he kicked the door with the heel of his boot. The bolt jumped from the impact, releasing for a moment, before latching back into place.

"Was that a sigil?"

He shrugged. "Without a network, it's the best I can do." Wincing, he put a hand to his ribs. It came away wet with blood.

He'd torn his stitches. Any push on his power was a risk. I moved toward him to check.

"It's fine." He held out his arm to keep me away. "I strained a bit. That's all."

The dark liquid streamed down the walls, dripping to the floor. It rolled together, forming larger droplets, and then shapes.

I gasped with the horror of recognition. "It's Azazel, isn't it?"

It was the creature Michael had fought and banished a few weeks ago, when Damiel had sent it to attack us, his way of sending a message. Once a leader of the Nephilim, the half-human offspring of fallen angels, Azazel had the ability to form himself from multiple shapes. His full size was that of an eighteen-wheeler—composed of demon flesh.

Michael gave me a nod in response. Kicking one more time, he jammed his sword to block the latch from falling into place and ripped the door open.

"Let's go," he said. "Now!"

I charged ahead of him, sprinting down the dark brownstone corridor. Michael followed, slamming the door, though I doubted it would stop Azazel. I was right. The slick droplets seeped through the gap underneath and congealed into an army of rats.

Azazel's rat forms sped down the hall after us as though they were escaping an inferno. I had hardly covered any distance at all before I tripped on the first of them, slipping as they collapsed into a slick substance. I yelped, almost losing my balance. I only had time to steady myself against the brick walls for a second before the foul-smelling things scrambled on top of each other right in front of me, blocking the way out.

I stood there, frozen, as they melded and merged into a humanoid shape. The last time I'd seen Azazel, he'd been huge—was he really only human-sized now?

His sword drawn, Michael clutched my arm and pulled my attention to the river of blackness surging around us. He slashed through the narrowest part with his fiery blade, and the creatures disintegrated.

"That way." He twirled me on my heels. "Back the way we came. Don't stop."

I hesitated. Rats quickly closed the gap his sword had made. Beads of sweat had formed on his brow. Beneath his jacket, a poppy-red stain pooled on his shirt. He was tired and injured, nowhere near his full strength, and each strike of his blade made it worse.

He swung again, pushing me through the gap before it closed. "Go! I'll join you as soon as I can."

"I can't leave you!" The river gushed between us, growing into Azazel's humanoid form. It stood almost nine feet tall now, widening as more rats joined. Surely we'd have a better chance fighting this together. There had to be something I could do.

"Go. Please," Michael urged, taking a swing at Azazel's head, knocking the rats and turning them to dust. "I need to know you'll be all right."

He took his second swing and I ran. Michael's counterattack held the creatures off. From the entrance of another brick-lined hallway, I couldn't help but look back. Azazel's humanoid form filled the corridor, splattering Michael with an acidic slime that oozed down his chest, smoking as though it burned. The last time they had fought, Michael had been in top form, somersaulting over the beast and slicing off its many heads, his wings keeping him aloft. Now, his wings were inaccessible, and his reflexes quickly dulled.

Michael lunged and cut off one of Azazel's arms. No sooner had it dropped to the floor than the other liquid parts of him formed a new one. Azazel's real size was ginormous, and using a smaller form simply gave him extra mass to work with, bulk that he didn't need in such a confined space.

As Michael sliced, Azazel struck him across the face, throwing him off balance. Forming another arm, the demon leaned its head in and bit Michael's shoulder. With a yelp of pain, Michael thrust his blade desperately into Azazel's chest, but the demon seized his sword arm and broke his grip. The weapon fell, and Azazel kicked it away. And with it went any chance Michael had of surviving. He swung with fists now, jumping up and hanging off a loose water pipe, blood streaming from wounds both old and new. Using his feet, he kicked his opponent, but though Azazel was human-sized and shaped, nothing else about him was mortal; he was clawed and fanged like a wild animal, and he never formed skin. In its place, an oily liquid both glimmered and sucked the light from the room. His claws scraped Michael's chest, shredding skin and the fabric of his already bloody shirt. Michael cried out.

I had to do something. I knew we weren't supposed to use it, but if I connected to the network, perhaps I could access enough light to push Azazel off Michael, before Raguel could figure out where we were. Maybe I could even get the fallen sword. It was risky. I had no idea how long I had before Raguel found us. A minute? I had to try. If Michael were at full strength things would be different, but Azazel was winning.

Closing my eyes, I reached with my mind for the grid work of light and found shadows. I reached again. Still nothing. It had to be blocked. Tears stung the backs of my eyes, threatening to drown them. But this was not a time for crying. I had to act. Without the network, we had nothing. I couldn't stand by and watch Michael get hurt, and jumping into the fray was suicide. I needed to be smart. All I'd be was a diversion at best. At worst, I'd distract Michael and Azazel would hurt him even more. There had to be something I could do.

With Michael injured and Turiel gone, I was Rhys's ward now, right? What if Rhys could still feel me the way Michael could? Did he need the network for that, or was it another type of connection? I focused on Rhys in my mind's eye, calling up an image of his face, and amped up my feelings of distress.

My cell phone chirped, making me jump. A quick glance in Michael's direction told me it was the first he'd noticed I was there. Azazel struck again and Michael barely escaped in time. Holding my breath, I answered my cell on the second ring. "Yeah?"

"Where are you?" Rhys's voice crackled over the line. "I can't see you."

I checked the phone. The number read "Unknown". I didn't think the phone had a signal down here. "How—? Never mind. We're in the Seattle Underground. Michael's fighting—"

Before I could finish my sentence, Rhys appeared in the corridor, about ten feet away.

"Over there." I pointed to Michael, his fighting arm shredded by Azazel's claws. Sword drawn, Rhys brushed past me and charged Azazel, catching the demon unaware. With the quick, efficient strokes of a seasoned warrior, Rhys sliced off the demon's head before it could take another bite. The head disintegrated. Michael collapsed to the ground.

Rats scrambled up Azazel's body to form another head, but I didn't care. "Michael!" I rushed to his side and dropped to my knees beside him.

His arms shook with fatigue as he pressed himself into an upright position. He mumbled and motioned for his sword, which lay in the soot and grime not three feet away. I scurried around one of the rats and grabbed it. The weapon hummed as I tossed it in Michael's direction, and he caught it by the hilt.

Rhys swung again, sending creatures everywhere, and then turned to the largest mass. But even that quickly scattered along the corridor, returning to its many rat forms. "Azazel, as Watcher of this realm, I banish you back to Hell."

The corridor's brick walls tore open, shredded fabric that formed a mouth of darkness. A flash of purple light filled the corridor, gathered the shrieking Azazel, and swept him into the hole. Then the tear in reality seamed together as though nothing had happened. A peaceful stillness filled the air.

Michael dragged himself to his feet, using his sword for balance, and gave Rhys a nod. "How'd you find us?"

"Mia used the network to call me." Rhys sheathed his sword, scanning the area. "Let's get out of here, before Raguel gets back. He must know we're here."

Rhys then reached for both our hands and teleported us out of the underground tunnels. If it were up to me, I'd never be anywhere near them again.

CHAPTER TWENTY-SEVEN

We arrived in what had to be one of the Luminarium's smallest healing rooms. Two chairs and a long, narrow cot absorbed half the floor space. A silver-white orb glowed above our heads, and crammed into the corner was an immaculate sink that must have been carved from the same substance as the walls. We guided Michael to the mattress, and he grimaced with pain as he eased himself down. Rhys tended to him immediately, shrugging him out of his jacket and unbuttoning the shredded, blood-soaked shirt. I reached for the next button, trying to help, but my fingers shook so much I couldn't get a grip.

Noticing my trembling hands, Rhys tossed Michael's jacket at me. "Put this in the sink," he said and continued examining Michael.

Zadkiel rushed through the doors, pulled one of the split-backed chairs up to the cot, and joined in the healing. Gold light beamed from his fingertips as he waved them over the weeping gashes. The wounds obediently stopped bleeding and knitted themselves together.

I crept forward and hovered beside them. "Is it okay to heal him like that?" Last time we'd been here, Michael's wings had extended behind him in full splendor. Now, a faint blue glimmer was all that remained. He was definitely weakened. "I thought healing him would make things worse."

"These wounds are fine. We just can't heal the one from the sword," Zadkiel said with a sigh. He was probably tired of having to explain everything to Michael's human girlfriend, which only made me miss Arielle and her infinite patience even more. His brow creased, he asked, "Where's Turiel? I thought he was with you."

"Grabbed the sword and ran." Michael shook his head in disbelief. "Sanctimonious pr—"

"Save your breath," Rhys cut him off with a frown. "You need it."

"Turiel did what?" Zadkiel's voice boomed. The light faded from his fingertips as he curled them into a fist.

"Wait," Rhys said. "Last I heard, Turiel was going in alone." He nodded in my direction. "What were you doing there?"

"They needed my help to get in."

"Raguel warded the room against angels, but not against humans," Michael explained.

Frowning, Rhys continued floating his hand over Michael's sliced chest, sealing the wounds. "Why would Raguel let humans in? His minions are demonic. Surely he could block humans."

Zadkiel loosened his grip and closed his eyes, relaxing his shoulders. His chest rose and fell as he centered himself. Energy burst from his fingertips, and he resumed the healing in silence.

As the angels worked, the color slowly returned to Michael's face. He swallowed before he spoke, his voice pained and raw. "The sword uses our weaknesses against us, right Zadkiel?"

Still focused on what he was doing, Zadkiel glanced at him. "Without a doubt."

"If Raguel knew Mia could get in, he'd have to know I wouldn't leave her alone." Michael sat partway up and propped himself on his elbows.

Rhys scanned Michael one last time from head to foot. Satisfied that his patient was sound again, he stood. "You think it was a trap?"

"Well, with Mia there, I was…distracted."

A flush burned my cheeks and neck with the memory of his 'distraction'. I could still feel the heat of his mouth on mine. With everything going on, it seemed like forever since he'd kissed me like that—and in front of Turiel, who clearly didn't approve of us. In any other relationship, it was normal to make out with your boyfriend—it was what people did. But aside from the fact that Michael was an angel, which made any display of affection taboo, our actions today could've gotten us both killed.

Zadkiel's shoulders stiffened. "Do you think Turiel knew it was a trap?"

"I think he was overcome by the sword," Michael said. "Its presence was powerful."

I scowled at Michael. "Yeah. That sword is powerful, all right." Still trying to shake the memory of his kiss, how foolish I'd been, I backed away to lean against the sink. I'd wanted to believe he'd kissed me because he'd wanted to, not due to some distraction caused by a cursed sword.

He gave me an apologetic look. "I didn't mean…"

"Turiel's always had a hunger for power," Rhys offered. If he noticed the tension between Michael and me, he was choosing to ignore it. "But taking the sword for himself?"

"It's unconscionable," Zadkiel growled. "Angels' lives are at stake."

"*Nemeraii* preys on any area of sin in us, right?" Michael turned to fold his long legs off the side of the cot. The drying blood on his torn shirt had stained deep rust around the edges, but at least his newer wounds had closed. A smudge of demon slime lit the bridge of his nose. I wanted to rub it off, but the angels' headquarters was hardly the place for affectionate gestures. "Which means Turiel was played like I was."

Rhys raised an eyebrow, and I could tell he wanted to know what Michael meant. Trying not to feel insulted by the idea that kissing me meant Michael was being 'played', I averted my eyes so neither of them could read an answer in me.

"I was hardly a match for Azazel in this state." Michael paused as though he'd just realized another detail, and ran his hands down his face. "If you hadn't come, Rhys, I don't know what would've happened."

I shuddered, trying to stave off the chill that permeated the marrow of my bones. Michael could've been killed.

Almost half of the angels I knew were gone. Turiel had disappeared, Arielle was mortally wounded. With Michael injured, who knew how much more the remaining two, Rhys and Zadkiel, could take? Until a few months ago, I'd never known that angels existed. Now, I wondered if there were enough of them to go around.

"Never mind what could have been," I said. "What now?"

"First, we have to find Turiel and destroy the sword." Rhys walked over to the chair he'd sat in and leaned against its high, wooden back. "Then, we've got to prevent a war."

"The three of us?" Zadkiel said, folding his arms over his chest. "Without either of our commanders?"

"We don't know that for sure," Rhys said. "If we destroy the sword—"

"That shouldn't be up to us!" Zadkiel snapped. "We should have told the council as soon as we discovered the sword's whereabouts. It's a matter of all our safety. For all we know, Turiel could be working with Raguel."

"Turiel?" I couldn't hide my surprise. Turiel was so uptight he was the last angel I'd suspect of tricking us. "His actions didn't seem deliberate." Guilt pricked my cheeks. Michael and I had been kissing, and Turiel had called for us to join him. What if he got so disgusted that all he could do was walk away?

"As much as I'd hate to admit it, and I do," Michael added, "we can't unfairly accuse him. He could have tried to come here and been stopped by Raguel on the way." Michael leaned forward on the small bed, the stains on his shirt a vivid reminder of his injuries, that I'd nearly lost him again.

"Well if he's not with us, he could be against us," Zadkiel insisted. "I don't trust him."

"You don't have to. I'll notify the councils," Rhys offered. "In the meantime, Mia, see if you can locate the sword again. You had some success before."

Zadkiel nodded in response, gave Michael one final quick look over, and headed for the door. Rhys trailed behind.

I rolled my eyes at their turned backs and plunked into one of the empty chairs. Fatigue weighed my limbs, as if lack of sleep had finally caught up with me. And Michael—wearing torn, blood-stained clothes and covered in black demon slime—couldn't be faring any better.

"Who do they think I am?" I whispered. "I can't turn these visions on and off at will." There was no way I could predict what Turiel would do. Prophet or not, I had no idea where to start.

"You can do a lot more than you think." Rhys's voice came from the doorway behind me. "And the sooner you realize that, the more help you'll be."

His words shocked me awake. I hadn't expected him to still be there, let alone hear me. I was still getting used to this whole prophet business. As flattering as it was to think I could actually help angels, *what if I got it wrong?*

Michael eased himself up and crossed the room to the tiny sink, where he twisted the tap and started to scrub his hands. With a shrug he added, "Rhys is right."

"Oh really?" I grumbled as he splashed water on his face. "How am I supposed to locate the sword?"

"I'll help," he said, drying his hands on a towel.

"But you're exhausted."

"It's easier here. You'll see. It only takes a bit." He headed to the door and closed it. With a wave of his hand at the silvery white orb over our heads, the light dimmed in the room. He took a seat on the other side of the bed and reached across the blanket. It was still spotted with his blood. "Take my hands."

A buzz of energy flowed between us the moment his warm, strong fingers connected with mine. My eyes widened.

"Just let yourself relax."

"But I'll fall asleep if I do that," I said, immediately realizing that would never happen. The buzz between us was far too strong.

He grinned. "I'll make sure you don't."

I closed my eyes, focusing on my breath the way Arielle had taught me. At the thought of her, my throat tightened. I swallowed, and a new sense of determination came over me. Maybe I was tired, but not nearly as tired as Michael, or even Rhys and Zadkiel, who watched over us around the clock. Everyone was doing their best, and if I could do anything to help, I would.

I'd never worked with Michael this way before. His energy was heady and sweet with a tinge of something else. It was the 'something else' that worried me. It washed over me in a wave, pulling me in with an undertow that made me want to kiss him so badly that it was all I could do not to open my eyes.

"Sorry," he whispered, his voice thick with—was it desire? "It'll pass, I promise."

Could he feel the intensity of my emotions? My face flushed instantly and I wished things weren't so damn awkward between us.

"Another distraction," I muttered.

"That's not true. Look at me." His blue eyes locked with mine, filled with all the fire I seen when he'd kissed me. The energy between us flared. "I always want to kiss you." He looked down at our hands. "It's just…"

"What? What is it, exactly?"

He swallowed, stroking the backs of my wrists with his thumbs. The heat building between us ran all the way down my legs. His voice shook. "I need it to be my choice. Not Raguel's."

He wanted a sense of self-control. I could understand that. Making out in front of Turiel wasn't exactly my proudest moment either. Especially since it would only sabotage our chances of being together.

I squeezed my eyes shut, and with newfound determination, focused on the task at hand: finding *Nemeraii* and destroying it before it was too late.

It took a while to settle myself. Under the surface, my fears for Arielle, for Michael, chewed at every thought. But eventually, a calming energy flowed between us, washing away my concerns, and my mind grew silent.

With that stillness came the kaleidoscope of color that usually happened when an angel was working with me. I struggled to both focus and relax at the same time. The next thing I saw were giant trees, spruce and Douglas firs that rose hundreds of feet high, their trunks as wide as cars. Turiel sat on a high branch. His halo flickered and dimmed around him. He gripped *Nemeraii*, admiring its sheen even in the cloudy sky. For this, he had risked Arielle's life and Michael's, angered Raguel, and betrayed all the other angels. What about this sword had been worth all that?

"I see him," I said to Michael. "He's in the forest. On a giant tree."

"That could be anywhere around here," Michael said. "Is there anything else to go on? Can you see the city or where he is?"

I tried to get a sense of my bearings. "It's raining. Same as here." The dense cover of the trees had blocked some of the rain, but it streamed along branches and dripped through the needles. "And the forest is old growth."

"Anything else?"

I tried to back away for an aerial view, but couldn't. In the vision, Turiel suddenly jolted as though someone was coming, and my shoulders jumped in surprise. Had he noticed me?

Then the image around me flickered and paled. I struggled to get it back until a dull ache formed between my brows. I opened my eyes. "I think he saw me."

Michael frowned. "If he did, he won't stay there long. We'll have to hurry." His focus shifted as he connected to whatever telepathic channel the angels used up here, probably to share the news.

Within a few seconds, Rhys stepped into the room. "There are two old-growth forests nearby."

Zadkiel stood in the doorway behind him. "We'll split up and each take one."

"In case you forgot," I said, "he's armed with an angel killer sword."

"Take me with you," Michael said to Rhys.

Rhys shook his head. "You should rest."

"Please," Michael insisted. "I can't just wait here."

"And I can?" I asked.

"Not with me," Michael said. "With *Nemeraii* there, I—"

"I know, I know," I cut him off. I'd still be a distraction.

"If Turiel's on the move, the prophet's the best at tracking him." Zadkiel pointed at me, his expression unreadable. "I'll take you."

My mouth fell open in shock—since when was Zadkiel on my side? Recovering, I gave him a nod.

CHAPTER TWENTY-EIGHT

Zadkiel transported me to a secluded grove of giant spruce and firs. The ground around us was dense with ferns and bushes as high as my waist. A silvery mist obscured the moss-covered tree trunks, obliterating our view of anything more than a few feet away. Rain dripping from the branches above pelted my hair and clothes and iced me to the core. Wasting no time, Zadkiel strode noiselessly through the soggy underbrush in search of the main trail. I struggled to keep up. My tennis shoes sank and slipped on the muddy ground. And while the river itself was hidden by fog, the sound of rushing water echoed around us. We were close to the place from my vision, where Turiel had perched high in the treetops. The hairs on the back of my neck stood up, and I comforted myself with the thought that the same fog cloaking Turiel from our view also shrouded us from his.

I followed Zadkiel over a fallen log that stood almost three feet tall. On the other side, the mist billowed so thick it shimmered and blinded me. Zadkiel had been completely enveloped by it. I stepped down and landed on a rock, losing my balance. Flailing, I reached for a nearby branch, but instead touched someone's arm. A pale hand clamped over my mouth, and I slammed into a body as solid as iron. He thrust me around a tree so fast I bashed my elbow on its giant trunk.

"Mia!" Zadkiel's blade made a swishing noise a few feet away as he drew his sword.

I sucked air in through my nose and tried to pull myself free. With a twisting motion, I craned my neck and saw not Turiel but Raguel. He spun me around to face him and pressed his fingers to his lips. Before I could cry out, he waved a hand and my tongue tightened in my throat. Dammit! What was it with fallen angels abducting me and taking away my ability to speak? Did he have the same thing in mind as Damiel?

"Don't flatter yourself," Raguel said through the network, letting me know he could hear my thoughts. *"You're not my type. You'd break far too easily."*

His hand wrenched my shoulder and he shoved me away from the tree, deeper into the fog. The damp cloak of mists swirled around me and seeped into my tendons and bones. While Raguel moved with stealth, a twig snapped beneath my feet, earning me a scowl and another shove. My foot caught in the tangled underbrush and it was all I could do to stay upright.

Zadkiel called my name again. If I squinted, I could make out the shadowed edges of his form in the mist circling the tree, where I'd just been.

At that exact moment, my phone rang. Snarling, Raguel seized my arm and, with a popping sound, we were gone.

***

We arrived in the middle of a pyramid-shaped room, where white walls arced to an apex high above our heads. Each wall was cut by an empty, black iron walkway as high as the ceiling of my house. Triangular windows served as alcoves, portals to a pallid gray sky.

Damiel never teleported. How come Raguel could?

"Damiel was my servant. He had a fraction of my power," Raguel answered.

Crap. He can still hear me! I unplugged my mind from the network and focused on the walnut floors beneath my feet. Except for crumpled newspapers and a few empty boxes, the room lay empty.

Raguel straightened the cuffs of his white shirt, and his fingers twisted a silver cufflink. His well-tailored gray suit was spotless and hardly creased. My coat was soaked and my damp jeans clung to my skin, the knees caked with mud. On the floor beside us lay a tiny figurine in a lacy white skirt, one of those ballerinas that twirled inside of jewelry boxes. Had the girl it belonged to lived here? If so, where had she gone?

"Excuse the mess," he said, as if in explanation. "The tenants moved out in a hurry when they could no longer afford the rent."

What price did he ask? I shuddered at the thought.

With another wave of his hand, the catch in my throat released. I coughed and cleared my throat.

"Where are we?" I demanded.

Raguel motioned to one of the triangular windows. I moved closer to take in the view spanning from Safeco Field to the Port of Seattle, and all the way out to the West Seattle Bridge. Traffic roared on the streets below.

"The best view in the city." He grabbed my arm, making me jump, and dragged me to another window.

"Oww!" When I tried to pull away, he tightened his steely grip.

Outside, all of Puget Sound—from the ferries to the Olympic mountains—lay below.

He released me and paced across the room, his gait confident, relaxed, completely in control. With the flick of his hand, he'd already silenced me. If I made a move, he had more than enough power to immobilize me—the way Damiel had. I wasn't going anywhere, and Raguel knew it.

I rubbed my arm where his fingers had been, sure he'd

left bruises. "We're in the Smith Tower?"

"Such a common name." He clicked his tongue in disgust. "I'll have to change that."

I followed him back to the center of the room and stopped when he did. "What do you want with me, when you have all this?"

"It's not you I want." He stood beside the tiny ballerina figurine. Sliding his foot to the side, he crushed the doll beneath his shiny brown Oxford, slowly, deliberately, as though he wanted to wipe away its very existence. "But you're going to help me get it."

For a fraction of a second, his irises reflected a red glint that sent icicles to my toes. I wanted to reach for the network, for Michael, but doing so would be pointless. He was no match for Raguel.

At first, it was only a susurration barely louder than the traffic noises outside. But as it grew closer, hundreds of wings darkened the sky around us, blocking any natural light and casting eerie shadows across the floor and walls. Tingles rippled my scalp as the *hamsa* necklace thrummed into overdrive, until I was sure it was going to break. Then all the windows exploded open at once, and a swarm of soldier demons burst through. The wind from their giant, leathery wings blustered through the room, blowing my hair and clothes and sweeping the shreds of paper and dust into tiny tornadoes.

The soldiers lined in formation around us, filling the room in a flurry of dark skin and red eyes. My heart hammered wildly, and their presence stole the breath from my lungs. Grotesque and twisted, their appearance drew the gaze away, the way people averted their eyes from atrocities. I strained to face them, to not let them see my fear.

My mind blanked, not white, the way it did when Turiel searched it. This time it deepened to a crushing charcoal, as though I were about to faint. With a spinning sensation, my knees buckled. I braced myself for a fall that didn't come.

"Now," Raguel's voice rang out, its color as red as the gleam in his eyes. "I am going to let you into the network soon. I want you to call Michael. He will come."

"Why?" I asked.

In response, Raguel nodded at one of soldier demons closest to me. It marched forward and clutched the back of my neck with bony fingers. Pain incinerated every nerve in my spine. I drew my breath in gasps, unable to think clearly. Raguel's voice boomed in my head. *"I am not Damiel. Questions will not be tolerated."*

Raguel was no stranger to inflicting pain. He was the one who'd tortured and broken Michael—or had someone else do it. *If I called Michael, then what? There was no way out of this. Raguel would destroy him.*

Another searing pain shot through me so violently that my eyes watered and blurred the sight of the soldier demons. They stood as still as terracotta warriors charred by hellfire. I choked back a sob, refusing to make a sound. I tried to wall out the sensation, the invasiveness of it, building a fortress in my mind the way I did with the network when I didn't want to hear it. The soldier demons shifted their attention to me, scoping their prey.

Raguel nodded again, and an agonizing electrical jolt snaked up to my brain, ceasing all thought. Then came Raguel's voice in my head. *"Do it."*

With the next tremor of pain, any protection or will I had of my own crumbled like a sandcastle in the waves. Instinctively, unthinking, I reached for the network and cried out. *"Michael!"*

His response came instantly, panic and surprise in his thoughts. *"Mia? It's not—where are you?"*

I tried not to tell him, but another jolt came. My jaw slackened, my teeth chattered, I convulsed. The one message I swore not to share came through me in a short staccato—a telegram of thought. *"Raguel…Smith Tower."*

In the fraction of a second before Raguel shut the

network down, I could feel Michael's response—electric, panicked—but there was no way I could stop it. I couldn't take it back.

What had I done?

The soldier demons shifted formation, surrounding Raguel. Two of them grabbed me. When I tried to wriggle free, they tore off my coat, their touches both fiery and cold at the same time. I convulsed again, this time not from hurting.

A black, cloudy haze—the kind I used to see around Damiel—rose in the room. A swarm of darkness blurred my vision and scalded my eyes. I coughed it from my lungs, sputtering, until I finally decided to hold my breath, trying not to inhale. My insides liquefied. *Am I dying?*

Michael had been racked. Had this torture not worked on him? Wasn't this suffering enough to change him? I didn't know how much more I could take. What *had* Michael endured?

With a popping sound, a brilliant light burst into the room, blinding me. I coughed out oily black phlegm as the corrosive coal-colored dust scattered everywhere. I blinked and the brilliant light became forms: Rhys and Michael with their swords drawn, prepared to fight.

The soldier demons held their position around Raguel and the two that were holding me tightened their grip on my arms. At least the smoke had cleared.

"Michael," Raguel said, nodding in his direction. "Brought a friend, I see." If he was concerned by the other angel's presence, he didn't let on. "I rather hoped you'd come alone."

Rhys stepped forward. "Name your terms for her release."

Raguel laughed, more of a cackle. With a flick of his wrist, the ground disappeared beneath me and I was airborne, hovering two stories above them in the apex of the room. A gasp escaped my lips. I swallowed back a scream.

He motioned to Michael. "I deal only with him."

Michael uncloaked his wings, but the strain of doing so showed on his face. Though he appeared calm, I knew him well enough now to see the panic in his eyes. Rhys's wings were already uncloaked as he leaped into flight, but several soldier demons took to the air, blocking him. He swung at them midair.

Two dozen soldier demons to two angels. The odds weren't good.

With a flick of his wrist, Raguel sent me flying into one of the iron walkways along the wall. I hit it so hard the metal tore my shin right through my jeans. Still buoyed aloft by Raguel's magic, I grabbed the railing and struggled to climb in.

Michael took to the air to help me but, like Rhys, he was cut off by soldiers and had to draw his sword and fight. He managed to take one out, slicing off its head before stabbing another.

"Stop!" Raguel commanded, and suddenly whatever held me aloft gave way and I dropped. Slippery with sweat, my hands gripped the iron walkway. My feet dangled.

In spite of myself, a scream escaped my lips. I fought not to look down.

Facing the walkway, my back was turned to the action, but the rustle of wings ceased. I heard the soft brush of shoes on the floor as the angels landed, the clicking of claws as the demons made contact with the hardwood floors.

My fingers slipped. Pain scorched the tendons in my arms. I wasn't strong enough to lift myself up. Any second now, I was going to fall.

"Let her down!" Michael growled.

"She's going to do that all on her own," Raguel said.

A blinding twinge from my fingers traveled straight through my arms. They trembled with weakness. There wasn't even a soldier demon below to cushion my fall, only wood. Perspiration slicked the tips of my fingers, the last points of contact. I pressed harder, but couldn't hold. The now slippery metal slid beneath my fingertips. With the sudden rush of air, I screamed.

And stopped moving. Suspended again, I was spun around, my arms splayed out to the sides, not of my own volition. I bit the sides of my cheek to keep from crying as I realized that every move I made, even my own fall, was beyond my control. No matter how much my eyes burned, I refused to break down. I would not give Raguel the satisfaction.

Michael stiffened until he became perfectly still, his face a wooden mask. Not even his fingers twitched, as though every ounce of him strained to stay calm. He blinked, his eyes blank with shock, and swallowed hard. "What do you want me to do?"

"You're going to bring me Damiel and the sword."

Michael took a step closer, and the soldier demons closed in around Raguel—pawns in a chess game, protecting their king. "And you'll let her go. You'll let this all go," he said, motioning to the room. It wasn't a question.

Raguel gave him a nod. "You have my word."

"Michael, no!" Rhys clasped Michael's arm and jerked it. "If you give him back that sword, what about Arielle? There's no saying how many of us will die. And you know the cost of handing over another angel who has come to us for sanctuary and redemption."

Michael pulled his arm free from Rhys's grip, his gaze glued to Raguel. "Mia will be safe and unharmed?"

"Yes. See?" With a flick of his wrist, I floated gently to the ground. My legs shook and collapsed beneath me, and I dropped to the floor, gripping it with my fingers as if I could hold myself down.

Rhys grabbed Michael by the shoulders and shoved him toward the window. "What you're thinking is an act of betrayal. It's unconscionable."

Michael bowed his head. "It's her or Damiel...you

know I can't let her get hurt again."

Rhys spun at Raguel. "You're insane! Damiel has chosen the higher path. He's in a protected sanctuary. Your plan won't even work."

"Leave Damiel to me," Raguel said. "I can handle him."

"No!" Rhys raised his sword to Michael's throat. "You can't do that. I won't let you."

"I think it's time for you to leave now." Raguel raised his hand and a bolt of red flame shot from his fingers, hitting Rhys. And with a pop, he vanished. Raguel turned back to Michael as though nothing had happened and said, "Now, where were we?"

Michael glared at Raguel. "I'll do it."

Raguel's victorious smile sickened me. He was even more sadistic than Damiel. "A wise choice."

Michael's shoulders squared, his face as cool as carved stone, he took a step closer to Raguel. If I hadn't remembered it myself, I would have never known the control Raguel had held over him so long ago. "But Mia comes to a place of my choosing, safe with my peers, not yours."

"Oh no, it doesn't work that way. If you think I'm going to let you teleport her to angel territory, where I can't reach her, you're gravely mistaken."

As one of the soldier demons closed in on him, Michael's right hand tightened around the handle of his blade. "Mia will stay on neutral territory, then. Neither Heaven nor Hell."

"I don't think so." Raguel tugged at his cuffs again, ignoring the soldier demon, who stood perfectly still, awaiting his master's command. Had Michael been a slave like that once? *How could he even bear to watch?* "I don't think you're in a place to negotiate with me."

And with a flick of Raguel's wrist, I was airborne again. I couldn't help but scream.

"Stop it," Michael snapped. "There's no need to punish

her any further. I said I'd do it."

"Of course you will. You rebelled against God the moment you chose a woman to love before Him. And then you sullied her memory when you chose to join me. You even betrayed me the moment you left. Double-crossing. It's what you do."

A cloak of shame hovered over Michael. He folded his arms across his chest as if he were trying to block it out. "Do you want your sword back or not? Because if you harm her—"

"We have an agreement then." Raguel lowered me with a flick of his wrist.

I landed swiftly this time, catching my breath. Michael knew the cost. If he did this, Arielle would die and he would lose everything. His angelic power, his friends, not to mention his own ascension. "Don't do it, Michael. It's not—*I'm* not worth it."

The adrenaline coursing through my system kicked in. I broke into a run. Michael stepped toward me, opening his arms. I got two steps before I hit an invisible barrier that hurled me back, like the one blocking Raguel's office, only this one worked on me.

Michael tested it, but it threw him back as well.

"Return what's mine to me, and I'll return what's yours," Raguel said. "And leave you to decide if it was all worth it." He raised his hand and red flames shot from his fingers. "You have one hour."

He pointed at Michael, and with a loud snap, Michael was cast from the room.

CHAPTER TWENTY-NINE

The second Michael left, darkness enveloped me in a thick, corrosive smog that stung my eyes and burned my lungs. I collapsed to the rough-hewn floor, coughing, and covered my nose with the sleeve of my sweater. The clouds left a residue of fine black powder that itched as it clung to my still-damp clothes and hair.

As far as I could tell, I was alone. When I strained to listen, the muted roar of traffic on the streets below reached my ears. Tracing the floorboards with my fingertips, I found the tiny, broken ballerina figurine that Raguel had crushed. I rolled it between my fingers and its sharp, ragged edges poked into my skin, the plastic lace of its skirt unmistakable even in the blackness.

Where was Michael right now? Had Raguel sent him back to the forest for Turiel? What if he found him? Michael was exhausted and alone, and Turiel was armed with a deadly sword. What about the other angels? I could no longer count on them to be on our side. Rhys's objections had made that perfectly clear. They would do everything they could to stop Michael. I know Rhys had said it wasn't my fault, but if I hadn't thought to redeem Damiel in the first place, Raguel would never have been freed. And Arielle wouldn't be lying in some bed, taking her last breaths. If she weren't near death from her injuries, she would have helped. She cared about Michael, and I believed she cared about me, too. *Nemeraii* had to be destroyed—not returned to its owner—or she was going to die. There was no way Michael could sacrifice her life for mine. She was his commander, his sponsor, his closest and most trusted friend. Risking her would cost him everything.

Even if Michael did get the sword from Turiel, then what? Rhys had said the plan wouldn't work, that Damiel was protected. Either way, I'd be left here. No matter how much Michael wanted to save me, how much he gave up—if he even succeeded in this quest—there was one thing I knew for certain: Raguel would *never* keep his word.

And Michael was a rogue angel now. He'd cast everything aside for me. What would prevent Raguel from taking him back to Hell?

Nothing.

The clouds around me grew thicker by the minute, their stench as foul and dank as sickness and death. I kept my arm over my nose and mouth. With each breath coming shorter and faster, I didn't even know how much oxygen, or time, I had left.

With a press of air came a popping sound. Footsteps as light as a cat's padded across the wooden floorboards, heading my way.

I tried to call out, "Who's there?" but all that came out was a cough.

The steps ceased.

"Raguel?" I sputtered the word out, then scolded myself. *Who else would it be?*

A familiar voice called my name. But in my fog, I couldn't make out who it belonged to.

Another footstep and the swishing of leather. A soft breeze followed by a high-pitched shriek, and the cloud of blackness around me became translucent. I gulped in the fresher air, squinting to make out the shapes in the room. A slim, angelic form strode across the floor, his wings tucked behind him.

"Turiel!" I gasped. "What are you...?"

Ignoring me, he spotted the serpentine minion a few feet away, strode toward it, and removed its head. The creature dissolved into a space beyond the floorboards. My smoky prison vanished, but I coughed up more smog.

Turiel leaned over, his silver bangs falling over his eyes, and helped me to my feet. "Serpent demon," he muttered. "A strong one. It had you convinced you were trapped."

"I wasn't?"

"It was all in your mind. But you can cough, anyway. It'll help your body adjust."

"What are you doing here?" My jeans were spotted with black dust. I swept my hands down my legs, trying to clean them, but it was pointless. At least the stinging had stopped. "Where's Michael?"

"There's no time. We've got to go." He grabbed my arm.

"No." I was about to pull away before he could teleport us out of there, but then I realized nothing had happened. We hadn't moved. "Shouldn't we be someplace else?"

"We should be." He frowned in concentration as he tried again. "It seems I can't transport you out. You've been blocked." Still holding my arm, he strode toward the nearest window and dragged me along with him. "We can still fly." He unlocked the window and tugged it open.

"No." Though he'd just released me from a serpent demon, I couldn't forget the way he'd abandoned Michael and me to deal with Azazel in the tunnels. Alone. "You took off with the sword!"

"You don't understand." Letting my arm drop, he took a step back. His white uniform jacket was still spotted with dust and demon slime. "With Zadkiel's help, it's been mostly disarmed. All that's needed now is a prophet's blood."

My blood? Was that what this is about—some kind of sacrifice ritual? Had it come down to this? My life in exchange for Arielle's. My life for Michael's.

I knew it was futile to run, but I dashed for the exit anyway. Turiel followed. The door didn't budge, even when I slammed the full weight of my body against it. I pounded the wooden boards with both fists.

Turiel moved so close behind me his breath made the hairs on the back of my neck stand up. His voice softened. "It's not what you think—"

I spun to face him. "Really? What is it then?"

He stood perfectly still except for the slouching of his shoulders; his eyebrows knit together under his bangs. "When Zadkiel found me in the forest, I didn't want to be found. The weapon could bring me such power. I thought about using it, killing so that I could keep it—but I didn't." He dragged his hands down his face, and when his eyes met mine, they were filled with anguish. "I understand now, how Michael could be so tempted. I know I always looked down on what he did, on the weakness of the flesh, but I knew nothing of my own greed, or the lust for power." Clasping his hands together, he bowed his head in shame. "Or of love."

This was a big deal for Turiel. Considering he'd always judged Michael so harshly, he wanted to make amends. But now wasn't the time, and I wasn't the one who should hear it. Michael should be. "Okay, I get it. Is Zadkiel all right?"

"He bade me come here to get you out. He's gone to help Michael and Rhys."

"He sent you?"

"Yes." He clutched my sweater at the elbow. "Now, please, we have to—"

A thunderous crack deafened me as Raguel entered the room. "Turiel!" Raguel smiled and greeted him as though he were an old friend. "Come to bring me my sword, I see."

Turiel stepped in front of me and spread his wings, blocking my vision—or was it Raguel's view of me? "You know what they say: fool me once, shame on you."

"And look who's come back," Raguel said. "*Nemeraii* is conditioned to return to her master. I guess that means the shame's on you."

He must have circled us, because Turiel stiffened and rotated on his heels to keep himself positioned between Raguel and me. Turiel's wings were a different color than Michael's, the feather filaments a silvery white. Tucking them behind his back, he raised both his arms. In one hand, *Nemeraii* glinted a red fire; in the other, his blade of blue light hummed its cool presence. I ducked in line with Turiel's wings, hoping that if I couldn't see Raguel, he wouldn't set his sights on me. I wasn't his broken toy to toss around.

Instead, it was Turiel's turn to be flung. An explosion of red flames sent him crashing into the white-beamed wall behind him. His wings collapsed, and for a moment he lay completely still.

Then his wings stiffened, and he shook off the blow the way a stunned bird recovers from slamming into a window. With a grimace of concentration, he leaped to his feet.

Raguel took a step forward, sneering at Turiel. "*Nemeraii* weakens any angel with her presence. Give her to me and I'll let you live."

In response, Turiel tightened his grip on both swords, raising *Nemeraii* overhead, while the other protected his chest.

Raguel didn't flame him again. This time, he drew a sword of his own that materialized into his hand as though pulled from the air, and made a crackling, staticky sound. Longer than *Nemeraii*, it was carved of ornate gold filaments and had a slick, black glow—as though it were cloaked in shadows.

Turiel swung first—right then left—but Raguel blocked

him easily. Raguel then swung his blade around, forcing Turiel to cross both his swords to block him. When that happened, *Nemeraii* sparked and the two weapons repelled each other like the same polarities of a magnet. They broke apart and weakened Turiel's stance.

Raguel swung low, slicing Turiel's chest. A red stain tinged with gold pooled on the angel's white tank.

"I told you she'd obey her master," Raguel purred.

Huffing, Turiel spun around and struck twice. Raguel pivoted back. With Turiel's next stroke, he lost control and swung *Nemeraii* wide. The veins in the hand holding it blackened. When Raguel thrust, Turiel jerked away and deflected a stab. The blow landed and opened a gash along his upper thigh.

Turiel tossed *Nemeraii* behind him and reasserted his grip on the intention sword. With renewed vigor, he swung again. Raguel blocked.

Neither of them noticed me, or how close I was to the discarded weapon, only a few feet away. Keeping low, I scrambled for *Nemeraii*, grabbed it, and retreated to the corner of the room.

Turiel fumbled his next attack and staggered, nearly missing another blow. It was clear now that *Nemeraii* had weakened him, and discarding it hadn't been enough. I had to act. I had to break the power of its curse. But how? Did it just need my blood? If so, how much would it take? Intention swords were designed to not hurt people, and *Nemeraii* had been made from one. Could it even cut me? I touched the tip—it was sharp. Closing my eyes, I tried to connect to that force I'd used to free Damiel. But as I suspected, it was blocked along with the rest of the network. Without Turiel's help, I was blind. I'd no idea what to do.

I watched him battle, but his movements became sluggish, as though he were fighting in water. The hand that once held the angel killer hung limply at his side, its veins black under too-white skin.

Quickly, I lifted the weapon to my finger and pricked the tip. As soon as my blood touched the blade, a shrieking filled the air, capturing Raguel's attention. Shoving Turiel harshly aside, he turned from the fight to me.

For a moment, I held my breath, thinking he'd fling me into the air, but nothing happened. His gaze collided with mine. And a deafening silence screeched in my ears. My heart pulsed.

"Mia, Mia, Mia. Pesky little human…" Raguel tsked. He did not blink. I could swear he moved closer and yet he remained in the same spot, poised with his sword. Powerful, yet immobile.

The throbbing of my heart intensified until my whole body vibrated. The thudding grew stronger and finally I broke from Raguel's intoxicating gaze.

Something was happening. The angel killer turned to charcoal in my hands.

Did I destroy it?

Startled, I dropped it to the floor. At that point, Turiel lunged between us, gripping his one weapon with both arms. *Has his strength returned?*

Raguel swung high and sliced Turiel's throat. Paralyzed by the horror in front of me, I held my breath as Turiel lurched forward. His gold-tinged blood spattered on the floor. Stumbling, he twisted to strike Raguel and missed.

Red rivulets streaming down his neck, Turiel spat gobs of blood and gulped air as if he were going to speak. But before he could, Raguel swung again, slicing clean through the angel's neck, and Turiel's head dropped with a golden flash of lightning. His blood wailed a song of lament, as his body collapsed to the floor.

"No!" I screamed.

Raguel gripped my throat, his face twisted in vengeance, and hoisted me off my feet. "Shut up."

Turiel's form melted and withered before my eyes. His wings, once glorious, lay in a heap, like broken branches.

Then, light blazed from him as bright as the sun, igniting his broken body. Golden flames exploded through the room in a supernova that rocked Raguel on his feet. He covered his eyes, visibly weakened by the light, and lowered the arm holding me. I pointed my toes, straining to touch the ground.

All that remained of the body were three silver-tipped feathers and a bloody outline of Turiel's broken wings.

With another popping sound, the air rippled, and Michael, Rhys, and Zadkiel stormed into the room, weapons first. Michael called my name and dashed toward me as the other two angels charged Raguel.

Raguel lifted me again. His fingers tightened as I fought for breath. Gripping his hand with both of mine, I tried to free myself, but my feet swung wild and useless beneath me. Breath wheezed in my throat as my lungs screamed for air. The room blurred through my tears. The angels froze.

"Not so fast, boys." Raguel didn't even turn to face them. "You make one false move and I might snap her little neck. Sometimes I don't even know my own strength." He winked and directed their attention to Turiel's blood congealing on the floor.

The angels took in Turiel's outline and lowered their swords. A clamor of leathery wings filled the air, and dozens of soldier demons burst through the windows. A blur of shadows by my sight, they surrounded us and blocked the angels' path to Raguel.

"That's better." Letting me down gently, Raguel patted my hair as though he were a concerned parent and I were a child who had skinned her knee. His touch and fake smile repulsed me to the core. "There, there," he sneered. "All better now."

I staggered away from him and struggled to regain my balance and breath. Unable to face Michael, I hung my head in shame and traced the shape of the broken ballerina in my pocket.

Raguel spun on Michael. His presence growing more

powerful by the minute. He glanced around the room. "Where's your little friend, Damiel?"

"Not coming." Michael's hand was at his sword. "The wards protecting him in Heaven are strong. Reinforced since you came back. No one can break them without his consent. But you knew that, didn't you? Or have you completely forgotten the law?"

"Your laws. Not mine," Raguel spat. "But you had no problem breaking these same sacred laws for the girl, right, Michael?"

He stiffened, preparing for the worst. "You got your sword back. Isn't that enough?"

"*Had* my sword back." Raguel motioned to *Nemeraii's* charred remains on the floor. "She destroyed it, with your friend's help." He flipped his wrist once again in the direction of Turiel's blood stain in the corner. "Or should I say your ex-friend. So sad."

Rhys and Zadkiel exchanged glances. Was it me, or did their shoulders drop with relief? At least the sword was no longer an issue.

In one quick motion, Raguel grabbed my arm. "You know the price of failing me," he said coldly. "Are you going to take your punishment? Or let her take it for you?"

I finally had the courage to look at Michael. Words, however, failed me. Michael had told me once that there was no happily ever after for us. He'd been right. I just hadn't wanted to believe him.

"Mia…" His voice caught. I squeezed the broken ballerina harder. I was not going to cry. That would only make things worse.

"It's up to you, Michael." Raguel said, tapping his foot impatiently. "May I remind you that my sword, unlike yours, can hurt humans. Are you willing to take that chance?" The tip of his blade pressed menacingly close to my temple. I tightened my grip on the doll in my pocket.

"Stop!" Michael said. "I'll do it."

And with his words, the angels and soldier demons

ceased fighting and turned their attention to Raguel and me. Raguel lowered his sword and smiled. Blood hissed in my ears.

"You yield?" he asked.

"Yes," Michael said, his voice breaking. "I yield."

Raguel shoved me away and I stumbled into the arms of a soldier demon, who gripped my shoulders with hands as cold and lifeless as lead. It was happening again. Michael was sacrificing himself to save me. Raguel would cut his wings, take him back to Hell and torture him, and there was nothing I could do to stop it.

"On your knees, then," Raguel said.

Michael folded his arms across his chest, his expression cold and defiant. "Call off your minions first. I won't do it until she's safe."

Raguel nodded to the soldier demon, who released me. I took a step toward Michael and our gazes locked. He shook his head.

Rhys stood at my side; his approach had been silent. "It's up to Michael now," he whispered. "There's nothing else we can do."

Nothing we can do. How many times had I heard that? As if everything was predestined and nobody had any choice, not even angels. Or was Michael eternally doomed for loving me?

"Now, kneel." Raguel said, pointing his blade at Michael's throat. "And lay down your sword."

Michael dropped to his knees and placed his weapon on the ground in front of him.

"No!" I rushed forward.

Rhys caught my arm and whirled me around to face him. "Stop. It's his choice."

"How can you even say that?" I shoved Rhys away. "After everything he's been through with Raguel, you know he can't go through that again. How could you even let him?"

A malicious grin tugged at Raguel's lips. "What's this?

True love?"

"Can you even remember what love feels like? Or are you just so used to ruling with fear that you forgot?"

"Mia! Don't!" Michael snapped.

"No. Go on." Raguel stepped behind him, poised and ready to strike. "Let's see what this *girl* has to say."

"If you want Damiel, why don't you get him yourself? If he can be redeemed, surely—"

Raguel roared at me, his harsh, hammering laugh a punch to my stomach. "Was Damiel turned with such a crude promise of *redemption*? Your tricks won't work on me. Damiel will pay for what he's done." He shoved Michael with his foot. "If he doesn't, Michael will."

I was going about this all wrong. When we'd redeemed Damiel, I'd used his own sin of envy against him. That sin made him fallible, easier to trick. Arielle had told me once that Raguel's sin was pride. But it wasn't pride anymore, was it? Now, it seemed he was so overcome with wrath and greed that all he wanted was vengeance and more power—any way he could get it. While Damiel had one sin, Raguel had three.

Michael reached for his own weapon, but before he could wield it, Raguel jammed the tip of his sword against his Adam's apple. Michael froze in submission.

Zadkiel drew his weapon, his deadly sights set on Raguel. "You take him, Heaven will fight back. Make no mistake. It will be war."

The soldiers moved in, poised to block Zadkiel with swords of their own. Raguel raised his hand and they froze. "That, my old friend, is exactly what I'm hoping for." Lifting his blade, he nicked Michael's chin, and droplets of blood trickled down his neck. Then, with a nod from Raguel, the soldier demons attacked Zadkiel and Rhys.

My stomach filled with ice. Raguel was going to do the same thing to Michael as he'd done to Turiel. I couldn't let that happen. There would be no more sacrifices today, not on my account.

Shifting forward again, my foot brushed something solid and flat. *Nemeraii* lay on the ground exactly where I'd dropped it. Clearly it had been destroyed, blackened to charcoal, a burnt husk of its former glory. But charred as it was, its edges still seemed sharp, and a deep purple glow flickered around it. With everyone's gazes fixed on Raguel, nobody saw me bend down and pick up the sword and hide it silently behind my back. What would a defunct angel killer do to a fallen angel like Raguel? I was about to find out.

I leapt into the fray without a clue about what I was going to do next. I'd handled Michael's sword once, and it had been light as air. This weapon weighed more than I could easily lift. Its touch was so cold it burned my hands. But I refused to let go.

Unlike the angels', my movements weren't swift. My footfalls creaked along on the wooden boards. When Raguel spun to face me, I thrust. The blade in my hands pierced him between the ribs. A lucky shot. Not a killing blow, but the strange purple light shook Raguel just enough to throw him off guard.

I leaped back and almost tripped. Raguel pulled the charred blade from his chest, and the weapon turned to dust in his hands. Michael sprang to his feet and charged, slicing Raguel's shoulder. When he huffed out his breath and slumped forward, for a moment, I thought Michael had won. But then, with demonic strength, Raguel spun around, swung high, and Michael ducked barely in time.

When Raguel and Michael locked swords, the soldier demons closed in on the other angels, and a battle began. Though individual soldier demons were hardly a match for Rhys or Zadkiel, Raguel was still strong. Even with *Nemeraii* destroyed, I was no longer sure Michael could defeat him. I was still reeling from Turiel's death; Michael's was unthinkable.

"No! No war!" I yelled. "Raguel, I'm the one who

redeemed Damiel. You want revenge. Take me."

Focused on Michael, Raguel didn't even look at me. I hadn't hit the nerve. So much for appealing to wrath. He wanted power, angels he could turn into minions and control. He wanted his harvester of souls, and my soul wasn't nearly as powerful as that. Though he may have been filled with greed and wrath, pride had been his first sin. I had to up the stakes. I cleared my throat and swallowed my fear. My voice came out steady and strong. "I stabbed you and destroyed your precious *Nemeraii*. Are you going to let yourself be bested by a human *girl*. A prophet?"

At my words, Raguel glanced at me. It had worked! He hadn't known I was a prophet, and I didn't even know what it meant. But clearly, prophet trumped human. Taking advantage of the distraction, Michael swung, but Raguel was so fast. He blocked and slid his blade under Michael's ribs. Soldier demons seized both Michael's arms. Blood dripped from his mouth.

"Let him go." I rushed toward Raguel, despite the fact that every nerve in my body had switched on. Every ounce of survival instinct I had screamed at me to run the other way. "I'll go instead."

"No. You don't know what you're saying," Michael insisted.

But I did know. If I did this, my life would be over, and thoughts of what would come next chilled my blood to ice. It was my turn to do for Michael what he had done for me so many times before. Perhaps if Raguel took his revenge on me, it would appease his pride and force some kind of peace.

"A prophet? You've been holding out on me." The gleeful expression on Raguel's face turned my legs to water, as the weight of what I was doing set in. "Do you submit freely?"

"Don't," Michael whispered. "Please."

I couldn't speak. My mouth formed words but nothing

came out. I tried to nod, but my head wouldn't move. I wanted to help them. Why wasn't my own body obeying me?

Raguel laughed, and the sound crept spiders down my neck. "Well, well, now things are getting interesting." He nodded in my direction. "Kneel."

I dropped to my knees. That much I could do. Blood rushed to my kneecaps as they bruised on the hardwood floors.

"You don't want her. I'm the one you want!" Michael said.

"The more the merrier for my little collection," Raguel replied, his footsteps and voice drawing closer.

Michael made a feral sound and broke free of the grip the soldier demons had on him. He charged Raguel. Their swords clashed. Blue light met greenish black smoke. Instead of the clang of metal, the swords gave off the hum and click of broken machinery, or bamboo swords. I watched as though I'd been frozen, the way Damiel had paralyzed me in that cabin. I couldn't move. Had Raguel enthralled me?

I didn't want Michael to sacrifice himself, but by trying to stop him, I'd made things worse. Now they were fighting and, despite his newfound fury, Michael was going to lose. How could I think it would be any easier for him to allow me to take the fall than it was for me to let him?

Raguel fought clean and fast. He wasted no time taunting Michael, the way Damiel had, and his skill was unmatched. Michael struggled to block Raguel's blows. His halo flashed light, as though he'd drawn energy from the shattered network barely in time. Raguel knocked Michael's sword from his hand. When Michael lunged for it, he took a slice to the ribs. Groaning in pain, he swung around and raised his weapon as Raguel ran him through. The two of them collapsed into each other. Their swords pierced each other's chests.

Michael's gaze locked with mine, and the grief, anguish,

and love in his eyes strangled my heart. His voice was barely a rasp. "I'll never forget you."

A bolt of purple flame shot through the room, and both Michael and Raguel disappeared in an explosion of black smoke. Freed from paralysis, I screamed and dashed through the smoke to the place the two of them had fought. Noxious fumes seared my eyes and lungs.

Zadkiel and Rhys approached and the smoke cleared. The soldier demons had gone. Michael's body lay on the floor limp, unmarked, and deathly still.

"Michael?" I dropped to the floor beside him. He had to be exhausted. Asleep. I dug my fingers into his shoulders and shook him. "Hey! Michael?"

Rhys crouched beside me, catching my arm before I shook Michael again. "He's gone, Mia."

"But… How?" Dread burned in my throat. Part of me knew what had happened. But it was too terrible to consider. I swallowed it back. "He's right here."

Rhys dragged an arm across his forehead, leaving streaks of black soot. "His body is, yes, but his soul…" He shook his head, unable to finish his sentence.

I traced Michael's chest and felt the faint rise and fall of breath beneath my fingertips. "See? He's breathing! He's alive!" Tears filled my eyes and I choked out a sob. "What's happened to him?"

Zadkiel's features hardened as he turned to Rhys. "We should get him to the hospital. She can take him."

I didn't want to move. It was as if all the blood had been drained from my body and replaced by cement. The worst possible thing had happened. Worse than being beaten. Worse than death. Michael's body was still here, but, his soul—the very essence of him—had been taken to Hell.

CHAPTER THIRTY

The two angels teleported me and Michael's body back to his room. They changed him out of his shredded, blood-stained clothes and healed his wounds, while I rushed to the bathroom to clean off the demon dust that clung to my skin and hair. When all visible evidence of what we'd been through was gone, Rhys and Zadkiel carefully placed Michael on the sofa, and I called for an ambulance—the way a normal person would do. Invisible to everyone but me, they stood at my side as I spoke to the paramedics and told me exactly what to say. The story was that Michael and I had been watching TV and fallen asleep: I woke up and he didn't.

The paramedics let me ride in the ambulance, because I wouldn't leave his side, even when his parents were called. His body was unmarked. With *Nemeraii* destroyed, its scar was gone. So it was easy for the doctors and nurses to believe that he'd relapsed into his coma. Especially since he'd had such a miraculous recovery last year, when he remembered what he really was. It was always easier to dismiss a miracle and believe the worst. To them, what else could it be? How could anyone know what had been done to his soul?

But I knew. I had seen the torments he had already suffered. And while there were two angels watching over me, Rhys and Zadkiel hovered as mute, armed guards who didn't know how to touch my grief. They could hardly deal with their own.

Besides, they had a war to plan. Taking Michael wasn't enough for Raguel. He needed to be stopped. And I was just a girl, one stupid, stupid girl who had enough knowledge of this other world to really screw things up. If I hadn't called Michael to the tower, or worse, stepped in and tried to fix everything, he might have had a chance. *Some prophet I am!*

I sat in one of the green vinyl chairs in the visitor's room and watched Michael's parents arrive. A doctor approached and they huddled like football players, his mother covering her face so no one would see her sob. I couldn't approach. What would I say? Their grief would only make me choke out the truth—a truth they'd never believe. And Michael would never forgive me for putting them at risk. At least they had each other.

Who did I have now?

My mom was at home sleeping off her night shift, and I wasn't ready to talk to her yet. Soon, she'd need to know, but I couldn't tell anyone what I knew. All of it was madness.

I texted Heather, not sure I could call her without turning into a sniffling mess, and asked, "Can I get a ride home?"

She texted back right away, "Where are you?"

"The hospital."

"OMG. What happened? R U OK?"

Grief clawed at my chest as I wrote the next line: "Michael's in a coma." But it was too much, so I deleted it and typed: "I'll tell you later. Room 293." I hit send and leaned my head back against the wall, searching for something to hold on to.

A faint voice called my name. Its soft tone sent a flash

of goose bumps down my arms. *Who was it?* I searched the room. The other visitors weren't even looking my way.

"Mia?" The voice came stronger now, with the soft tones of a violin.

"Arielle! You're all right!"

"Let's just say I'll be better soon." I could hear the smile in her voice. After a moment of silence, she added, *"I know how much you loved him."*

"I'm so sorry—for everything!" I forgot and said aloud.

I felt an arm around my shoulder and looked up to find Katharine, Michael's mother, sitting beside me. Her own eyes filled with tears. I leaned in to hug her and breathed in her floral scent. It only made me cry harder.

"Shh," she said, patting my back. "The doctor told us he had a relapse. You did everything you could. You called the ambulance. He's in good hands."

No. He's not. He's in Hell and there's nothing I can do to get him back. The thoughts rushed through me, but I couldn't reveal any of them.

Releasing me, she squeezed my hands. "Do you need a ride home?"

I shook my head. "My friend's coming. Can I see him now?"

His room was filled with machines that beeped and clicked like a giant robot. As I approached his bed, Michael felt different. When people sleep, you can still feel them, their presence, in the room with you. Not now. Though technically his body was alive, his soul—the essence of him that I'd known for millennia—was gone. That part of him was someplace far away, being tortured and broken at the hands of Raguel. And the thought filled me with an overwhelming surge of anger. Crazy rage that threatened to choke any love I felt right out of me. Anything was better than this, than being left here without him.

Soon, the angels would be going to war, as Zadkiel had promised. But all I knew was that I had to get Michael back. Raguel was pure evil, but he had to have a weakness that could be exploited. A reason—beyond the sins of pride, wrath, and greed—for wanting Damiel back. And I was going to find out what it was.

The beep of the cardio monitor kept time to my sorrow. Every pulse a reminder that I—that *we*—had lost. Again.

I held Michael's cold and unresponsive fingers in mine. All his strength was gone.

"I know you're suffering right now, and that it's my fault. But, please, *please* don't give up." My voice broke. Tears burned my eyes. I blinked them back. Of all people, I had no right to cry.

I forced a smile, hoping Michael could hear me, knowing full well that it was impossible, but as long as his heart still beat, there was hope. "I'm going to make it better, okay? I don't know how yet, but we're going to get you out of there. I promise."

I wasn't sure if it was my mind playing tricks on me, but for a moment, it seemed as though the heart monitor beeped a little faster, and his eyelids flickered. Had he heard me?

"Michael? Are you there?" I squeezed his hand, but his body stilled. His heart resumed its slow, steady pace, an indicator of minimal life.

Hope had fluttered through me so fast I couldn't trust my own memory of it. Digging into my pocket, I found the broken ballerina, a broken doll—the one thing I refused to be. I tossed it into the garbage and leaned in to kiss Michael one last time.

BONUS MATERIAL

Read one of the hottest scenes from Michael's perspective.

Legitimacy (from Chapter Nineteen)

I was so wiped out from fighting that not even my usual fix of a long, hot shower could wash away my exhaustion. What kind of *djinn* could take out the network like that? Was it a weakness in the network itself? If so, how could we prevent this from happening again? I'd listened to the Host struggle with these same questions over and over, until finally, I tuned them out to give myself some peace. After all, Arielle had told me to rest; I was officially off duty.

I towel dried, careful of my newly scabbed wound, and tugged on a clean pair of jeans. The shower had fogged up the glass and heated the small room, so I left my chambray shirt open to cool off and stepped out into my living room.

Mia kneeled on the couch with her long, dark hair pulled into a damp braid. Loose tendrils curled across her cheek. The pose gave her an air of innocence, but she

271

looked haunted. Her face was pale, her brow furrowed. I was used to the dangers of my world, creatures like the *djinn*, and even I'd been overwhelmed by this one. It all had to be too much for her.

"You all right?"

Her shoulders jerked in surprise as she noticed me. Then her gaze softened and I held my breath as I felt the warmth of desire pooling through her, weighted by sadness. My hair fell into my eyes, so I shoved it back and slid beside her on the couch, drawn to her and yet not wanting to impose myself. She needed comfort right now, reassurance. An angel, not a man.

"First Jesse and Dean, now Fatima." She bit her lip. "Who else is going to get hurt?"

Despair lurked around her, tugging at her attention as she tried to make sense of what had happened. I had to coax her back to the light. I placed an arm around her shoulder and a chaste kiss on her cheek. "It's not your fault, Mia. You know that, right? Evil has nothing to do with you."

I tried to remember back to a time when evil used to jar me that way, but couldn't. I'd become acclimatized to it, the way a sailor gets sea legs.

Flyers swarmed outside the windows, blocked by our sigils. In one swift, agitated movement, Mia leaped to her feet and closed the blinds. "How can we possibly keep them all safe? What if they go after my mom? Bill? My dad?"

"We've been watching your immediate family since Damiel came back. They're fine."

"You have?" She spun to face me, frowning, her tone accusatory. "Why didn't you tell me?"

Didn't she know that all I wanted was to protect her? "It's what we do." I stood and fastened the lower buttons of my shirt. If it were up to me, these dangers would never exist. "I never gave it much thought."

She sighed, and the tension dissolved from her

shoulders. "What if I stayed here with you and never went outside? Do you think these flyers and stuff would forget about us and go away?"

Something constricted in my chest and drew me to her side. I placed a hand on her lower back and felt the heat flush through her. A stray curl covered her cheek. I swept it away, my thumb brushing her soft, plump lip. "And how would we entertain ourselves, cooped up in here?"

"I'm sure you'll think of something." She caught my thumb in her teeth and smiled. The light and heat in her forest green eyes unraveled me. I wanted her. All of her. *So much for the angel.* I drew in my breath, unable to tear my eyes away. *Hold it together.*

Resisting the urge to press my thumb into her mouth, I reached under her braid and caressed the nape of her neck. Our bodies grazed each other, sending electric sparks through my skin. It felt the way the network did, only sharper, more blissful, intoxicating. As carefully as I could, I grazed my fingers along her throat and collarbone, wanting to go lower, waiting for an invitation. My celestial energy blazed, reminding me of what I am. It tingled through both of us, as though her body were already joined with mine. I could feel her response, the heat of her, how much more she wanted. And my heart roared like thunder.

God help me. I cannot go further. Not yet.

Her arms circled my waist and she kissed my bare chest, igniting an inferno of desire. Involuntary tremors quaked through me. I wanted her more than anything in this world. I always have. Unable to resist, I pulled her closer, tilting her face up to meet mine. When our mouths finally met, she let out the softest moan.

Guiding her, I inched backward and eased us down on the sofa. I lifted one of her legs, then the other, trying to wrap them around me. Sliding into my lap, she straddled me, pressed her thighs into the sides of my waist, and I was almost undone. I huffed out my breath against her neck and drew in her scent. *Pull it together.*

Our kisses deepened, and I caressed the exposed skin at base of her spine. When she melted into me, my energy pulsed so strong, I thought we'd catch fire, sending up a flare so bright that both Heaven and Hell would see it. Enthrallment, they would say. And I could feel the lust like a force, begging to take me over, and consume her with me. I struggled for control, to hold that force back.

My hands weren't enough contact. I explored her neck and throat with my lips, tasting the salt and sweetness of her. Her palms rode my bare chest and back. My skin erupted into goose bumps, reaching for her.

Her cotton shirt bunched up, a wrinkled barrier between us. I wanted it gone. I played with the top button. "May I?" I could hardly speak. To enthrall was to take without asking. I would always ask.

She nodded, her eyes black with need, and I fumbled open the top button. She did the rest. I pressed my spine against the back of the couch, wanting to explore every inch of her, but afraid. How endless was my need for her? So far, it hadn't abated for millennia.

She leaned in for another kiss and I enveloped her mouth with mine, drinking her in. With gentle strokes, I caressed her rib cage, unable to resist the silkiness of her skin.

"Tell me if you want me to stop," she whispered as she shrugged out of her shirt. Then she reached around to unfasten her bra.

Stop? Now?

My hands shook as they slid up her back. At her bra clasp, they pressed against her fingers, holding them in place. "I never *want* you to stop."

She gave me a questioning look. She knew my limitations well, and she'd loved me anyway. "But?"

I sat there, not moving, catching my breath, as I fought to regain self-control. All I wanted was her. And she wanted me back. There's a poem I'd heard once: "The pain of loving you is almost more than I can bear." I thought the guy who wrote it was nuts. How could loving someone hurt? I understood now. My heart constricted, my limbs grew tight. I would die for her. And yet I no longer desired to love and live in fear. It was time for us to be together, but it had to be done right. I'd been to the high councils, and they'd heard me out. I was no ordinary angel. I was half human. She was half prophet.

If there was ever going to be a case for us to be accepted by the other members of the Host, we needed legitimacy.

"These are stolen moments. I don't want to have to hide anything about us." My heart still raced. "I can't."

"You're not in the network right now, are you?" She pulled back, checking around the room, as though she were looking for the network there.

"That's not what I mean. I want it to be right between us. No suspicion from colleagues. No having to hide the way I feel." Unable to stay away, I wound my arms around her and pulled her in for another sweet, lingering kiss. "You've seen a fraction of my world. There's councils, high councils, courts, more layers of legislation than you can count, and laws that, believe it or not, hold the universe in place. But I've petitioned them, as high as I can, for an exception to be made."

"What kind of exception?" She leaned into me, and my body ached from the contact.

"I didn't tell you before because I didn't want to get your hopes up. These things take a long time. It could mean—"

Her kiss was filled with so much love and passion, and more than that: hope. The thought that we could be together, really together, fueled me, and I kissed her back even more hungrily than before. My lips explored every inch of exposed skin until her body shook with desire. And then I pulled her close and simply held her, my body trembling, too.

ACKNOWLEDGEMENTS

First of all, I want to thank you for buying and reading this book. Without your support as readers, *The Angel Killer* wouldn't exist. I also want to thank the many bloggers who read and reviewed *The Watcher* and helped spread the word via Goodreads, Amazon, and your own sites. Without you, the Internet would be a lonely place for authors and booklovers alike. Among those bloggers, I want to give a shout out to the members of the "Angels on the Street Team," who blogged, tweeted, and shared my book to all their friends and followers.

I also owe a great deal of thanks to my beta readers, Elinor Svoboda, Jessica Rust, Blair Duncan, and Cara Anderson, who've read this book in its infancy, and through its gangly growth spurts to the maturity of publication, giving me both the honest feedback and the encouragement I needed every step of the way.

Next, I want to thank Maggie Bolitho and Lynn Crymble, my critique group and cheering squad. This book would still be in its infancy stages without your loving guidance and amazing feedback. I'm so lucky to have found you both!

Thank you to all my friends who have supported and encouraged me through the emotional journey of writing and editing a book. Thank you to all my colleagues in Training in Power for your encouragement. And thank you, Faye Fitzgerald for your metaphysical teachings, which have been instrumental in my life and helped me to move through all kinds of blocks, including (and perhaps, especially) writer's block.

Matthew, thank you for every late night reading, for listening to me, and for every meal you prepared so I could have time to write. I could not have done this without you. Dianne, thank you so much for your genuine enthusiasm. And Dad, what can I say? You've done so much! Thank you for spreading the word, for speaking to libraries, and for even driving to Bellingham to pick up books when they wouldn't ship across the border. And thank you for reading my stories when I was a kid, knowing how much it mattered to me. You're the best Dad a writer could have!

I've also had some amazing friends who've been my champions throughout this journey: Tina Gilbertson, Leanne Walsh, Marilyn Foreman, and Crystal Braunwarth.

A huge thank you also goes to Melissa Keir, at Inkspell Publishing, for making this book a reality. Thank you for taking all of us authors under your wing. Thank you, Rie Langdon, for your careful, concise edits. It was great working with you again. Najla Qamber, thank you for designing such a gorgeous cover. It was a thrill to work with you. Also, I wanted to give a shout out to my author colleagues at Inkspell who have been so supportive and welcoming all along.

ABOUT THE AUTHOR

A Canadian-born author, Lisa Voisin spent her childhood daydreaming and making up stories, but it was her love of reading and writing in her teens that drew her to Young Adult fiction.

A self-proclaimed coffee lover, Lisa can usually be found writing in a local café. When she's not writing, you'll find her meditating or hiking in the mountains to counteract the side effects of drinking too much caffeine!

Though she's lived in several cities across Canada, she currently lives in Vancouver, B.C. with her fiancé and their two cats.

Find her:
Website: http://www.lisavoisin.com.

Facebook: https://www.facebook.com/lisavoisinauthor

Twitter: https://twitter.com/lvoisin @lvoisin

Blog: http://lisavoisin.wordpress.com

ALSO BY LISA VOISIN-
BOOK 1 IN THE WATCHER SAGA

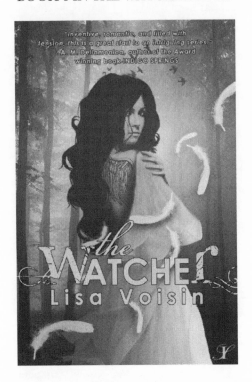

Millennia ago, he fell from heaven for her. Can he face her without falling again?

Fascinated with ancient civilizations, seventeen-year-old Mia Crawford dreams of becoming an archaeologist. She also dreams of wings--soft and silent like snow--and somebody trying to steal them.

When a horrible creature appears out of thin air and attacks her, she knows Michael Fontaine is involved. Secretive and aloof, Michael evokes feelings in Mia that she doesn't understand. Images of another time and place haunt her. She recognizes them—but not from any textbook.

In search of the truth, Mia discovers a past life of forbidden love, jealousy and revenge that tore an angel from Heaven and sent her to an early grave. Now that her soul has returned, does she have a chance at loving that angel again? Or will an age-old nemesis destroy them both?

Ancient history is only the beginning.

AMAZON